Alan Brierley May Have Retired

GRAHAM CUTMORE

Copyright © Graham Cutmore, 2024

All rights reserved.

Graham Cutmore has asserted his right under the Copyright, Designs and Patents Act 1988 to be identified as the author of this work.

This book is a work of fiction and any resemblance to actual persons, living or dead, is purely coincidental.

ISBN: 9798328298384

Monday 2 November

Does anyone keep a diary anymore? They still sell them, so I suppose some people must, though they also still sell talc and bath salts, and I'm not convinced anyone has used either of those since 1982.

Of course, these days a lot of people keep a record on social media instead, but no one's life is really like that, is it? No one's life is really all holidays, family meals out, prestige sport events, gigs by famous artists, winsome children and grandchildren, and playful, cute dogs. Is that genuinely our ideal, anyway? Wouldn't a life that was just a procession of outings and social encounters, without any challenges or setbacks, lack substance and quickly become boring? I think we humans (though I'm certainly not setting myself up as a spokesman for the species) generally need a balance: not too many insuperable challenges obviously, and as little unmitigated pain as possible please, but also more than just acres of vacuous, analgesic contentment.

So I think diaries are still useful. And the audience is in any case different from social media: I suspect I will be the only person who ever reads this diary, at least while I am alive; I certainly hope so. Which means I can be candid, and frees me from the straitjacket of trying to impress other people. The diary can be a sounding board, a way of processing experience and challenging thoughts and beliefs. If someone doesn't recognise my portrayal of them, or disputes my recall of what they said, what of it? What is true? We all have different realities, don't we?

This won't be Instagram then. Nor, it goes without saying, will it be a modern-day Samuel Pepys, with a grand, sweeping overview of the political machinations of the time.

Mine is a smaller life. But live it I do. And today is my fifty-eighth birthday!

The alarm went off, as it always does, at six thirty this morning. It woke me from a deep sleep in which I was having some sort of dream that seemed to require a lot of concentration, but which immediately made no sense as soon as I was awake. I felt confused and not at all ready to get up and start the day. My bedroom was still completely dark, I thought I could hear rain outside and I quickly realised it was Monday. It then also dawned on me that it was my birthday, but that knowledge didn't lead to any improvement in my mood. I pushed the large snooze button, which allowed me to doze for a very precise nine minutes until the alarm sounded again. I felt no better the second time. I levered myself out of bed and mechanically showered and made breakfast.

I always leave home long before the postman comes, but I wasn't expecting anything today. Lisa sends me a card most years, but texted me yesterday to say that she had forgotten, what with the kids and everything, and that she hoped I agreed it wasn't worth sending one after the event. I called her to say that was fine, but her phone went to voicemail and I left a message saying that perhaps she would like to ring back when it was convenient for her.

Getting to the station was a bit of a struggle. Rain was coming at me diagonally, though luckily I had thought to put a pair of waterproofs over my suit trousers, which kept me dry. Some of the wave of schoolkids coming in the other direction appeared to find them quite comical, and one of them made some sort of remark that I didn't catch but which made her friends laugh, but, as I have explained to my work colleagues, they aren't supposed to be a fashion statement. Lisa says I should drive to the station, but my car doesn't take kindly to being exposed to the elements all the time.

Plus it costs more than ten pounds a day to park there, and the daily round trip must be good exercise for me.

The train was on time this morning. I had to stand, someone was making a phone call in a voice that was so loud you could make out every word from the other end of the carriage, and I could hear the music leaking from the earbuds of the person next to me; but it's a means to an end, and I have got used to the discomforts over the years. On a whim, and possibly to cheer myself up, at the end of the journey I went into the supermarket by the station and bought some birthday doughnuts.

I walked through the office and said good morning to everyone as I got to my desk. Hardly anyone replied; a lot of people wear headphones these days, which maybe explains it. Ade does, but he pushed them onto his neck and smiled and wished me a happy birthday and said he would get us both a cup of coffee, which I thought was a kind gesture. By the time he got back I had struggled out of my waterproofs and was offering the doughnuts round, though I made sure there were two left.

Ade is a really good lad. He's thirty years younger than me, but we get on really well. He seems to be climbing the career ladder in our company very quickly, which is great to see. His parents came here years ago from Nigeria. I know that because I asked him after we had been working together for a couple of months and had talked about all sorts of things. I could feel Kevin, my boss, glaring at me, and the next time Ade was away from his desk Kevin said to me that you can't ask things like that. And Sarah said that Ade is as British as you are, which is true as most of my family seem to have come from Ireland but, like Ade, I was born in the U.K. Anyway, since then I've told Ade a little bit about Ireland, and he's told me quite a lot of interesting stuff I didn't know about Nigeria, which is now on the list of countries I'm hoping to visit when I eventually retire.

The doughnuts were all gone by ten o'clock and a few people had come over or emailed to wish me a happy birthday, which was nice. One asked if it was a landmark birthday, which worried me a bit because, looking in the mirror, I concluded that they could only have meant sixty. I would have been happy to put my hand in my pocket for some birthday drinks, but that tradition seems to have died out in our office: people are much healthier than they were when I first started work, which can only be a good thing, but I do miss being able to mark the occasion. Never mind.

I sat down with my coffee and doughnut and started reading and replying to some emails. And then, at about eleven, a lot of people started drifting away from their desks into a meeting room. There was nothing in my calendar and I asked Ade, who said he thought it was a managers' meeting. I usually go to those, but when he came back Kevin explained that it was a new initiative to streamline the meetings, which were thought to be becoming unwieldy, and in future he would give Ade and me a summary of anything that had been discussed that we needed to know about. He said there was nothing today.

The day dragged a bit, as they often do lately. Despite that, I often feel that it is taking me longer to get things done than it used to. That's a bit of a worry: I know I'm not ancient yet, or senile, but the brain does seem to slow down gradually or get less agile as you get older. The main advantage I have over younger colleagues is experience, but you need to be able to deploy it quickly or your knowledge can become invisible, and you with it. Should I care with only a few years to go to retirement? Maybe not, but I suspect that I do.

After lunch there was a lively discussion about football across the office, and that slowed me down even further, even though I wasn't really taking part. Of course, these days we have the option to work from home if we want peace and quiet, but Kevin isn't all that keen on it, and if you live on your own as I do there is only so much peace and quiet that you want.

In mid-afternoon Kevin, who had been in and out of his chair all day, announced that he had inadvertently double-booked himself, had two meetings at the same time, and he asked Ade if he would do the easier one, which was with Finance in twenty minutes. Ade looked a little surprised that Kevin hadn't asked me, but I gave him an encouraging look and said I would help him if he needed it. He didn't. Kevin came back briefly after his meeting, and had a quick conversation with Ade before running off to his massage appointment. This is a recent initiative from HR, as part of their stress and mental-health programme, and has been very popular. It's available to everyone, but I haven't done it so far, though I keep telling myself that perhaps I should: I don't want to become one of these older people who don't keep up or, worse, dwell in the past.

As the end of the day approached, I felt a rising sense of panic that I hadn't really produced a proper day's work, and I felt uncharacteristically despondent on the way home. Partly, I think, because it was my birthday and I would have liked to celebrate it in some way with other people; and also because the fact of a birthday reminds me of the march of time, that I am still on my own, and that I have spent a further twelve months working for the same company. Thirty-nine years now, since I left school!

A little bit of excitement when I got home: there was a light on in the flat across the way that has been empty for months, and I could hear a woman's voice. Outside the door was what looked like some sort of metal case, with meshing around the sides. The door to the flat opened and a couple of quite weedy looking men of about my age scuttled out and pushed the case into the flat. One of them caught my eye and, as I smiled and attempted to raise my hand in greeting, looked away as if he were embarrassed for some reason. I don't imagine that removal companies would employ people with physiques like that, so I assume they are family.

I had an impulse to fetch a bottle of wine, knock on their door and suggest a double celebration of their new home and my birthday, but of course I didn't do anything. But who knows? Maybe I'll make new friends there.

A couple of good things to end the day, though. Lisa did call, and although it was quite a short conversation because the kids were yelling for attention in the background, it was nice to hear her voice. Jasmine came on the line and, prompted, wished Grandpa a happy birthday and, unprompted, asked if I had bought her a present for my birthday! Lisa and I laughed about that. She didn't mention Christmas, as I had hoped she might, and I didn't either. I did say that it was lovely to hear her voice on my birthday and would be even nicer to see her soon, and the kids. And Neil, of course. Lisa said it would be great, but it had been bad enough with one child, it was manic now that she had two. She suggested we play it by ear. I said 'OK' as I didn't know what else to say.

Then, just as I was starting to get ready for bed, Sunil texted to wish me a happy birthday. He usually remembers, and this time he was apologetic for having left it so late in the day. I employed Sunil as my assistant over twenty years ago now. He was and is a smashing fella, and was a great assistant too until he left to further his career. He now runs his own company and is a bit of a star in our market. It seems to upset Kevin when I have lunch with Sunil, though I don't know why it should. It amused me (and Sunil when I told him) that Adam, our CEO, now sends round staff emails saying that discrimination in all its forms will not be tolerated in our company and should be called out wherever it is found. When I employed Sunil, who was one of the first non-white people in the company outside the post room, Adam called me into his office and angrily told me I was up to my old lefty tricks and should have asked him first. Adam still says that Sunil is a wideboy, but in my view Sunil is one of the narrowest boys I have ever met. One of my big regrets is not going to his wedding. Anne and I were asked, but she was worried that it might be gender-segregated and she would end up trying to make conversation with a lot of women she didn't know. I wasn't sure but, as I said to Anne, I could hardly ask: if someone is kind enough to invite you to their wedding you can't make conditions: you either go or you don't. So in the end we made some excuse which I hope was believable. If it wasn't, Sunil was gracious enough not to let on.

Another day done, and, encouragingly, enough to write about in my new diary. Let's see what my fifty-ninth year holds.

Monday 9 November

Where to start!

The day began normally enough. The usual Monday-morning struggle with the alarm clock, but only because I was still asleep when it went off. The weekend had been a bit too quiet so, truth be told, I wasn't that reluctant to go to work.

I can't even remember anything about the commute now, except that I was hoping that the train would slow down a little as it arrived at the terminus, so that I could finish the chapter of the book I was reading. I love reading, especially narratives that take you to a completely different place. There are too many books in the flat, though. But how do you decide which ones to get rid of?

I felt unusually hungry on the short walk to the office. I thought about last week, but ran my hand over the bulge that my stomach makes under my work shirt and concluded I couldn't make a habit of buying doughnuts. But fruit would be OK, I decided. And I could eat a little less at lunchtime so that I didn't put on weight. I went into a small supermarket, found the fruit aisle and liked the look of their display of bananas. It appeared you couldn't buy less than four, but that was OK, because they weren't that expensive and looked like they would last a couple of days.

Once I got to the office, I said good morning to everyone and sat down in front of my computer. Kevin didn't reply and Ade wasn't at his desk. I felt so hungry that, as I waited for my workstation to boot up, I immediately ate one of the bananas, which was just at the right stage of ripeness. It occurred to me that the others might last two days but probably not three, and also that Ade likes bananas – he often has one with his lunch – so I left one on his desk while I went to get a coffee from the machine. While I waited my turn to put my cup under the nozzle I noticed a new poster on the kitchen wall. In large blue letters it read: "Banter at others' expense. It's not funny. It's harassment." That pulled me up a bit. There was something oddly aggressive about the typeface and colour and size of the thing. I instinctively looked round to see if anyone was watching me. I felt a little uncomfortable for some reason, though I couldn't pinpoint why I should. Over the years I have definitely been more banted against than banting, particularly as the supporter of a football team that hasn't won a domestic trophy for four decades and isn't going to on current form. But I suppose that isn't what they are getting at.

When I got back to my desk, Ade was looking at the banana with a perplexed expression on his face. I smiled and pointed at the fruit.

"I had a spare one," I told him. "I thought you might like it."

Ade immediately brightened. "Thanks," he said. Then he put the banana in his drawer and went back to reading through his emails.

I quite enjoyed the rest of the morning. Kevin recently volunteered me to give some training to some of the newer recruits. I wouldn't exactly call it mentoring, as we are a technology company and technology and the culture that go with it change so quickly that some of these bright kids already have knowledge and skills that I have never had. But the basics of programming don't change that much, plus there are tips I can give on setting and handling customer expectations that you can only really get from experience. So I learn from them as well as passing on my knowledge. Some of them call me 'Uncle Alan', which made me feel a little old at first, but it seems to be intended as a term of endearment, so I've sort of adopted it. Today one of them asked me how we got on for data storage before the cloud, and another one chipped in that I had everything on vinyl, which I thought was a good one. For Secret Santa last year one of them got me a model abacus, which they said would remind me of the old days. They're a good bunch.

Lunchtime came round really quickly. I went out to get a sandwich and a proper cup of coffee and then sat at my desk catching up on the news online. There weren't many people around. A lot go to the in-house gym these days, or sit in a recreational area where, apart from eating, you can also play pool and table tennis. I've been up there a couple of times but never felt that comfortable. I like to read the news, anyway. It can be depressing, but I think you should know what's going on in the world. It worries me that some of the youngsters don't, and don't want to either, but their logic seems to be "if you can't change it, why make yourself miserable?" and I sort of get that.

My phone rang. It was the Head of HR's secretary, who told me that her boss wanted to see me and had made an appointment for me at 2:30. She said no, she didn't know what it was about. I said 2:30 was fine with me and went back to reading about a group of people who had been murdered by another group over a tiny detail of theological difference.

Nikki, the Head of HR, kept me waiting for almost ten minutes. The door to her office was closed, but I could hear her holding a conversation via speakerphone, though I couldn't make out any of the words. There was nowhere to sit, so eventually I went and leaned against a cupboard. There were four people from HR at their desks; one smiled at me and said that Nikki wouldn't be long. Two others were engrossed in their phones. The fourth was staring attentively at his screen and didn't appear to be aware of my presence. The screen had one of those clever covers that stop you seeing anything from the side, so I couldn't tell what he was doing.

Nikki finally finished her call, came out, shook my hand and apologised for keeping me waiting.

"Sorry about that," she said. "Something always comes up at the wrong moment. Best laid plans..! Josie," she shouted towards the young woman who had smiled at me, "could you join us please?"

Josie slowly got up from her desk, smiled at me again, followed me into Nikki's office and closed the door behind her.

Nikki motioned me to one of two chairs in front of her desk and Josie took the other. Nikki sat down in her own seat, which creaked as she leaned back in it. A giant computer screen obscured one half of her face from view.

Nikki took off her red-framed glasses and rubbed her eyes. "You've been with us a long time, Alan," she began. She replaced her glasses, referred to her screen and then to a batch of papers in front of her. "Thirty-nine years. Is that really true?" She looked at both me and Josie for confirmation. Josie nodded.

"Yes," I replied. "In those days the whole industry was Bill Gates, Steve Jobs and me. I don't know what happened to the other two."

Josie smiled. Nikki looked first at her notes, then at Josie and me, with a confused expression on her face.

"Right," she said. "Now in all that time I am sure that you have seen a lot of changes. Not just in technology itself, which is the lifeblood of this company of course, but in social attitudes as well, particularly as they relate to the workplace."

I agreed that I had.

Nikki moved an empty coffee cup to one side and leaned forward slightly. "Now," she went on, "this company is, rightly, proud of its record on diversity and inclusion, and it is a large part of my role these days to drive the agenda and identify deliverables in that space."

I nodded politely.

"And, of course," Nikki continued, "that does mean taking everyone with us and ensuring, bluntly, that our older members of staff do not, however unwittingly, continue to hold onto outmoded ways of thinking."

I looked blankly at Nikki and then at Josie. Josie smiled again.

Nikki shook her head regretfully. "I'm afraid there's been a complaint, Alan."

"Really?" I was genuinely surprised. "About me? Who from?"

"Obviously I can't tell you that."

"I see." We sat in silence for a few seconds. "Can you tell me what they are complaining about then?" I asked finally.

Nikki had a pained expression on her face. "Racially insensitive behaviour towards a co-worker," she replied, as though reading from a charge sheet.

It took a couple of seconds for the words to sink in. Then my head spun. "Someone's accusing me of racism?"

"No, not explicitly racism, but 'racially insensitive behaviour'."

I sat back and clasped my hands in front of me. "Specifically?" I asked quietly.

"Specifically," Nikki consulted the paper in front of her, "leaving a banana on the desk of a BAME colleague."

I laughed at the absurdity of it. "No, that's nothing," I explained. "Ade likes bananas, as do I. I had a spare one, so I gave it to him. Or left it on his desk as he was in a meeting."

I thought that would be the end of the interview, but Nikki only shook her head. "That's all very well, Alan," she said earnestly, "but did you not consider or appreciate the optics of that action?"

"The optics?"

"Yes."

I thought about that carefully for a few seconds before I replied. "As you say, I have been here a long time," I began, "but basically I have always been happiest as a coder. That's what I do best."

Nikki gave me a joyless smile. "Vital for our business," she said.

"Right. And this is relevant to your question; I haven't just gone off at a tangent. Now one of the basics of coding, pretty much any coding, is the 'if statement': if a is true, do b; if a is not true, do c."

"OK." Nikki looked perplexed. Josie appeared to be trying not to laugh.

"So," I went on undeterred, "here is my scenario and 'if statement'. I have a spare banana because the shop doesn't sell them in ones. So rather than waste it, which would be against the company's environmental policy, I look for a colleague to give it to.

"If I give it to Ade, who is the obvious candidate, as he sits next to me and I know he likes bananas, then someone, clearly not Ade himself, may say that looks racially insensitive."

Nikki nodded.

"But if I decide not to give it to him solely because he is black, then aren't I a) discriminating against him because of the colour of his skin and b) making the connection in my head between black people and bananas? Which I didn't and don't. Wouldn't that be far more racist?"

I sat back in my chair and looked round to see if Josie agreed with me.

Nikki looked at the clock on the wall behind me. "This company is very committed to all its staff," she told me, "and we understand that cultural changes can sometimes be challenging for older colleagues..."

"Wait a minute." I felt my hackles rise. I had just given a reasoned response. Surely Nikki owed it to me to address the points I had made? I mean, if she could show that I was wrong, then fine. But she just ploughed on:

"...which is why we are introducing enhanced diversity training for colleagues over forty-five." She started writing on a pad, like a doctor writing a prescription. "And I would like you to be one of the attendees for the first course. You look worried, Alan. It's not that terrifying: just a day in a classroom with some diversity scenarios and role-play, letting people see the real-life results of certain attitudes and prejudices."

I was determined to sound calm, not to say something silly that I would regret. "And what if I don't?" I asked gently.

Nikki looked up. "It's compulsory training. Under your contract of employment you have to do it."

A couple of seconds of eye contact and silence.

"And if I don't."

Nikki leaned back in her chair, took her glasses off and placed them on the desk. "Let's not go there, Alan," she said. "You've been here a very long time and must presumably be having thoughts of retirement."

Nikki's even expression suggested to me that the interview was over. I got up wearily and made for the door. "Have you ever heard of the BNP?" I asked on the way out.

Nikki looked blank. Josie said that music wasn't really her thing.

I had to smile at that. "I don't know how far back your HR files go," I told them, "but the BNP were a neo-Nazi group, and almost made it big back in the day. At that time the company wasn't at all keen on anyone doing their bit to try to stop them."

I went back to my desk. Ade smiled and looked slightly embarrassed; I smiled back but didn't know what he knew, or what to say. Sarah eyed me suspiciously from her desk. Kevin began to talk about an ongoing coding project in a brisk business-as-usual voice, which meant he knew what was going on but was trying to avoid getting involved. I tried to do some programming for the rest of the day, but I kept making mistakes and my mind kept going back to the discussion with Nikki. I felt dirty, but I didn't know why I did, or why I should.

I kept looking at the clock, and it was a relief when it was time to go home. Sarah had gone ten minutes earlier, and now Kevin got up, wished us a good evening and headed towards the lifts.

Ade waited until Kevin was out of earshot and turned towards me. "Shit, man," he said, "you've been looking like death all afternoon. What's going on?"

I started to explain, but hadn't got far before Ade stopped me. "Two things," he said. "We need a beer, and you urgently need to meet my girlfriend."

The pub wasn't busy and we easily found a table. It had been Ade's suggestion, but it is a bit of an old man's place to be honest - wooden bars and real ales, fruit machines and a dartboard - and I guessed he had selected it as somewhere that I would be comfortable. He also tried to buy me a drink, but I insisted on getting the first one in.

He was scrolling through his phone when I got back from the bar with the glasses. "Cheers, man," he said. "So what did Nikki say exactly?"

I told him. Probably at too great a length. I need to stop doing that.

"That's bullshit," he said definitively.

I shrugged. "Did anyone talk to you?" I asked.

Ade nodded. "Josie called me. I told her it wasn't a thing. I mean – you know it wasn't me, right?"

"Of course. Who do you think...?"

"Sarah?"

"Do you think so? I don't think she likes me very much, but wouldn't she have asked you first?"

Ade shrugged. Neither of us spoke for a couple of seconds.

"You seemed a bit perplexed," I ventured, "when I came back and you were looking at the banana."

Ade nodded again. "I didn't know it was from you."

"Yeah. But you weren't thinking it could be...?"

"Something racist? Yeah, sure."

"Really?" I was surprised. "In this day and age?"

Ade smiled indulgently but quickly adopted a more serious expression. "Sure," he said adamantly. "Anywhere, any time. Why not? Racism is alive and well in this country."

I nodded. "Yes, I get that. But in a professional office with intelligent people, you'd think..."

Ade exhaled quickly. "I don't think that matters. They're just cleverer about it."

I thought about that. "So, was I being insensitive?"

"No," Ade replied. "Well, not deliberately. Just a little naive maybe."

I smiled ruefully. "That's what you want to hear when you're fifty-eight," I said.

We both laughed.

"So," Ade asked, "are you going to do the course?"

"I don't know."

"Really?"

"I want to sleep on it."

"Ah, here she is." Ade was standing up and beckoning to someone behind my back.

I turned and saw a young woman in a grey jacket and skirt and white blouse making her way towards us. She looked bewildered by her surroundings, as though she had never been in a place like this before. Some of the older guys were watching her walk past. I went to get her a chair and she smiled at me and sat down. At the same time she glowered at Ade as if to ask him what had possessed him to choose this as a venue.

Ade made the introductions. "Alan, this is Eniola, my girlfriend," he told me. We exchanged a limp handshake, and I was about to tell her that I had heard a lot about her, but I realised that that wasn't true. "I'm with her while I'm waiting for a nice white girl to come along," Ade went on. Eniola barely reacted; she had obviously heard the line several times before.

"And this," Ade told Eniola, "is the old white supremacist I was messaging you about."

I must have looked embarrassed. "Ignore him," Eniola told me, "he thinks he's funny."

"Eniola is a solicitor," Ade said, trying, I thought, to conceal the pride in his voice. "Employment law specialist."

I stuttered something about her not being at work now, and that I couldn't expect free advice. Then I insisted on buying her a drink, which took a while, because the barman had never heard of the first two things she requested (nor had I) and I ended up with a glass of tepid white wine that Eniola sipped politely.

She listened to the story, which I tried to make shorter this time, and immediately said that it was a blatant case of age discrimination. She offered me her business card and said that if I needed representation I should call her. I took it, thanked her and said that I would think about it. I wanted to ask how much it would cost, but it seemed rude in a semi-social setting, so I kept quiet.

Ade made polite conversation with me for a couple of minutes while Eniola continued to sip her wine, surveying her surroundings as though checking where the exits were. I realised that they both wanted to leave, so I drank up as quickly as I could, politely declined Ade's offer of another one and said I was sure they didn't want to waste their evening with an old timer like me. They made all the right protests in response.

"Anyway," I said as I got up and started to put my coat on, "got to go. Those crosses won't set fire to themselves, you know!"

Ade laughed. Eniola looked puzzled. "Seriously," she called out as I waved goodbye to them, "give me a call."

There was another large box outside the door of my new neighbours when I got home. It looked like it might be some sort of theatrical costume trunk and I thought it would be interesting to get to know someone in the entertainment business. After the day I had had, and despite having voluntarily given up the company of Ade and Eniola, for their sake, I quite liked the idea of chatting with someone, so was tempted to ring the bell on the pretext of letting the new tenants know there was a box outside and introducing myself at the same time. I hesitated for a moment, and then thought I could hear a raised voice from within the flat, and then something that might possibly have been a slap, or maybe just something falling over. I decided it would be better to come back another time.

I got something to eat and fitfully watched television for the rest of the evening. To my own surprise, the more I thought about it, the more it seemed to me that I didn't want just meekly to give in; that I should give Eniola a call.

Thursday 12 November

Can diary-keeping be a jinx? I had hoped keeping a diary might prompt me to lead a more interesting life, but this really isn't what I had in mind.

Events have moved very quickly. I'm not sure this is what I want. On the one hand, you can't just let people walk all over you. On the other hand, routines acquired over a number of years give a certain comfort, don't they?

On Tuesday morning Josie from HR sent me a calendar invitation with the date and details of the course they wanted me to go on, 'Diversity and Inclusion for Seasoned Staff'. 'Seasoned' seemed like a strange word: it made me sound like a cutlet. I ignored it for an hour then sent a 'tentative response' saying I wanted to get some advice.

Nikki called. I asked her how she was and got no reply. She said that I was of course entitled to take legal advice if I wanted to, but the company, and she personally, would be very disappointed if I did. In a tone that told me that I was out of my depth and wasting her time, she suggested that I come and see her again on Thursday morning (today).

I went out of the office and stood with a surprisingly large group of smokers in the chill autumn air and rang Eniola's number. She sounded pleased but not surprised to hear from me. She said I should come round to her office before work on Wednesday, and we could discuss what my rights were, what our strategy was, and what we were trying to achieve. I agreed, thanked her and hung up. I found that I was shaking, but didn't know why. I thought about asking someone for a cigarette, though I haven't smoked in years.

That evening I wanted to ring Lisa to ask her if she thought I was doing the right thing, but I guessed she would be too busy with the kids and changed my mind.

Nikki only kept me waiting five minutes this morning. She exchanged a limp businesslike handshake with Eniola, briefly glanced at me then wearily invited us to sit down. Josie came in again a few seconds later.

"Hopefully we can clear this up quickly," Nikki began with a cold smile on her face.

"That would be good," Eniola agreed.

Nikki ignored her and continued to address me. "The long and short of it, Alan, is that you have a contract or employment with us, and under that contract we are entitled to require you to undertake any training we believe would be beneficial to your role."

"Within the law," Eniola interjected.

"Of course within the law," Nikki agreed testily, still looking only at me.

"You couldn't send Mr Brierley on a course about paedophilia."

Nikki finally gave Eniola her attention. "Why on earth would we..?"

"Because it would be defamatory," Eniola went on calmly and slowly. "Because it would imply that Mr Brierley had engaged in that sort of behaviour."

"There's no..."

"In the same way that the course you are trying to send him on is defamatory because it implies he is a racist."

"It is simply a way to ensure..."

"Which would be bad enough on its own. Without the additional implication of this course, as it is constructed, that all people over a certain age are automatically racist. Which is flagrantly discriminatory. And therefore unlawful."

Nikki looked at us for a few moments, then down at the keypad of her computer.

"What do you want?" she asked baldly.

Eniola looked at me and I nodded. She cleared her throat and addressed Nikki directly. "My client would like the rescission of the requirement to take this course, a written apology including the assurance of no future victimisation, the payment of his legal expenses and five hundred pounds for the stress it has caused him."

I nodded again. Eniola had suggested we add the five hundred pounds as something that we could then negotiate away. She said it was a good tactic. I had agreed, though had wondered whether it might be prove to be the proverbial red rag.

Nikki stood up and offered her hand again. "Thanks," she said curtly. "We'll be in touch."

At half past four we were back in Nikki's office. This time Josie had been replaced by a middle-aged man sporting a salt-and-pepper beard and dressed in a suit whose creases emphasised how close he was to bursting out of it. It appeared that the company had a lawyer as well. Eniola had warned me this might happen; she now wore a combative if slightly apprehensive expression on her face, as though she were trying to work out if there was anything she hadn't thought of.

The lawyer spoke first, slowly and deliberately. "Based on previous discussions," he began, "the company thinks it would be better for both parties to part company, preferably amicably." He craned his neck to look at Nikki, who nodded in agreement.

"What are you offering?" Eniola enquired bluntly.

The lawyer dismissed the interruption with a brief wave of the hand, without looking in Eniola's direction.

"So, Alan," he went on, "you have been here for a very long time. Which means that you have a large number of years in the old final-salary pension scheme. What the company is therefore generously proposing to do is top it up so you can retire now as though you had worked to sixty."

"It's a good offer," Nikki said. "Very good. Because the company appreciates all your years of service."

"We'll consider it," Eniola replied non-committally.

The lawyer looked at her over the top of his glasses. He handed us each a copy of the draft legal contract. "By tomorrow please."

"I'm not sure if this is what I want. It's all a bit sudden."

I was sitting in a coffee bar with Eniola, where we had been considering my options for the previous half an hour.

"I did advise you this could happen," she told me patiently. "The thing is we can't force them to employ you if they don't want to. We can only get damages from them, and I would have to advise you that the extra pension they are offering is probably worth a lot more than that."

I nodded. "I was really just hoping they would apologise, and then go back to normal," I explained.

"But you were adamant you wouldn't back down. We did talk about Plan B."

"I know," I agreed. "I'm not blaming you. It just seems strange, after almost forty years, that it comes to an end like this, over a banana." Hearing myself say the word, I had to laugh at the absurdity of it.

Eniola smiled. "Yeah," she began softly, "but it's not really over a banana, is it?"

I smiled ruefully. "No, you're right. It's not."

"So we accept?"

We must have sat in silence for about a minute, though it seemed much longer. I took a sharp intake of breath. "Yes, we accept."

For the next few seconds I experienced a euphoric realisation that all the petty worries of office life for as long as I could remember had suddenly evaporated. And it was a big world, and a beautiful one, and at long last I would have the time to explore it, as well as the means.

But very rapidly the euphoria faded and gave way to vertigo. What was I doing in this place, on my own, with nothing and no one to support me? At least the office gave my life some sort of framework. Was there still time to change my mind? Should I?

"And," Eniola noted, tapping the contract approvingly with her forefinger, "they've agreed to pay my fees."

Friday 13 November

My last day at work after thirty-nine years, two months and I'm not sure how many days. I know I started in September.

Even this morning I didn't realise it was my last day. I thought they would want me to work my notice (which is, or I should say was, only three months) or at least spend some time handing over or documenting ongoing projects plus the training I was giving to the kids, but at the moment I handed over the signed "compromise agreement" (strange phrase) this morning, I appear to have turned into a block of asbestos that needed to be removed from the premises as soon as possible.

Josie was sent to stand by the door while I cleared my desk, which didn't take long; I've never really been one to bring my personal life to work. Ade shook my hand and we then did a sort of man hug thing that neither of us quite got right. Kevin was mysteriously absent, though there was nothing in his calendar. Sarah looked straight ahead at her screen. Most of the others looked embarrassed; a few muttered something about arranging some future drinks. "When the dust has settled" was a frequent phrase. What dust was there, I wanted to ask, and when would it settle?

Josie accompanied me down in the lift. She came through the barrier with me then asked for my pass and work phone. I handed them both over, then all but insisted that she shake hands with me. She complied but looked so embarrassed that I felt guilty for asking.

Then, at eleven o'clock in the morning, I left the company's building for the last time. There was still a group of smokers huddled in the alleyway next to the front entrance, some of them the same people I had seen on Tuesday. I quickly gazed at the marble facade of the building, reflecting the autumn sunlight, then headed for the station.

But it seemed too early to go home. I got on the tube and then got off at Oxford Street. I went from shop to shop with a half-formed idea in my head that I should buy myself some sort of retirement present. I looked at some watches, but they all seemed so expensive for what they were, unless I went for something no better than I already have, which would be pointless. And did I need a watch any more anyway? I had lunch in a department store cafe, which was the only place I could find with any spare tables. The pie tasted home-made, but not in a good way, with cheap ingredients, like hospital or school food.

I headed home at around four. For some reason I didn't want to travel in the rush hour, bump into people I knew, talk about leaving work.

I got back to the flat around five.

My new neighbours were at home. Or at least one of them was – I'm not really sure how many of them there are. Ahead of me as I got out my key to let myself into the block was a short, middle-aged guy with untidy curly hair. He was pressing one of the buttons and someone had just buzzed him in. He looked embarrassed to see me. I smiled and waved my keys, as if somehow that would show him that I lived there and wasn't trying to break in. He was carrying a small paper bag, which aroused my curiosity. I took a furtive glance and saw what looked like an expensive box of chocolates inside. The man seemed keen that I should go up the stairs first, so I obliged and then let myself into the flat. Looking over my shoulder at the last minute, I saw the man standing awkwardly by the door of my new neighbour. The door was ajar, but he wasn't going in. I caught his eye again, but he quickly looked away. Very strange.

Alone in my flat, I spent quite a lot of time after that trying to work out who the visitor might be, and what was going on. A relative bringing a present? But then you would wrap it, wouldn't you? A first date? Not at five o'clock. I tried to snap out of it – I told myself I wasn't going to be one of those retired people – assuming I have indeed retired – with nothing better to do than spy on the neighbours!

I watched the early evening news, though can't remember what the main story was. I felt semi-detached from myself, as if I knew something major had happened to me but couldn't quite believe how different life was going to be. Thirty-nine years of the same routine is a lot, even if it did seem like yesterday that I started.

I got something to eat (predictably fish and chips as it was Friday) then cleared away and sat down again.

I was going to text Lisa, but remembered that she keeps telling me to use WhatsApp – "No one texts anymore, Dad!" – so I did that. 'Guess what?' I wrote. 'Your old dad has only gone and left his job. Call you over the weekend? Lots of love xxxx.'

Sunil also appears on my WhatsApp contacts list, but I wasn't sure of the etiquette of WhatsApping people without asking them first, so I texted him instead.

He replied very quickly. 'WTF man! Away for the weekend, but will call you on Monday.'

I watched TV for the rest of the evening. I got a bit bored at one point and thought that perhaps I should instead be starting to make plans for the future. But then I thought that after so many years, and a traumatic week, I deserved the evening off. And possibly the weekend as well. By Monday I would have a better perspective on things.

I had a couple of bottles of beer, though I wasn't sure if I was celebrating or not.

A couple of times during the evening I heard footsteps on the landing, and two voices, the same woman's voice each time but different male voices, I thought. And a few muted thuds. The spyhole in my door was no use as my neighbour's door is outside of its field of vision. Daphne, my previous neighbour, was there for years and hardly made a sound; she was polite enough but never responded to any of my overtures of friendship. I hope I'm going to get on with the new people/person, particularly if I'm going to be spending more time at home.

I decided to have an early night.

Lisa replied on WhatsApp just as I was getting into bed. 'Noooo! What are you like, Dad? Frantic with the kids, but will try to call over the wknd. Xx'

I was asleep by eleven.

Monday 16 November

I've only just realised that I haven't been making diary entries for weekends, which perhaps reveals how much my life has revolved around work in recent years, even if I didn't realise it.

I could have made an entry especially for my chat with Lisa yesterday, but I'll pick it up here.

She sounded worried, I thought. I wasn't sure whether about me or about something else. "Oh Dad," she said, when I had explained the circumstances as briefly as I could, "what have you done? Couldn't you have just done the lousy course? And what were you doing giving a banana to a black guy in the first place?" I gave her the same logical analysis of that as I had given to Nikki, largely with the same result. "That's not how it works these days," my daughter told me in exasperation. "I sometimes wonder if you should be let out on your own, Dad. I know you mean well, but..."

"It was time to go," I told her. "I didn't like it anymore, I didn't fit in. Everything had changed, it was becoming uncomfortable."

Lisa was silent for a couple of seconds. "You don't think this Abe was trying to get rid of you, do you?" she asked.

"Ade," I corrected her. The idea hadn't occurred to me. "Why would he want to do that?" I asked, "we got on very well."

"Well, career advancement, I guess," Lisa replied. "He wants to move up, you're in the way. You give him a pretext to complain about you, then he gets his girlfriend to push you down a path where you get boxed in and have to leave."

I thought about it for a moment. "No, I'm sure that's not the case."

"People take advantage of you, Dad. You're too nice."

"Well, if that's the worst thing people can say about me," I laughed.

Lisa sighed. "What are you going to do now, then?"

"Well, I don't need to do anything," I replied cheerily. "They've paid up my pension, which is much better than anything your generation is going to get."

No response.

"And on Monday," I went on, "I am going to sit at my desk and make a plan. I can travel – I have never been to most countries. Or develop some hobbies. Or do some voluntary work – they're always on the lookout for more people. Or write something – everyone has a novel in them, they say. And if all else fails I could always try to get another job. There's no retirement age now, and I'm only fifty-eight. I still have contacts and I have skills. You see – I have given this some thought."

"Oh, Dad!" was all my daughter replied by way of encouragement.

"Or," my heart sped up a little as I said it, "I could spend more time with my grandchildren. That would be great."

"Right." Lisa sounded unenthusiastic, but then she seemed to change her mind. "No," she continued, "that would be good. Let me talk to Neil and get back to you."

"Whenever you like."

"Best not when Mum's around."

"We're grown-ups, but yeah, probably better."

"I'll send you some new photos."

"Please do."

"Bye."

"Love you."

I woke up at the usual time this morning. I tried to get back to sleep but didn't succeed and eventually got up around eight. Everything takes longer when you don't have a deadline, so it was almost ten before I sat down at my desk with a cup of coffee, a pad and a pen. I'd spent more time than I intended watching a TV news channel, until it occurred to me that I was watching one of their reports for the second time.

I clicked the pen open then wrote "Lisa visit" and underlined it. That was one thing that did appear to be part of my future plans, something to look forward to.

What else? Travel. I underlined that as well. Where did I want to go? A lot of places, surely? I've been to the US a couple of times and quite a lot of western European countries, though often only to one place in each. When Lisa was growing up, we mostly had Mediterranean beach holidays, which was easier, though doesn't really constitute travelling, does it? Since I've been on my own, I've mostly been having one week away a year, with the same singles' holiday company, more so that I have something to say when people ask me where I've been on holiday than because I actually enjoy it in most instances. The change of scenery seems to do me good, but more noticeably during the first few days after I get back than at the time. I wonder if other people get that. Africa or South America would be completely different, but would I find going there a pleasurable experience? Should I make myself go even if I don't enjoy it, to make myself seem more interesting, particularly to women? It was my lack of adventurous spirit that killed off my relationship with Margaret, which was a shame because I really liked her, and hated being on my own initially after Anne left. Margaret and I went to Egypt, and I just wasn't at ease with the two of us going off track, hiring a car, venturing into local markets where everyone's in your face trying to sell their goods. Margaret, on the other hand, was in her element driving, navigating, bartering, trying any food she was offered. She said I was a package-tour kind of guy, which stung but was probably true, and we split up soon after we got back to the UK. Margaret said there were other issues too, though I think that was the main one. Lisa says she never liked Margaret anyway.

I looked at the website of the singles holiday company I use (I call them NoMates, though that isn't actually their name) and filtered on South America and Africa. Not that many possibilities, though they do have a trip to Machu Picchu and a Kenyan safari. Both over four thousand pounds though. Still, as a retirement treat, I could, couldn't I? I read on. I hate the matey, first-person-plural prose of these things: "then after a hard-day's rhino watching we soak up the rays for a couple of hours before partaking in a cheeky margarita or maybe two and enjoying a well-earned feast under the stars!" The accompanying picture showed a lot of people in their sixties: bald men with paunches and women with identical short iron-grey hair, all wearing sunglasses and raising their drinks to the camera.

I couldn't face it.

I got up and made another cup of coffee. There was a pop music quiz on the radio that kept me away from my desk for twenty minutes.

I sat down again. Travel was still staring at me from the paper. I tapped the pen against my bottom teeth. A thought came to me. Why not just go? Next week, just stick some stuff in a rucksack, take the train to Paris, find somewhere to stay, enjoy the sights, move on when I felt like it, see where I ended up. Yes, the idea really appealed to me! The silver backpacker! It was sort of intrepid as well, wasn't it, only with toilets?

A week today, then. Time to book the train, cancel whatever needed to be cancelled, buy a rucksack, study some maps, work out how I was going to have access to money en route. Time to deal with anything else that occurred to me.

I felt so pleased that I decided to give myself the rest of the day off. I watched some TV and read a book. I checked my emails and messages a few times to see if anyone from work, or anyone else I know in the wider IT market, had contacted me. No one had. Still, I figured my ex-colleagues had only seen me on Friday, and the news would take time to travel outside the company.

Sunil called me in the afternoon, as he had said he would. He's always been a good lad. He didn't have that much time because he was at work, but it was nice to talk to him. He told me he'd been at his second home in Normandy for the weekend. I almost told him about my travel plans but decided in the end not to. I related the story of my sudden departure from work as concisely as I could.

"Well," he said after I had finished, "everything has to come to an end, I guess. It's the end of an era though!"

Curiously I found that wasn't what I wanted to hear. The last thing I wanted for the moment was to go back to work, but I also didn't want people assuming it wasn't even a possibility.

"You don't think Ade was trying to get rid of you, do you?" Sunil mused aloud.

I was about to say that my Lisa asked the same. "No, I don't," I replied. "He's a good lad."

"Then his girlfriend."

"No, I don't think so."

"Fair enough. Listen, I've got to go now, but let's have lunch in a couple of weeks. After the dust has settled."

"Yes, I'd like that," I replied. More settling dust. I decided not to try to make a firm date because I didn't know how long I was going to be away for.

The other piece of excitement for today's diary entry is that I finally met my new neighbour. There seemed to be quite a lot of toing and froing at her flat again today and a few random unexplained sounds – like bumps and swishes – and a raised voice, enough to pique my curiosity without seriously disturbing me. Mid-afternoon I left my flat to go to the station to find out how to cancel my season ticket just as a figure was coming out of the door opposite. She turned as she heard my door open, and I saw that she was a woman in her late thirties, I would say. She was dressed in a running suit but had not put the hood up. She had very long (particularly for a woman of her age) very dark hair pinned back severely into a ponytail. Her face bore the signs of dark make-up having been removed in a hurry. I thought she was naturally good-looking though. She glanced at me neutrally without really acknowledging me. I decided I should introduce myself.

"Hi," I said, holding out my hand, "I'm Alan. From next door. Well, obviously."

There were the beginnings of a smile about her mouth. She took my hand – hers, I noted, was quite small, and the handshake quite limp as if she wasn't quite sure about it.

"Ella," she said. "Pleased to meet you."

"Likewise. Successfully installed in the flat?"

"Pretty much."

"Good. Just you?"

"Sorry?" She looked as embarrassed as I felt. What must she think: some old bloke trying to find out if she was alone!

I tried to ignore it. "Well, great to meet you, Ella. If you need any help or local knowledge..."

"Thanks, I will."

"Enjoy your run."

I opened the fire door for her and watched her disappear down the stairs, putting her hood up as she went.

That had been a bit awkward, I thought, but not unsalvageable. And I would be genuinely happy if she did ask for my assistance. One thing seemed odd to me though: the way her gaze had been surreptitiously darting around as she looked at me, not as though she were eyeing me up (in your dreams, Alan, you're fifty-eight) but as though she were measuring me for something. Perhaps she's in the clothing trade. Little clues to build on.

Monday 23 November

The day arrived! New Adventurous Alan setting off on his European odyssey!

I didn't sleep very well, which was annoying, because with a busy and tiring day ahead what you really need is to feel refreshed before you start. But I am a worrier. And what was worrying me at three a.m. on a Monday morning was...well, a number of things. Had I cancelled everything you need to cancel if you don't know when you're coming back? Had I packed everything I would need? Had I packed anything I wouldn't need? It seemed perfectly possible. Should I leave the heating on? Or the water? How should I make the flat look occupied to deter burglars?

It had been surprisingly difficult to find the right rucksack. I looked at some online, but you couldn't really tell how big they were, so in the end I went to one of those outdoors/ camping shops in an out-of-town shopping centre. They had a big range, but none that struck me as perfect for my needs. What I wanted, I told the intermittently interested salesman, was the biggest one I could comfortably carry. Preferably, I joked, a sort of tardis: bigger on the inside than the outside. He proposed one with a large metal frame that, even empty, was so heavy I almost toppled over backwards when I put it on. I went for a grey and crimson one a couple of sizes smaller, that the salesman advised wouldn't take more than a week's kit. Well, I reasoned, neither could my back, and there must be launderettes in France, or anywhere else I got to, or opportunities to buy cheap clothes.

But it was depressing how little would go into the thing. Even putting in one spare pair of shoes was a struggle. The fact that I was going off at the end of November and would need warm clothes didn't help. Not for the first time I thought that perhaps I should delay my trip till spring. But the train ticket was booked and non-refundable. And, I told myself, that was Old Timid Alan thinking. Seize the day!

I left home at seven, slightly behind schedule, having had second thoughts about turning off the water, because I wasn't sure if it needed to be on for the heating, which I was leaving on at 10C.

It's years since I have been on Eurostar, and in that time they have moved it from Waterloo to St Pancras. I don't know why that is – perhaps the French were upset by Waterloo, though I imagine it would have been cheaper to rename the station than move everything. Luckily, I thought to read the ticket, or my journey wouldn't have got off to a good start.

I found my allocated aisle seat, which somewhat awkwardly turned out to be at a table of four with a French couple and their teenage son. But was this awkward? Maybe over the next two hours and sixteen minutes I would get to know these people. The next problem was my luggage. I didn't want to put it in the containers at the end of the carriage in case it got stolen, but some of it hung over the side of the overhead rack and the French man glared at me, even though I had deliberately positioned the rucksack so that if it did fall off it would hit me. But that seemed too real a prospect, and in the end I did get up and put it in the container, thereafter craning my neck every few minutes to ensure it was still there.

The French family were conversing – arguing if their tone was anything to go by – in French, so I settled down to watch the grey, overcast English countryside through the opposite window. I really enjoy reading, but much to my chagrin there hadn't been room in the rucksack for anything but a small French phrase book, and I had arrived at St Pancras too late to get a newspaper. I put my earphones on and listened to the radio on my phone. The signal went as soon as we entered the tunnel so I listened to one of the ten downloaded albums on the internal memory, quickly realising I was bored with all of them and should have added some fresh ones before I left. With nothing to see, I closed my eyes and tried unsuccessfully to nap. It was quite soothing in the dark of the tunnel, but I was also uncomfortably aware that the closer we came to France the more apprehensive I was becoming.

Someone came through the carriage with a trolley selling snacks and drinks. I hadn't eaten since breakfast, so I bought a cappuccino and a ham and cheese baguette. It was quite difficult to eat it without sharing the crumbs with the rest of the table; in my attempts to avoid that, a lot of them ended up in my lap and then untidily on the floor. As I let the French teenager out to go to the toilet his arm caught my coffee cup and spilt the third that I hadn't yet drunk. His parents apologised in French and I smiled back at them. Fortunately I had enough paper napkins to clear up.

Without warning we were back in daylight and heading at pace through the French countryside. The same grey, overcast skies prevailed as in England, and it occurred to me that the flat landscape wasn't that different either, the most notable differences being the architecture of the farmhouses and the occasional road, where you could see that cars were driving on the right.

We stopped at Lille, which I haven't been to before, but it wasn't possible to form much of an impression of it from the station. I checked my phone to see if it was working and was pleased to see that it had automatically connected to a French network. I was hoping someone I knew would call: "Where are you Alan? Sainsbury's? B&Q?" "Well, funny you should ask – I'm in Lille!" Then we were off at high speed again, and it didn't seem long before we were slowing down once more and pulling into a long platform at the Gare du Nord.

I nodded and smiled at the French family as we stood up to get off, and the mother slightly awkwardly reciprocated. I collected my rucksack, which seemed to have got heavier since

I had taken it off, descended gingerly onto the platform and headed for the concourse.

I was relieved that I had, following much internal debate, decided after all to book a hotel for the first night in advance. My map indicated it was within walking distance.

It was starting to spit with rain as I came out of the station onto a main road. And I was feeling quite thirsty. I decided I should stop and reward myself with a beer! I could see two almost identical cafes with large red awnings projecting over the pavement, sheltering a scattering of metal tables and wickerwork chairs. I chose the nearer of the two. I wanted to go inside for the warmth, but when I looked through the door I saw a couple of young guys in bomber jackets shaking hands with the barman, who appeared to know in advance what they wanted to drink. One other table was occupied by a woman on her own and someone else was playing a fruit machine. I wasn't comfortable as a lone foreigner going into that atmosphere, so I ended up sitting outside. After ten minutes waiting to be served I gave up and went to the other bar, where as luck would have it the waiter was just coming out. I ordered "une bière" from him and smiled enthusiastically when he suggested it should be "grande". He returned with it a couple of minutes later, the glass arranged slightly theatrically on its own on a large silver tray, froth still running down the sides. I paid for it immediately, adding a further tip to the service charge, which I thought the waiter would appreciate. But he seemed more interested to know what I wanted to eat, and when I indicated that I didn't he looked a little put out and went away.

The view wasn't great: there were a lot of grey nineteenth-century buildings with crumbling facades, some covered in graffiti, and one or two tired-looking shops, including a beauty salon with bleached photos of old-fashioned hairstyles in the window, and a tattoo parlour displaying gothic images on a largely blacked out frontage. I tried to relax and drink my beer slowly, but the rain, driven by a strengthening wind, was starting to penetrate under the awning. A stray dog came past then halted just behind me so that I could hear it panting. I tried to drink more quickly, though it wasn't easy as the beer was very gassy and surprisingly heady too. As the alcohol ran into my veins, I began to feel a bit more positive: I told myself I should find my hotel, leave my luggage and strike out into more interesting parts of Paris for the rest of the day.

I drained the glass and strapped on the rucksack again. I was slightly disorientated, so I put the hotel address into Google Maps and followed the instructions. They took me off the main road, down a narrower side street and then down a series of what were really just alleyways, so that I began to worry about having my phone on display and wondered if I would be able to retrace my steps if I needed to. But then the app told me I had reached my destination. I looked to my left and saw an unprepossessing doorway with the hotel name above it and the badges of various hotel guides attached to it, each with its differing star verdict.

I went inside; the entrance vestibule was dark and smelt musty, as though of cigarette smoke ingrained long ago. There was a woman in her sixties, or maybe even older, behind the reception desk, dressed in a black dress and with her hair in a practical bun. She had no English and did not appear to take kindly to anyone who did not speak fluent French. Eventually we established that I was early and that my room would not be ready till later. I completed the forms she proffered in any case and then, remembering a sentence from my phrase book, asked whether it would be possible to "déposer mes bagages". It was, for a fee that I paid, I hoped, without sighing too loudly. That done I asked where the nearest Metro station was. The woman waved her arms in the air. "Partout!" she advised before retreating into the office behind her with my completed paperwork.

If Metro stations really were "everywhere" it seemed to be surprisingly difficult to stumble upon one. After wasting the best part of forty minutes, I eventually resorted to Google Maps again. I was pleased that I had done my homework on the Metro network, what ticket to buy and so on, and soon found myself on a train heading south towards the city centre and suddenly feeling much more chipper. I had never been to Paris before and had a long list of places I wanted to see; if they were unashamedly touristy, who was to know or judge me? The Eiffel Tower, of course, the Louvre and the Tuileries, the Arc de Triomphe and Champs Elysees, Montmartre, the Latin Quarter, the Jardin du Luxembourg, the Pompidou Centre. I also wanted to take a boat down the Seine. There were a couple of other things I was less sure about: whether Notre Dame had yet reopened to the public after the fire, and whether I wanted to go to Pere Lachaise: however eminent the people buried there, I really don't like visiting cemeteries and never have.

"Fermé le lundi". I hadn't done my homework as thoroughly as I had thought, and now discovered that all the main attractions were closed on a Monday. I tried not to feel too disappointed: I told myself they wouldn't be closed tomorrow, or the next day, and I was completely the master of my own time – this wasn't just a brief interlude before returning to the office.

In which case I could have a nice afternoon just getting my bearings. I got off at Etoile and walked down the Champs Elysees. I took some photos, including my first ever selfie, in front of the Arc de Triomphe. I thought it would be nice to send it to Lisa there and then, but there was a problem with the signal.

It was still disappointingly blustery, but you could get something of the atmosphere of the city just by visiting the shops, without having to buy anything. In one department store I went into the cafe and treated myself to a large coffee and a generous slice of 'tarte aux pommes'. It was quite exciting to hear French spoken all around me and to note the little cultural differences between us and our nearest neighbour: the effortless style of some of the women; expressive facial and hand gestures; maybe also a general sense of impatient activity.

Soon there wasn't much of the afternoon left. Almost by accident I found myself close to the Seine. I saw a small group of people walking down a narrow gangplank towards what was described as a "Bateau Mouche". My phone translated this unhelpfully as "fly boat" but it was fairly obviously a tourist river craft. On an impulse I joined the queue, but when I got to the front the unshaven young man watching people board shook his head dismissively, pointed to a kiosk on dry land and tapped at his watch to indicate that I would need to hurry. At the kiosk the woman selling the tickets asked me twice to confirm that I only wanted one ticket, which was embarrassing, but I managed to make it back to the boat in time, just as they were beginning to ease the knot on the mooring rope.

The trip didn't seem to last very long. It was the last trip of the day, so maybe the crew wanted to get home. It was also starting to get dark. There was a well-worn tape that was giving information about the sights to be seen to left and right in several languages. I found that I wasn't paying much attention to it. There was an Arab couple with their two young girls sitting on the bench opposite me. The younger girl stared at me; I smiled back, but when that elicited no reaction I looked away, turning to face the front window. The mother seemed to be eyeing me curiously as well now. Was it that strange that I was on a tourist boat on my own? Perhaps to her it was.

I was almost relieved when the boat docked. The father of the family motioned to me to leave before them, and I nodded in acknowledgement and obliged. The unshaven young man was staring skywards as I exited the boat mumbling my thanks.

It was now six o'clock. What to do next? There was no longer any natural light, though like all great cities Paris had started to illuminate itself, which gave it a certain allure and cheered me up. I hadn't seen any good restaurants in the vicinity of the hotel, so I reasoned it would be best to eat now and then make my way back. My guidebook suggested the Latin Quarter for good food, but if it was as cool and trendy as the book implied, I imagined it would be full of young people and I would stick out like a sore thumb. Perhaps another night, as I got to know the city better. So I headed back to the Champs Elysees then branched off into the adjoining side streets that I hoped would be less busy and less expensive.

In this area there seemed to be two types of restaurant: those that were completely mobbed, and had queues, and those that were completely empty. Some of the desperate proprietors of the latter called ingratiatingly to me and tried to entice me in, but I couldn't cope with the idea of having a whole restaurant to myself. I also couldn't bring myself to join one of the noisy queues because I didn't think they would want me taking up a table on my own when they had more lucrative groups waiting behind me. Suppose they flatly refused to seat me? From what I had heard of Paris, and seen since my arrival, I didn't think that was at all impossible.

I walked round for over an hour, trying to find the Goldilocks restaurant that would be just right, but failed to find it. The busy places got busier and even some of the empty ones started to fill up. I felt cold, dispirited and hungry. I ended up back on the Champs Elysees where I went into a fast-food restaurant and bought a burger with large fries and a cola. There were no free tables so I had to eat it standing up, having found a small perch next to the sauces, serviettes and stirrers. I felt self-conscious and tried to eat too quickly, which almost caused me to choke, and gave me indigestion for the remainder of the evening.

I went for a slow walk afterwards because I didn't want to get back to the hotel too early. The shops were open and bustling, night life getting into its stride, landmarks strikingly lit up. I could see the appeal, but didn't feel part of it on my own.

I was back at the hotel before nine. I collected my rucksack and the key to my room from the same dour woman I had met earlier. The room was small and dimly lit, with the smell of a chemical that was trying to mask the smell of something else. The view out of the window was of a fully enclosed brick and concrete courtyard.

I tried to watch television but there were no English channels, and only three in total with both sound and a reliable picture. I wished I had found room in my rucksack for a book to read. For the first time in my life I downloaded one onto my phone, a whodunnit that I thought would be easier to read in an unfamiliar format than the more serious stuff I usually go for. I also got an absurdly overpriced beer out of the mini-bar. The book proved to be more difficult to understand than I had hoped, mainly because I couldn't flick back a few pages as I would normally do to pick up some aspect of the plot that I had missed. The small screen started to give me a headache as well, and I was actually relieved when I started to feel drowsy around ten o'clock. I told myself that having had a long and tiring day it was no shame to have an early night, and gratefully turned the light out.

Tuesday 24 November

I am by nature a positive and optimistic person, as well as a believer in the restorative powers of a good night's sleep. I woke up this morning feeling surprisingly refreshed and, once the confusion of finding myself in unfamiliar surroundings had dissipated, much more upbeat. The first day of any such voyage was bound to be a little bumpy, I told myself, and it was just a matter of adjustment and ensuring that Intrepid Alan always got the better of Timid Alan.

I showered, once I had finally found a compromise between the flow and temperature controls that allowed me to get reasonably wet without scalding myself, then headed down for breakfast. It was clear that there were far fewer tables in the restaurant than rooms in the hotel, and a small queue had formed, which was not moving very quickly. But, I told myself, I had all day. I had all year. And next year!

It was finally my turn, and I was shown to a table for two. I asked for coffee and orange juice and was instructed to go to the buffet, which was set out on the other side of the room, atop two or three tables covered with white tablecloths. When I returned a couple of minutes later with some fruit and a couple of croissants, I was pleased to see that my drinks had arrived. More unexpectedly, though, there was a young man with a long ginger beard sitting in the seat opposite me, his body turned at ninety degrees in order that he could conduct a conversation in what sounded like Dutch with a couple sitting at the next table. I noted that they were all wearing shorts, which seemed odd at the end of November, but then some young people don't seem to feel the cold. I didn't feel particularly comfortable eating in the presence of the young man, whose voice was getting louder as his gestures became more elaborate, and I thought that if that had been me I would have asked first before sitting down. But then I told myself that people are different, and there was no harm done.

I wished the Dutch group a good day as I left the table; the young woman gave me a small smile but the young men just looked surprised. I went to reception to ask if it would be possible to stay another night. The same woman as before – didn't she ever have any time off? – shook her head gravely and pointed to a sign reading "Complet". With low expectations I asked if she could recommend anywhere else. She couldn't. How about my luggage – could she store that for me temporarily, for a fee obviously? That wasn't possible either. "La gare," she said: I should use the station's left luggage facility.

I went back to my room and quickly put everything into my rucksack, trying to find a system to keep dirty clothes away from clean. I then went back down to reception again, checked out and had no difficulty ignoring the receptionist's none-too-subtle attempts to direct my gaze to the tips plate standing ready, and empty, on the counter.

It was a blustery day again, overcast but dry for the moment. My rucksack felt as though it had got heavier since yesterday, so I was relieved on entering the Gare du Nord to find that the left-luggage office was open, though there was a queue. When I reached the front there was something about the size, shape or weight of my rucksack that seemed to be inspiring a debate between the two attendants as to its admissibility; but eventually the one promoting its acceptance won the day, much to my relief, and the other conceded with a large shrug.

I got back on the Metro and decided to head for the Eiffel Tower.

An hour later, somewhat breathless but feeling pleased with myself nonetheless, I found myself on a viewing platform with a commanding view of the city of Paris. It was a little misty, but I thought that would look good in photos, and I managed to take a few that weren't too bad in the circumstances: it was a bit hit-and-miss as I had to hold my phone up in the air to prevent the crowd of jostling schoolchildren in front of me getting into the shot. I also took my second ever selfie, though if you look at it you can't really tell that I'm at the top of the Eiffel Tower as my looming face dominates almost the entire frame. I stayed on the platform until I had had a good look over the city in all directions, but then spent almost as much time in the gift shop, where I bought a couple of postcards - wondering whether to send them or keep them - and a bookmark.

Back at ground level I was surprised to find that it was almost lunchtime. I was starting to feel hungry and had been thirsty for some time. Once again there were a large number of cafés, brasseries and restaurants to choose from, if choose was the right word, as some had queues and none, as far as I could tell, had a small table free. I enviously watched couples and families eating their food and unhurriedly enjoying their leisure time.

I thought I spied a table for two through the window of one café – it was placed slightly awkwardly next to a pillar but it would do - and went in.

"Monsieur," said a man in a waiter's outfit.

"Bonjour," I replied.

"Combien de personnes?"

I could feel myself blush. "Une personne."

The waiter looked around. "Une? One person?" It sounded even worse in his fractured English. "Non. Désolé."

I hesitantly pointed at the table I had seen.

"Réservé. Bonne journée, monsieur."

As I left I held the door open for a young couple coming in the opposite direction. I deliberately didn't look round in case they were being offered the table I had wanted.

A few minutes later, with no other obvious option, I bought a very pricey hot dog from a small kiosk together with a bottle of Orangina. The sausage tasted as though it had been reheated, but it smelled OK, so I decided I was desperate enough to eat it. I managed to find somewhere to sit on the end of a bench. It afforded no shelter from the wind though, and I ate quickly with a view to being on the move again as soon as I could. I looked at the base of the tower and idly watched the queue of people waiting to get in and the constant trickle of people coming out. No one else seemed to be on their own though.

I hadn't expected getting food to be such a problem. Over the years I'd read several books by solo travellers, and they all seemed either to take eating alone in their stride or immediately to have got talking to people on adjoining tables who invited them to join them or, in some cases, back to their homes. How did you do that? I began to suspect that some of those authors hadn't been travelling alone at all or, if they had, had introduced some fictional encounters to help their narrative along. Or was I being churlish? Maybe it was me.

Anyway, the meal over, I was no longer hungry or thirsty, so my incipient despondency dissolved and my spirits lifted. I decided to get back on the Metro and visit Montmartre.

I hadn't realised until I got there that the Sacré Coeur is at the top of a steep hill. Happily, a funicular railway is provided, so I joined the queue for that. A little boy with the family ahead of me kept pushing against my leg. I made eye contact with the mother and smiled. She gazed back blankly, then seemed to notice that I was on my own, looked at me suspiciously and pulled the boy towards her.

The church was crowded with noisy tourists in a way that seemed, even to a non-believer such as me, to be on the edge of sacrilegious. Well, I thought, I couldn't be too snobbish about it as I was a tourist myself and part of the problem. I'm never very good with churches. I think unless you really know what you're looking at they're all pretty much alike: brown wooden pews, stone floors, pulpits, statues, tombs and carvings. Yes, I'm impressed by the great architectural feats of stonemasonry and the swooping vaulted roofs, the exquisite stained glass made with techniques lost to man, but I do think that - unless you read up on them and become a real expert on the detail - if you've seen one you've seen the lot. A bit like firework displays. So Alan is a bit of a philistine when it comes to churches. And they smell of death.

I was relieved to be back in the fresh air. I watched the street entertainers in the Place du Tertre and put some coins in the proffered hats. I saw some people posing for silhouette artists, who skilfully and rapidly cut out their profiles from black paper. The sitters all looked worried for some reason. I wasn't tempted to give it a go.

For the first time in the day the sun seemed to be trying to break through between the clouds. I bought an ice cream and sat down on a wall to eat it. A bedraggled looking man with what appeared to be a fairly recent cut on his forehead approached and asked me for money. I gave him a small amount, much to the disapproval of some of the other people around me, who all refused. I don't think I was being charitable if I am honest, just doing what I thought was necessary to get rid of someone who was too close to my face and my food. Is that bad of me?

I realised that I needed to think seriously about hotels and took my phone out. I was surprised, and disappointed, to see how few messages there were, and that those I had received were mostly forwarded amusing videos (none of which seemed worth looking at) rather than personal communications. Well, perhaps no news was good news.

I searched for hotels in Paris, but that produced an impossibly large number of results. I tried narrowing it to hotels near the Gare du Nord, as I remembered that I needed to go back in that direction to collect my rucksack. Again, a large number of results, but two stood out as particularly promising, with a large number of reviews and average scores of more than four stars.

I called them both: the first did not answer, and at the second the receptionist either couldn't hear me or couldn't understand me and rang off.

I decided it would be easier to go there in person. I walked down the steep slope rather than queue for the funicular again, and was surprised how much pressure that put on my knees. Obviously the old body isn't what it was. I headed once more for the Metro.

At the end of my journey I quickly found one of the hotels, but before I had even finished my carefully rehearsed French sentence the receptionist had told me that they were full. The second one was trickier to locate and required a little bit of phone map technology. Like so much of backstreet Paris, it looked from the outside as though it had been built about a hundred and fifty years ago and not really touched since. Despite being increasingly desperate for accommodation, I found myself in two minds as to whether I wanted there to be any free rooms here or not. I wondered why the online reviewers had apparently been so enthusiastic. Eventually I went inside.

There were three groups of people ahead of me at reception and one person attending to them: a woman about ten years younger than me wearing a cabin-crew-like uniform with a blue jacket, cravat and name badge on her lapel. Something either wasn't to her satisfaction or was displeasing the customer, a man in a white linen suit, who stood at the front of the queue with two small children that his wife was struggling to restrain. A printed form was being pored over and the receptionist and the man in the suit were pointing at different parts of it. Five minutes went by as the conversation became more animated. The receptionist appeared to be completely unaware of the growing line of people; I wondered if that was part of the training. Now she was making a phone call. Another five minutes went by. I looked round and saw a further three groups of people behind me, becoming just as restive as those in front. Someone called out something loudly in French; I don't speak the language, but it was fairly obvious it was something along the lines of "Hurry up!" or "People are waiting!" Someone else applauded.

I felt thoroughly miserable. The wall clock showed six o'clock and my wristwatch confirmed it. I scanned the room to make sure there wasn't a sign saying "Complet", which would mean that I was definitely wasting my time, but I couldn't see one. Now someone else had appeared behind reception, a man in a short-sleeved white shirt, who was holding up the printed form and pointing at one of the boxes on it with a ballpoint pen. The customer was jabbing at the same box with his forefinger. One of the children broke free and ran into the legs of the person behind. A second argument seemed to be about to break out.

Ten past six. I was beginning to feel very uncomfortable. I could be here another half an hour at least, and when I thought about it, I didn't want to be here at all.

I left the queue and headed towards the door, trying and failing to make eye contact with the reception staff as I did so. I heard some derisive whistling as the door closed behind me, but surmised it wasn't aimed in my direction.

I told myself all wasn't lost: I would collect my rucksack from the station and see if there was an accommodation office there that could help me. But then I really would have to be decisive: it was late November, not the time of year to risk being on the streets all night, certainly not at my age.

I rapidly reached the station and, to my relief, retrieved my rucksack without difficulty. But if there was an accommodation office, I failed to find it. Or maybe didn't look as hard as I should have. Almost as though my legs had a mind of their own, I found myself in the - thankfully rapid-moving - queue at the ticket office. When I reached the front, I heard myself ask when the next available ticket for Eurostar to London was and felt my heart rate increase as I awaited the answer. The laconic clerk said eight o'clock, but only first class, full fare. Otherwise, tomorrow. I took the first-class fare without even asking how much it was. It was a lot. But I told myself money wasn't a problem for me, not in the short term at least.

There wasn't much time before the train departed. I found an empty stool at a bar and perched on that while I drank the large draught beer that I had ordered. I felt a mixture of emotions: relief, definitely, but also embarrassment, bordering on shame, that I was 'giving in' so soon. But I looked around me in the almost full bar and couldn't see anyone else on their own. That, I thought, was my real problem: our society is built round families, or couples or groups of friends and just doesn't cater for singles. So I had learnt a valuable lesson: either I could change society – unlikely – or when I resumed my travels, and I was determined that I should, it would need to be with a companion.

I cheered up considerably on the train. First class was very plush and comfortable and made me feel special, which certainly helped, but also my natural state is one of optimism. It seemed to me that I hadn't lost anything: I had had a short break and seen Paris for the first time, and as for the tail-between-my-legs aspect of the thing, well, no one knew I had gone, so consequently no one knew I was coming back early. If I'd stuck it out and posted upbeat updates via my phone, I'd just have been creating a delusional image of having a great time, and where would that get me? Perhaps one or two people might have found me, temporarily, more interesting. But at my age, I reasoned to myself, it probably really is later than I think, so I should enjoy myself, whether that looks good to other people or it doesn't. Perhaps I'll make that my motto.

It's not always easy, though.

The tube was a bit of a let-down after first class on Eurostar, but it was functioning adequately enough, and I was home around midnight.

I noticed that my new neighbour's hall light was on as I came up the stairs and crossed the landing. I was half relieved (because I was tired) and half disappointed (because I would have welcomed a friendly conversation) not to run into her. I thought in the coming days I should make a positive effort to get to know her.

The flat felt as though I had been away much longer than I had. The smell of myself, my food, my toiletries, had dissipated. There was the pile of mail that, inexplicably, is always much greater when you go away. I quickly turned the heating on.

Unpacking could wait till tomorrow. I made myself a cup of tea and spent a few minutes in front of the TV catching up on the news, none of which was very interesting. Someone's resignation was being demanded, and some other hapless politician was being pressed to give a one-hundred-percent, cast-iron guarantee about something, as if that is ever the way the real world works.

I finished my tea and went to bed.

Thursday 26 November

I thought this was going to be one of those nothing days that I don't bother recording in my diary, but what follows suggests it turned out rather differently.

I allowed myself a lazy day yesterday after my travels the previous two days, though in fact by the end of it I was getting quite bored, and was pleased when it was time to go to bed.

The plan for today was to research "Plan B", being voluntary work I might like to do (travelling having been "Plan A"). I had sat down at the computer to start doing that at around ten o'clock. I was going to do a general search for voluntary work, then go from there to the websites of individual charities and organisations and make contact with any that took my fancy. Then, I thought, assuming that the weather stayed OK, I would go to the local shops and see if any of the charities there, which seem to be occupying an increasing proportion of the units, needed any assistance. The added benefit of which would be exercise and fresh air.

My online search was not proving to be as fruitful as I hoped. It turned out that a lot of charities were quite choosy about who they wanted, and apparently could afford to be: just because you were willing to work for them, even for nothing, didn't apparently mean that they would have you. As with a paid job, you had to have skills that were useful to them. I didn't think I would be much good with children. Possibly the elderly or people with physical or mental health problems of various types, but it appeared (rightly, when I thought about it) that you were expected to have certain qualifications or to undertake extensive training, and probably exams, before they would let you loose in those areas. Fund-raising? It turned out that was a specialist skill too, unless you just wanted to organise a coffee morning (who with?) or stand outside the supermarket rattling a tin (fair play to those who do, but I had been hoping for better things).

I decided to bring forward my visit to the high street: I wanted to get out of the flat, and the web would still be there in the evening when the shops would be shut. I put on my jacket and walked out into the hallway, closing the door behind me. Someone was visiting Ella again (I had heard them come up the stairs) and there was the same unaccountable swishing and thudding sound coming from her flat accompanied by what sounded like a muffled male voice. One day, I thought, I would ask her what that was all about. Just as I got to the top of the stairs, though, there was a very different sound: a high-pitched woman's shriek, followed by something being dropped. Then I could hear both voices, raised but not arguing. Then a door closing. Then nothing.

Being on your own can make you nosier, I'm afraid. I quietly let myself back into my flat but stood to one side of the door, leaving it ajar so that I could see Ella's door, but she hopefully would not see me. Nothing happened for what seemed like an age. Then the door opposite opened and a plump, bearded man emerged, apparently letting himself out and putting on a beige bomber jacket as he went.

"Thanks for nothing!" I heard Ella call out sarcastically after him, but her voice sounded a bit hoarse, as people sometimes do when they have hurt themselves. I heard the man disappear at speed down the stairs.

What to do? How to help without giving away my eavesdropping? I waited ten minutes (which seemed like an hour) then left the flat again, got momentarily caught in two minds and finally crossed the hallway and slightly timidly pressed the doorbell. Nothing happened at all for a while, then finally I heard footsteps. The door opened and Ella's face appeared around it. "I've just messaged you to canc..," she began in the same hoarse voice I had heard previously, before catching sight of me and stopping. "Oh, hello."

"Sorry to disturb you," I said. "I just wondered if you were OK – I thought you might have hurt yourself."

There was a lot of smudged black mascara under her eyes, which suggested to me that she had been crying. She seemed reluctant for me to see the rest of her, though I could see some sort of, presumably fashionable, leather collar around her neck and noted that she seemed oddly to have gained a few inches in height.

"It's nothing – well, I think I've hurt my arm, right at the top here." She clasped the top of her right arm with her left hand and winced as she did so.

"Oh dear," I replied sympathetically. "How did you – never mind. Do you want to go to A&E? I'm very happy to take you."

"Thanks, but I'm sure it'll be fine. I just need to put some ice on it for a few minutes, I think."

"Have you got some?"

"Must have. In the freezer." She attempted a weak smile.

"Well, if you change your mind. I'm just across the way. I'm just going out for an hour or so, but any time after that."

"Thanks. I appreciate it."

I smiled at her as the door closed.

I realised as I walked down the high street that although I always see the charity shops, I rarely actually go into them. I don't very often buy clothes, but when I do I am fortunate enough to be able to buy them new. My books are new too: I like the smell of bookshops and of new books. One of the little luxuries I allowed myself when I was working and earning reasonable money. Beyond that I don't collect anything in particular, and I'm not one of life's natural browsers.

I tried a few different shops. It turned out they weren't overjoyed at my offer of assistance, but more positively they weren't ruling it out either. I was given forms to fill in and referred to managers or, if they were not available, told that they would call me to discuss. To my surprise, a couple of places told me that they had a waiting list, but I wanted to sound positive and said if that was the case I was happy to be on it.

One manager, a very short woman who I guessed was about five years younger than me, said she was happy to interview me there and then, and led me to a kitchen area at the back of the shop. I realised quite soon that I should have given this some thought and prepared some answers in advance: not having been interviewed for thirty-nine years (and even then the questions were no more taxing than "Are you prepared to work for this little?" and "When can you start?") I was a little rusty.

The manager said nothing at all for a couple of minutes while she read through the forms I had hastily completed. She then asked me to describe my motives for applying for a job in this shop. I said I had recently left full-time employment after thirty-nine years and was now looking to do something useful in the community. She asked me to go on. I said that I liked working with people, which I thought would be good for shop work, and that I had an organised mind, which I imagined would be good for inventory and accounts and that sort of thing.

"You wouldn't be doing any of that," she told me bluntly and I had the impression I had inadvertently trodden on her toes. I nodded compliantly.

"This charity is an equal opportunities employer, and that is very important to this us," she continued. She noted that I had not listed any disabilities on my form. "What about mental health?" she enquired. "Have you ever sought help for that?"

I wasn't sure what the right answer was. "No," I said, which was at least true.

"Would you?" she asked me challengingly. She could see that I wasn't following. "Would you seek help for mental health issues, if you needed to?"

I thought about it. "Yes, I would," I replied, which I imagined was the only acceptable answer.

"What about family?"

I told her.

"That's fine." The manager appeared to be ticking something on the form. "More generally, are you a supporter of equal opportunities, Alan? It's particularly important for this charity because all the money we raise goes overseas, and we sometimes find with older volunteers such as yourself that after a short period they start questioning that and asking why we don't divert some of the money to areas of need in the UK."

I said I was happy to leave policy to whoever made policy.

"This charity," the manager went on, reading from a piece of paper on her desk, "does not tolerate any discrimination for reasons of race, ethnicity, gender, sexual orientation, disability or creed. Are you OK with that?"

I said I definitely was, though I drew the line at gingers.

It was obviously too early to make a joke. The manager fixed me with a cold stare and said that these were serious matters and older people had to understand that they were. I explained that I was making a joke at my own expense, as I used to be ginger, though supposed you couldn't really tell any more. To recover the position, I volunteered the fact that I was a proud and active opponent of the BNP in the eighties but she didn't seem impressed, or maybe didn't hear.

In a matter-of-fact way the manager thanked me for my time, then asked me to sign two forms: one agreeing to a criminal records check, and the other to the charity contacting my former employer. She noticed my hesitation with the latter. "Problem?" she asked.

I said there wasn't, in a way that I hoped implied that I was surprised by the question. I didn't think the company would actually refuse me a reference: if I knew how they worked, they would just supply a bland statement that I used to work there and hadn't stolen the toilet rolls. If they still remembered who I was.

The manager showed me out and gave me a limp handshake as I left the shop. I looked over my shoulder as I passed through the door to make sure she wasn't throwing my paperwork in the bin, and was relieved to see that she wasn't.

I felt a bit subdued on the way home. I wasn't sure that I wanted a job in that shop even if they offered it to me, though I supposed I would take it temporarily. And, I reminded myself, there were plenty of other opportunities.

To my discredit, I have to admit that I had completely forgotten about Ella and was therefore surprised to see her come out of her flat as soon as I started to cross the landing. She looked quite dishevelled: she was wearing an old pair of jeans and trainers and a black top that was riding up around her right shoulder. She was awkwardly holding a grey fleece in her left hand while simultaneously rubbing her upper right arm. Her hair looked as though she hadn't bothered to brush it, or hadn't been able to.

"Could I take you up on your kind offer?" she said surprisingly diffidently.

I said of course, and that I just needed to drop off the forms I was carrying and get my car keys. When I came out again, I suggested she probably should put her coat on as it is a bit of a hike to the garage where I keep my car. She said she didn't think she could: that was part of the problem. I offered to help and took the fleece from her but it took a couple of minutes of trial and error to get her into it. It helped a bit that she had once more lost the height she had gained when I had seen her earlier in the day. Initially I pursued her from behind like a matador with a cape, but that failed because she simply couldn't get her right arm into the correct position. Then I tried one arm at a time, but that ended with a passable Quasimodo impersonation but no nearer to getting the coat on. Finally we arrived at the successful combination, which involved putting the bad arm in first, then the other, then hoisting the whole thing over her shoulders in one move. As she used her good arm to try to free her trapped hair she seemed to become aware of the collar around her neck. She looked slightly embarrassed as she asked me if I could remove it, but I said it was all part of the service. She held her hair out of the way as I undid two or three small straps, below which there was just a Velcro pad that gave way easily. Ella eyed me curiously as I brandished the collar in the air, then closed her door before I could suggest I place the item inside her flat, so I ended up carrying it down to the car.

Ella understandably wasn't feeling very talkative as we headed round the back of the block of flats towards the garage: she mainly talked about the pain in her shoulder though didn't seem to hear my questions as to whether she knew what had caused it. I was hoping no one had parked in front of my garage as that seems increasingly to be a thing: hardly anyone bothers to put their cars away any more, even though the lease is entirely clear on the point.

I like to surprise people by opening my garage door with a flourish because, although apparently people expect Alan Brierley to have a Ford Focus (or, apparently, "something like a Morris Minor"), what he actually has is a smart red 1989 Maserati Biturbo Spyder. Ella looked positively crestfallen to see it, which I attributed to an ignorance of cars, and to the pain which was possibly clouding her judgment.

A little to my relief, it fired up first time and I couldn't resist giving it a little blip to hear the V6, even though Ella was waiting patiently to get into it. It is quite low, and as she couldn't steady herself with her right arm I got out and did my best to help her into the passenger seat.

The traffic wasn't too bad, which was also good as the Maser doesn't like standing still very long, and we soon arrived at the hospital. As the A&E sign came into view Ella thanked me for my help. It hadn't occurred to me she was just expecting me to drop her off, so I said I was quite happy to wait with her, unless she was intending to call someone else to come down and keep her company. That way, I said, she wouldn't need a taxi home. She didn't reply, so I assumed I had convinced her.

They don't let you park outside the entrance to A&E though, for obvious reasons, so I suggested she could be getting booked in and making progress up the queue while I went and found the car park. I helped Ella out of the car and took no notice of someone in a uniform who was shouting about not stopping there. The way I saw it, I wasn't obstructing anything, and sometimes you just have to ignore people, don't you?

The car park was multi-storey, newly built since I last visited the hospital. I drove round and round trying to find a space and eventually located one on the top, open-air deck, though a car to one side was too close to the line and I struggled to get out of the driver's door. I was almost admitted to the cardiac ward when I saw the prices for parking, which became ever more penal the longer you stayed. The arguments on this are well rehearsed. I won't add to them.

Suffice to say, though, that when I entered A&E I was hoping that miraculously the ward would be experiencing a freak lull that would mean an almost instantaneous turnaround: less than thirty minutes parking was absolutely free.

"Five hours," sighed Ella in answer to an unasked question as she caught sight of me. She had found a seat but there were no others free in the vicinity, so I stood awkwardly in front of her, wondering if the woman sitting opposite minded that she now had a view of my backside.

"That's bad, isn't it?" I offered.

Ella tried to shrug, winced and then held her shoulder. "Low priority," she explained. "It's not life-threatening, is it?"

Thinking, I have to say, mostly of the cost of parking I wondered aloud if we could go home and come back nearer the time, but Ella said it didn't work like that: five hours was an estimate, and if you missed your slot you were buggered.

I again declined her kind offer to leave her to it and suggested I should go and get us some drinks. I came back with two small plastic cups of brown: I can't remember now if it was tea or coffee and don't think it was obvious even then. Serendipitously the seat next to Ella was now free, and I gladly took it. I made smiling eye contact with the man the other side in the hope that he would realise that by sitting diagonally he was preventing me putting both feet comfortably in front of me, but it didn't have the desired effect.

Ella had taken up mindreading. "Excuse me," she said, leaning across me while holding her bad arm, "would you mind please giving my friend a little more room?" The man didn't look happy about it, but something about Ella and her expression clearly convinced him that it would be better to comply. He moved and I thanked both of them, berating myself for not having made the request myself. I was pleased that Ella had referred to me as her 'friend', even though I knew it was just shorthand.

The four hours and thirteen minutes before Ella was called did not pass anything like as slowly as I had feared. Conversation seemed to flow easily, though I did worry at one point that I was doing most of the talking. I told her about leaving my job (though not the exact circumstances which I thought could wait until I knew her better), some of my plans and that I had just come back from Paris, though not that I had cut short what was originally intended to be a much longer trip. I told her a bit about Lisa and the kids as well, and probably showed her a picture at one point. In return she told me that she was originally from Yorkshire and still had family there. She didn't seem all that keen to talk about work, though I gathered she was self-employed and her business had something to do with the internet. I asked her periodically if she was in pain and she always said she wasn't unless she forgot and inadvertently moved the affected shoulder. She asked me why I was smiling, which must have seemed insensitive of me, so I said I didn't realise I was. I had actually been reminded of an old Tommy Cooper joke, but I didn't explain that because I suspected Ella was too young to remember Tommy Cooper, and also that the joke wasn't funny if anyone else told it.

I went to the toilet after about three hours and when I came back Ella had inserted a pair of wireless earbuds and was listening to some music. It sounded like rap, which for some reason surprised me. So for the next couple of hours, until Ella came back from being diagnosed and treated, I was alone with my thoughts, with only the comings and goings of other patients, various posters and a clock on the wall for entertainment. A couple of real emergencies came through on trolleys, booked in by paramedics, and everyone turned to see; conversation in the room descended to a murmur. I looked at the posters hoping to see some inspiration for NHS voluntary work possibilities. I couldn't leave my seat without losing it, and wasn't close enough to make out any phone numbers, but resolved to do some research online. I consulted the clock increasingly frequently as the four-hour parking mark loomed, the threshold beyond which you become a public enemy whose financial resources should largely be confiscated, and then relaxed when it was past and there was nothing further I could do about it.

"Rotator cuff," said Ella in answer to another unasked question as she emerged from somewhere-or-other back into the waiting room. Definite hint of Yorkshire in 'cuff' I thought but didn't say.

"What is?" I asked uncomprehendingly.

Something about my reaction seemed to amuse Ella. She smiled. "The muscle at the top of the arm."

"Right."

"It's called the rotator cuff."

"Oh. I didn't know that."

"Obviously. Well, you do now. And mine is either strained or torn. They can't tell which without a scan, which isn't available right here and now."

"So?"

"So, they've given me this high-tech sling and some physiotherapy exercises to do. And if that doesn't work, I ring up and book a scan."

"Sounds a bit second-rate," I said, thinking aloud. "Shouldn't they do the scan anyway?"

"Welcome to England and an underfunded NHS," Ella said ruefully.

A couple of waiting patients and a passing nurse heard and nodded. That's one thing we agree on, I thought.

It was late and neither of us had eaten so we ended up in a pub on the way home with a meal of scampi and chips, which Ella had selected as the easiest thing to eat with one hand. I noticed a couple of things about her: firstly that men looked at her (those in couples furtively and the remainder more blatantly) and that although she was approaching middle age – though only approximately two thirds of my own age – there was undoubtedly something sexy, if you could still use that word, or sexual about her, even though she wasn't necessarily classically beautiful. Second, that she was fully aware of the first point and a bit standoffish because of it, at least to any man such as myself that she didn't find attractive and didn't want to give the wrong idea to. While we ate she expressed her gratitude for my assistance today, and was perfectly polite, but more than once I noticed that she was looking over my shoulder as I was talking to her. Well, it appears you've become an old bore, Brierley. Hopefully there is still time to do something about that.

Back at the flat I helped Ella her out of her jacket by reversing the procedure by which I had initially got her into it. I did wonder how she was going to get out of the rest of her clothes, but felt it would be entirely wrong to offer my services, however innocently and sincerely. She thanked me again and laid her good hand gently on my arm as she did so. I was surprised and a little embarrassed to find that my sense of touch had become so starved that I really appreciated that.

It took me a long time to become sleepy, so I watched a lot of low-quality TV before going to bed. It hadn't been a bad day, really. I might have found some voluntary work to do, or at least gained some useful interview experience. And, although of course I didn't wish Ella's accident on her, and hoped her recovery would be swift, I also hoped that I might have gained a new, and interesting friend.

Monday 30 November

Offered my second ever job!

I was surprised this morning to receive a call from the lady who had interviewed me in the charity shop. It was just after nine o'clock and woke me up. I hoped that wasn't obvious in my voice. I quickly steeled myself for disappointment because, well, I suppose you get more disappointments in life than triumphs, don't you? And it's as well to be prepared. But it turned out it was good news. Well, sort of. They couldn't offer me a permanent position, at least not yet, but they did need some extra assistance with the Christmas rush. Days here and there. Would I be prepared to do that, starting tomorrow?

I said I would. I was surprised at how keen I sounded. The lady said that in that case she would see me tomorrow at eight fifteen, some preliminaries being necessary before the shop opened at nine thirty. I started to ask what I should bring with me, but she had rung off.

I supposed it should have occurred to me that they would need extra assistance at Christmas time, though it had never come up at my interview, but with all the changes to my life in recent times the fact that the festive season was approaching had pretty much passed me by.

I had a leisurely breakfast to celebrate. I realised that I didn't even know what they would be paying me – if they would be paying me – but decided it didn't matter. The important thing, I was realising rapidly, was filling your days. Paris wouldn't occur every week, and not every day would have the excitement – wrong word – of a trip to A&E. The rest of the time you needed some structure and variety in a day and some interaction with other people. Or you could become a potterer, or watcher of daytime TV, or daytime sleeper, or drinker... I shuddered.

Looking in the shaving mirror I realised I needed a haircut. That would be my task for the morning. I would have to find a new barber, as for years I have been going to a place close to work, having a nice chat with young Caroline while getting pretty much the same cut every time. Would she notice I wasn't coming anymore? She would have hundreds of clients, so it was unlikely, I thought.

Coming out of the flat I caught sight of Ella's door. I hadn't seen or heard from her since the hospital trip and hadn't wanted to disturb her unnecessarily. I had heard her door open and close over the weekend and footsteps on the stairs, so assumed she was OK and out and about. After four days, though, I didn't think it would do any harm to enquire, so I wrote a note saying I hoped she was OK and to let me know if she needed anything. I vacillated over whether to add my mobile number, and eventually did. I posted the note through the door quietly on my way out.

It was more difficult to find a local barber than I had thought. There were several in the high street but quite a few looked off-puttingly trendy from outside. I didn't suppose they would actually refuse to serve me, but I could imagine the glances the staff would exchange between themselves, the metrosexual young men and spiky young women, as they decided who would get the short straw. At the other end of the spectrum was a place prominently advertising OAP discounts, with one such old chap already in the chair and two others, one with a comb-over and the other with what appeared to be a natural tonsure, patiently waiting their turn while flicking through magazines. A large middle-aged woman was doing the cutting. It reminded me too much of the places my mother used to insist on taking me to as a child: no-nonsense haircuts, odd-smelling hair oil and something for the weekend, sir?

After a quick stop for a coffee and cake, I finally found a place that looked OK. The girl on reception said it was better to book usually, and gave me a card, but there was a slot available if I didn't mind waiting a few minutes. I agreed without admitting that I actually had all day.

The woman who cut my hair was friendly enough. She was probably about Lisa's age. She seemed a little put out that I had washed my hair that morning, saying it was easier to cut it just after it had been washed, and insisted on using scissors around the sides where Caroline always uses clippers, but the result, I thought, looked good enough. They charged me for a cup of coffee I had declined, but I thought perhaps that was how it worked and didn't say anything.

I had a slow lunch watching the TV news and started to think about what I would require for the next day. I was surprised at how nervous I felt. It wasn't as though I were a school-leaver, or even needed the job to pay the bills, so I couldn't rationalise it.

I texted Lisa to let her know that I was starting a new job. I left it vague enough that I hoped it would pique her curiosity and that she would call me.

I dug out my passport and driving licence, which I guessed the charity might want for ID. I failed to find my national insurance card, but I know the number, so I just wrote it down on a scrap of paper and put it in my wallet. I found the P45 that I had been given on my last day of work.

I had started to think about what clothes to wear when my phone rang. I expected and hoped that it would be Lisa but it was an unknown number. However, when I decided to answer it, I was almost as pleased to discover that I was talking to Ella.

"Got your note," she said matter-of-factly. "Thanks. How are you?"

"Fine. Just found some part-time work, actually," I blurted out in a desperate attempt to say something interesting. "More to the point," I went on, "how are you getting on?"

"On the mend, I think. Slowly!"

There was a pause in the conversation. I didn't want it to end. I looked up at the clock. "Are you next door now?" I asked. She said she was. "I'm just putting the kettle on," I explained. "I just wondered if you.."

She seemed to think about it for a moment. "OK," she said finally. "Why not? I'm free for an hour or so."

I opened the door, quickly tidied up and then went into the kitchen. A minute or so later I heard Ella say "Hi!", and I told her to make herself comfortable and asked how she liked her tea.

When I came out and put the mugs on the coffee-table Ella smiled at me and brandished a packet of digestives she had brought, which I thought was a nice gesture. She was sitting in the chair I usually use, so I sat on the sofa to one side. She was still wearing the sling on her bad arm. She was also wearing what looked like jodhpurs and a long pair of black boots. Thinking aloud, I almost asked why – I couldn't imagine she was going riding with a torn arm muscle, and getting into those items must have been a struggle with one arm – but, noticing the direction of my gaze, Ella looked embarrassed, so I thought better of it.

"Managing OK, then?" I asked.

Ella reached forward to pick up the mug with her good arm. "Just about," she replied and pointed at the packet of biscuits. I took one and offered the packet to her.

"Able to work?" I asked.

"Mostly, yes..." Ella seemed to be looking at me quizzically.

"Because your business is mostly online," I said, recalling our conversation in A&E.

Ella nodded. "Completely, for the minute."

"Other stuff," I asked. "Shopping, cooking, cleaning?"

"Wonders of modern technology again. Home deliveries. Lots of takeaway pizzas." She smiled. "And I have someone to do my cleaning."

"Still, you have to pay for a cleaner," I offered, for want of anything better to say.

Ella seemed to find that amusing. "Right," she said. "Something like that."

I told her about my new job and Ella said she knew the place and was pleased for me. She said it was amazing what you could pick up at charity shops if you kept an eye out.

I noticed that her phone, which was on the coffee-table, kept buzzing. I would have preferred it if she had put it on silent, but to be fair to her she made no attempt to look at it. She left after about forty-five minutes and was already making a call as she crossed the landing. I couldn't hear what she was saying, but the tone of her voice was one of controlled anger, the same tone I had heard from her flat but certainly hadn't encountered in any of my conversations with her. I wondered if there was a less charming side to her, and found that I hoped not.

The rest of the day passed quite quickly. I had dinner and watched some TV and found myself preoccupied by the thought of making a good impression at the charity shop tomorrow.

Lisa didn't call, but she did reply to my text with one of her own saying 'good for you' and 'speak soon', which I found heartening.

Tuesday 1 December

Started my second ever job! Only eighteen days after I left the first.

I slept badly, which was really frustrating and annoying. I told myself it wasn't logical: I didn't need the job, I didn't need the money (if there was any) and it clearly wasn't going to be a responsible role, so what was my brain's issue? It wouldn't listen though. Something primeval, deep inside my brain, thought there was a danger of my being eaten, so refused to shut down. Oh well.

I got up earlier than I needed to, had breakfast, shaved and showered. I put on a proper shirt, with a collar, and buttons all the way down the front, and some semi-formal blue trousers rather than jeans, thinking that it was better to be overdressed than underdressed on the first day. I had gathered together my documentation, and was just about to leave for a leisurely walk to the shop when the nerves returned and I ended up paying a second visit to the bathroom. When I came out there was no longer any slack in the time I had allowed for the walk, so I grabbed my coat and papers and hurriedly left the flat.

Mrs Aldridge, the shop manager (I had learnt her name when she called to offer me the position), gave me a momentary smile as she opened the door to let me in, bang on eight fifteen. She led me to the office at the back of the shop and sat me down. She said I could call her Irene. She said we would do this as quickly as possible as it was currently very busy with Christmas and all. She took copies of my ID and said I needed to sign a form to say that I was voluntarily working for nothing and another one to say that I would abide by the charity's diversity and inclusion policy. I happily signed both. Irene then said they had contacted my previous employer for a reference but would let me start in the meantime. I gave my best poker face. She also said you wouldn't believe how many applications she got, mostly from unemployed youngsters trying to get some work experience on their CVs. She looked at me intently when she said that, and I wasn't sure whether I was supposed to feel guilty or grateful, so I just nodded.

She then introduced me to just such a young person, in the shape of Becky, who had come into the shop while we were out the back. She was in her early twenties, with long, straight blonde hair. We exchanged a limp handshake as Irene told me that Becky would be showing me the ropes this morning. Becky didn't look delighted at the prospect, but I put that down to her having her own stuff to do rather than any hostility towards me. I resolved to be a quick learner and, as they say in business now, to add value as soon as I could. What passes these days for a cash register turned out to be more complicated than I had imagined, particularly understanding how to make it work with both a barcode reader and a credit-card terminal, and I regretted leaving my reading glasses at home; however, having an IT background, I think I grasped it much more quickly than most of my contemporaries would have. Becky then showed me quickly what went where, which was fairly obvious, told me to refer any 'would-be donations' (as she put it) to her for the moment, and then joked she had left the most important thing till last: where the toilets and drink-making facilities were. I thought I would show willing by offering to make a round of hot drinks, and my offer was accepted. I took Irene's mug into her office and, without looking up, she thanked me and also said that I would need to go on a course on dealing with shoplifters; in the meantime I should inform her if I saw anything and under no circumstances attempt to intervene myself.

Becky didn't unlock the front door until nine thirty-five, which for some reason I found irritating, and a couple of people who had been patiently waiting immediately came in. One was a man in his seventies, I thought, carrying a large black bin-liner. Becky invited him to accompany her to the counter. The other was a lady probably a little younger than me, with a multi-coloured scarf around her head, who came over to where I was standing next to the Christmas cards and asked if we sold Christmas cards. On my best behaviour, without a trace of sarcasm, I said that we did and that there was a selection right here. The lady began to root round in the stack, and I stepped back so as not to crowd her.

"These seem very expensive," she said after a while.

"We think they are reasonably priced," I improvised, "as charity cards."

She looked at the price label again. "How much goes to the charity?" she asked.

That threw me a bit. "All of it, I think," I offered. "After production costs and overheads, I imagine."

The lady put the cards down. "I'll try Smiths," she said, and left.

Happily my sales virginity did not last long and I was soon doing a brisk trade in cards, wrapping paper and Christmas decorations. But I was embarrassed by the number of questions I was getting that I couldn't answer and had to deflect or refer to Becky. She meanwhile was having a difficult time with the man with the black sack, who clearly wasn't prepared to take no for an answer regarding his 'would-be donation'. Instinctively I wanted to intervene, to ask him to leave, but I supposed it wasn't my place on my first day, and I knew it could be interpreted as being patronising to Becky, or sexist, or ageist. I felt a bit shabby nonetheless, keeping quiet while the man became increasingly belligerent, and I was relieved when Becky eventually asked me to mind the counter while she went to fetch Irene.

There was an embarrassed silence while we waited for what seemed a very long time. I tried to peer into the sack and saw what appeared to be the collar of an old, threadbare jacket.

To my relief Irene was now heading swiftly across the shop floor, removing her glasses as she did so.

The effect on the man was immediate. "This is a fucking joke," he pronounced. And with that he dropped his sack on the floor and headed for the door. Irene tried to go after him, with the sack, but wasn't quick enough.

She came back to the counter, threw the sack on the floor and kicked it. "This really pisses me off," she told Becky, who looked as though she wasn't sure if she was being blamed.

Irene then turned to me. "A lot of the stuff we get offered is just rubbish," she explained. "The donors are just being selfish and trying to pretend they are doing us a favour. So now," she kicked the sack again, "we have to dispose of this stuff, which costs us money, reduces our funds. Where's the charity in that?"

Becky nodded in agreement. I said I understood and that I had seen bags dumped outside charity shops where there was a big sign on the door saying "don't leave donations outside".

"Exactly," Becky agreed with her arms folded. "They're just too lazy to go to the fucking tip."

"Bloody public," Irene muttered as she headed back to her office. Becky and I exchanged a smile at that. I offered to make her another cup of tea or coffee, but she said she couldn't drink it on the shop floor, and that it must be time for my break. So I ended up drinking on my own for fifteen minutes out the back. It was a novelty as drink breaks disappeared in the late eighties at my previous job, and I felt a bit guilty about it. Then my break ended and Becky had hers, which meant I was manning the shop on my own for the first time.

I found myself hoping that no one would come in. There was a constant stream of Christmas shoppers passing by the window, though, so that wasn't likely. I took up position behind the counter. Three people came in: one lady quickly made her mind up about Christmas cards and just as rapidly paid for them; another took more time in the same area of the shop and left without buying. The third was a man of about my age. He was looking at some porcelain figurines and picking them up to inspect more closely; I was desperately hoping he wouldn't drop one. He eventually selected one and came over with it.

"I like this, but I think the price is too steep," he said without preliminaries. The price sticker said £4.99, which seemed eminently reasonable to me.

"I don't have authority to barter, I'm afraid," I told him.

"Who does?"

"The manager."

"Can you get him then, please?"

I looked round at the closed door to Irene's office.

"How much are you offering?" I asked.

"Three quid."

I looked round again. I didn't want to disturb Irene again. "OK," I said. The man gave me three pounds and, as I carefully wrapped the figurine, I surreptitiously slipped a two-pound coin out of my own pocket into the till. I handed the package across and smiled.

"Where does this charity do its work?" the man enquired.

"Africa and Asia mainly, I believe," I replied.

"Not the UK?"

"No."

"Why not?"

I remembered my interview with Irene. "I don't really know," I responded. "Other countries are poorer, I suppose."

"Hmm," the man nodded. "Well, that's their look out, isn't it?"

I smiled and thanked him for his custom.

The morning went very slowly. It wasn't unpleasant or particularly boring, it was just that I hadn't realised how much my old job had become automatic over the years; now that I had to concentrate every minute seemed longer. Lunchtime eventually arrived, though. Both Irene and Becky had brought their own sandwiches, but it hadn't occurred to me to do that, so I went to the local bakery and queued up for a giant sausage roll and can of cola. It was quite nice to have some fresh air, though there was a biting wind and I did not stay outside for long.

I was surprised to find that for part of the time my lunch break overlapped with Becky's, so we were sitting at the back of the shop together while Irene, for the only time during the day, was out the front. Like most young people Becky was buried in her phone and didn't appear to perceive any awkwardness in not making conversation. But she was also quite willing to talk once I had initiated it.

"How long have you been working here?" I asked unoriginally.

Becky looked up and smiled. "About four months," she replied.

"Oh," I said. "I would have thought longer."

Becky looked a bit unsure, but not hostile. "Why's that?" she enquired.

"Well, just because you seem to know how everything works."

She laughed. "It's not that difficult, Alan."

"Well, no, I don't suppose... So, what's the plan, if you don't mind me asking?"

Becky replaced the lid on her Tupperware sandwich box. "The plan is to get a 'proper' job. So I'm doing this for a while, then I'm going travelling for up to a year, hopefully get some overseas work with this charity by being known to them already and," she lowered her voice, "doing the boring bit first."

"And the 'proper' job would be in the charity sector?" I asked earnestly.

Becky shook her head. "Oh, no. This girl wants some cash! Financial services hopefully."

"So why...?"

"ESG."

"Environmental, Social and Governance," I said, keen to show that I was keeping up with the times.

"Exactly. My successful friends say that's what you want to talk about at interview if you are going to have any hope of getting in."

"And once you're in?"

Becky shrugged. "I guess you have to do some mentoring in a school in a deprived area or whatever."

"And make a fortune," I suggested.

She nodded with exaggerated enthusiasm. "That's the idea."

I wanted to say that I found such cynicism in one so young depressing, but then I thought that maybe I was being unfair to Becky. She seemed a nice enough girl and had already helped me out several times that morning. She might be joking anyway or at least exaggerating for effect and, if not, maybe she was just being realistic: if companies that don't really care go in for token shows of concern about the wider world (my employer had been no different), then that, I suppose, is the game you have to play if you want a job. Even if you do actually have genuine concerns about the wider world. It turned out Becky has a master's degree in geography from a good university (I forget which now) and I think in my day that would have given you the pick of whatever job you wanted, 1980s recession notwithstanding. I don't think I would like to be young now, except that it would mean living longer overall, and sometimes I'm not even sure about that.

After our chat we went back to work. I thought I was getting the hang of things quite quickly, didn't end up subsidising any further purchases during the afternoon and was of genuine assistance to a number of customers, if I said so myself. But, to be truthful, the time still dragged a bit, and I found myself surreptitiously looking at my watch or the clock on the wall behind the till whenever I thought no one would notice.

And then my first shoplifter, about half an hour before we closed. He was hanging around the Christmas decorations section, and what drew my attention to him was that he kept looking towards the ceiling rather than at the display. I turned towards Becky, who nodded that she had seen him as well. She had started to move slowly towards him when he turned, walked briskly towards the door and left the shop. We went over to where he had been: it didn't look like he had taken very much, maybe a couple of rolls of wrapping paper and some tinselly bits. Becky said we wouldn't know until we did an inventory, and even then you wouldn't know exactly who had taken what as it was a frequent occurrence. She laughed when I asked if we would be informing the police, and laughed again when I said I was surprised that people stole from charity shops. I wondered aloud why the shop bothered having security cameras and Becky said it was in case one of us got stabbed. Once again I couldn't be sure if she was joking.

I felt a flood of relief when we shut the door for the evening, though it wasn't yet time to go home. I was shown how to use the cylinder vacuum cleaner, which I gladly did – there wasn't much on the floor except a bit of glitter – while Irene and Becky did some accounts work at the till. Irene then said that she would see me tomorrow, if today hadn't put me off. I said it hadn't, and that I was glad she wanted me back.

I felt quite happy on the way home. I had set out to get a part-time job and I had got one, and it seemed OK, and it was for a worthwhile cause. There was no pay, but I didn't need the money. But the upbeat feeling faded quite quickly once I got home, and by the time I had had dinner I started to feel really weary, but not as though I could easily go to sleep. I watched my phone in case Lisa texted to ask how I had got on on my first day. She didn't, but I think those kids take up all her time. So I channel-hopped on the TV, deliberately selecting programmes that did not require much intellectual application, until I was convinced that I would sleep if I tried; and then I went to bed.

Wednesday 2 December

My second day at the charity shop. Much the same as the first, except that I am having to get help from Becky less and less, which is encouraging, and the time passed much more quickly, though still somewhat more slowly than at my previous job. I'm sure that won't be the case for long.

An old chap came in asking if we were looking for any volunteers. I referred him to Irene, who thanked him for his interest but said we were now fully staffed. When he had gone, I said to Becky that I thought he looked quite lonely. She said he looked like a child molester.

Thursday 3 December

Day off! It seemed strange to have a day off after only two days of work, but Irene had told me that I wouldn't be working full time (and I hadn't wanted full-time work anyway). Apparently Gwen does Thursdays and has done for years. I got the impression that Irene doesn't much like Gwen, which I suspect has something to do with the fact that, as Becky informed me, Gwen managed the shop for many moons before her retirement and still retains ideas as to how it should be run.

So, a free day. I didn't set the alarm, but was wide awake well before eight anyway. I decided to get up and have a leisurely breakfast in front of the TV. The news was full of depressing facts and annoying people (and vice versa), so I flicked around until I found myself watching the pilot episode of a famous US sitcom. I hadn't seen it before and I like the show, so it didn't seem like a waste of time to watch the whole thing. Then I started watching the next episode, but it was from several series later, for some reason, which jarred a bit. I gave up halfway through.

After I had showered, I made a cup of coffee and sat down to decide what to do for the day. Christmas shopping was a possibility, except there's only really Lisa, Neil and the kids, and I'll need to talk to Lisa to find out what they would all like or I'll get something completely useless. Christmas card writing was a possibility, except that I didn't have any cards and thought I should really show loyalty to the shop and buy some from there.

It seemed a bit quiet, so I put the radio on. I hopped between a few stations because I couldn't find anything that was 'just right'. Most of the music stations were too inane and the talk stations too serious at one end of the spectrum and too full of opinionated idiots at the other. I turned it off. Immediately it seemed too quiet in the flat again, though in another way it was surprisingly noisy. At any one time I could always hear the whirr and grind of power tools, not necessarily in this building or next door, but close enough, and from various directions. Also snatches of very loud conversations, often on mobile phones, as people walked past. Dogs barking, often for several minutes at a time. And someone seemed to be in the flat downstairs, because you could just hear their television or radio and the odd mysterious banging noise at irregular intervals. The combination of silence and unwanted, unpredictable noise unnerved me more than I would have thought. Eventually I found a classical chill compilation on Spotify and listened, or half listened, to that.

I did some cleaning. Vacuumed the floors, cleaned the kitchen and bathroom, even had a go at dusting, which turned out to be more overdue than I had thought. It did look better, but even so I was relieved when I looked at the clock to discover that I had killed sufficient time to be able to have lunch. I watched an old episode of *Antiques Roadshow* as I was eating, then fell asleep in the chair. I awoke for a few seconds when I heard the buzz of someone pressing the button outside for one of the flats, but then dropped off again. Almost immediately, though, it seemed, I was woken again by a timid knocking at my door. I got out of the chair, my head still clearing as I did so. It sounded as though someone was making barking and yapping noises in the hallway, though my befuddled brain was telling me that couldn't be the case. I couldn't see anything through the spyhole, so I gingerly opened the door and found a man on all fours.

"Woof," he said, without looking up.

"Can I help you," I asked politely.

He appeared to flinch, like a large spider that thinks you're about to whack it. Then he slowly stood up, brushed what appeared to be imaginary dust off his jacket, and only then fleetingly made eye contact with me. I noticed that he had a drooping moustache and thick-rimmed glasses, and judged that he was probably in his forties. "Sorry," was all he said, and then he made for the stairs.

I've said before that being alone and having time on your hands makes you nosier. So when I closed the door I stood behind it, watching through the spyhole and listening as carefully as I could. I did not hear steps going down the stairs, but instead a quiet rapping on Ella's door a few seconds later. I heard the door open, there were voices for a few seconds, and then the door closed again. Ella seems like a nice woman, but she does seem to keep some very strange company!

I went and stood by the window. It was still light, and quite sunny as well. I had a brainwave: I could go for a drive; that would be enjoyable. I kicked myself that I hadn't thought of that earlier, when I could have had more time in daylight.

The Maserati started at the first attempt. I blipped the pedal a couple of times just to hear the note of the V6. I admired the clock, even though it appeared to be half an hour slow. I engaged drive, released the handbrake and headed off with a smile on my face for the first time today. There was a frustrating amount of traffic around though, which I guessed I should have expected in London on a Thursday afternoon near Christmas – I normally take the car out on Sundays. But I know the roads round here, so I patiently made my way to a dual carriageway, where I was able to get up to around sixty for a few minutes before I encountered roadworks and had to slow down again. It was getting dark by then anyway, and the Maser doesn't have great lights by modern standards. And you have to treat a thirty-year-old engine with respect unless you want eye-watering garage bills. But it was kind of fun nonetheless.

There was a tissue on the passenger seat, which I supposed must have been Ella's, as no one else has sat there recently. I know some classic car owners don't agree (heated debate on online forums!) but I always think it is nice to have someone with you when you go out for a drive. Lisa used to like it until she reached her teens and started worrying about the environmental impact of the engine, and then again for a while when she stopped worrying so much about the environmental impact of the engine, but Anne never really got it, except as a curious foible of mine that she was willing to indulge, at least for a while. It nearly had to be sacrificed for the divorce settlement, but happily at the time it wasn't worth much and in the end I got to keep it.

I was back home by four o'clock. I admired the car for a final time as I closed the garage door, but noted a few spots of grime on the bonnet and resolved to give it a clean on Saturday, if it doesn't rain.

I had a cup of tea and read a book for a couple of hours. Then I made dinner and watched TV for a while as I tried to find the energy to go and do the dishes.

The phone rang. It was Lisa's number. My heart leapt and I quickly answered.

"Hi darling!"

"Hi Dad!"

"How are you?"

"Great, thanks. And, miracle of miracles, both of the kids are asleep. At the same time! So hopefully I've got a few minutes. How's the new boy getting on at work?"

I told her, trying to make it sound as interesting as possible, adding some colour and humour, without becoming long-winded. I'm not sure that I succeeded. "Anyway, enough of that," I said, "how are the kids getting on?"

"Yeah, fine, Dad. Just a minute. Neil, can't you sort her out?" Inaudible response. "Really? Sorry, Dad, the little one's woken up, I'm going to have to go."

"Of course." I tried to hide the disappointment in my voice. The phone screen told me we had been talking for only six minutes.

"OK. Coming. Just one thing, Dad, before I forget. We were wondering if you would like to come to ours for Christmas?"

I felt myself flush for some reason. "I'd love to!" I replied immediately.

"Great. Discuss details nearer the date."

"And let me know what the kids would like. And you, obviously. And Neil."

"Will do. Got to go."

"Love you."

"Bye."

I sat staring at the phone for a couple of minutes. I felt such a surge of pleasure and relief: I hadn't fully appreciated just how much I was dreading spending Christmas on my own. I shed a couple of tears and was glad no one could see me.

The rest of the evening passed very quickly. I had an early night, intending and expecting to sleep well and awake refreshed for another day's work.

Tuesday 8 December

Just when I thought I was really getting my feet under the table at the shop, today turned out a bit differently.

Irene had a serious look on her face as I walked through the door, and asked me if I would mind accompanying her into the office. I turned towards Becky, who shrugged in response. In the office Irene asked me to sit down and, without further pleasantries, told me there was a problem with my reference. The way she then looked at me seemed to imply an accusation that, whatever the problem was, I knew all about it and had done it deliberately in order to give her grief.

I had an inkling of what the issue might be, but hoped I was wrong, and in response just tried to look suitably nonplussed.

"Our reference form," Irene informed me, "is in a questionnaire format. Where the former employer gives the 'wrong' answer to any of our questions, there is space for additional information. On your form, the question as to whether you were compliant with the company's policy on diversity and inclusion has been left blank. They have not ticked 'no', but in the additional information box they have written 'early retirement – compromise agreement.' Can you please elaborate on that?"

I leaned forward to try to see the form, but Irene seemed reluctant to let me see it. I didn't doubt that it said what she had told me; I just wanted to see if I could make out the signature or recognise the handwriting. I couldn't. Well, I consoled myself, maybe there was no malice in it; maybe whoever it was just thought they were giving a truthful answer.

I cleared my throat. I told myself I needed to avoid sounding angry, resentful or defensive. I told Irene the full story. I explained calmly why, in my view, it would have been racist on my part not to share with a black colleague fruit that in the same circumstances I would definitely have shared with a white colleague. I pointed out that Ade was on my side, to the extent that his girlfriend had actually been my legal representative. Not that I was suggesting in any way that she had to do his bidding. I decided to stop talking.

As with Nikki previously, Irene appeared to have heard nothing except 'black person' and 'banana'. I had the impression that I had inadvertently donned a pointy white hood with little holes for the eyes and mouth.

"This is really bad," Irene said finally, shaking her head. "Area is not going to like this. I'm very disappointed that you didn't share this with us when you first applied. I hardly need tell you that if you had we would not have taken you on."

I wanted to protest, or loudly take offence, but couldn't find the energy to do either. "Is there any sort of appeal process?" I asked meekly.

Irene seemed surprised by the question. She stumbled a bit over her words as she replied. She said that she would need to take up with Area and get back to me, but in the meantime I should go home.

I got up and quietly left, giving Becky a smile and a friendly wave on the way out. I hoped that her c.v. wouldn't be contaminated by having briefly worked with me.

I got back to the flat feeling very deflated. How was I going to fill the next two weeks until Christmas? And the New Year and beyond, because anywhere else I applied for a job was likely to have the same objection. That could mean literally thousands of days like yesterday before I…

Ella seemed to be having a heated argument with another man as I walked past her flat. It sounded as though she were saying that she was very angry at the quality of his work in the garden, but that didn't make any sense as we haven't got one. Equally oddly, though, he was saying that he was very sorry and promised to do better in future. Ella didn't sound convinced.

Maybe I'll subtly ask about that the next time we have coffee. If we do. I hope we do.

Unexpectedly Irene rang around midday. She sounded not exactly contrite but definitely more conciliatory than she had earlier. She said that there was indeed an appeals process. If I wished to avail myself of it then, on the basis of the presumption of innocence, I could continue to work at the shop until the panel had made its adjudication.

Effectively I was being offered the opportunity to work for nothing for an organisation that was accusing me of racism and, on that basis, would probably chuck me out in a month or two's time. I knew what any self-respecting response should be. "Yes," I said. "I would be happy to."

"That's great," Irene replied. "Could you come back this afternoon – poor Becky's been rushed off her feet all morning?"

Thursday 24 December

I have been looking forward to visiting Lisa, Neil and the kids above anything else ever since she invited me. It has kept me going during the problems with the shop and the solitary winter days I wasn't working and was largely amusing myself in the flat. A day ringed on the calendar when there wasn't much on any of the others.

And yet this morning I found myself wishing that I could push it back a few days. Possibly because it is always nice to have something to look forward to, but I also had a sense that maybe I had oversold it to myself, maybe it wouldn't be as great as I'd hoped. I realised that I hardly knew the kids: well, I had met Jasmine as few times ('met' seems a funny word with your own granddaughter) but not seen little Alfie since he was literally a new-born baby. I want them to like me, but kids are instinctive creatures, aren't they? If you try too hard it can have the opposite effect from what you intend.

I was a bit comforted to get a message from Lisa saying 'looking forward to CU later Lxx' as I was walking to the shop this morning. I had not been expecting to work today, but it seems Gwen's devotion to the cause doesn't extend to working on Christmas Eve! It was one of those crisp winter's days when the breath you can see in front of you is almost white. It was a visual treat to see all the lights and decorations in houses and shops as I walked by. I thought I could smell wood smoke, but maybe that was my brain playing tricks on me, trying to create an idealised Victorian Christmas.

Irene and Becky were both feeling festive. Irene had taken her glasses off and Becky was sporting glitter on her face and had tinsel around her neck. We all put on Santa hats and shared a mince pie and a glass of sherry before the shop opened, and we all wished each other a happy Christmas. Irene started to say something to me, which I think was intended to signal that whatever might happen in the New Year wasn't personal, but it wasn't coming out well, and in the end, to spare her embarrassment, I said I knew what she was trying to say and appreciated it.

It wasn't actually that busy. I suppose I shouldn't have been surprised: no one sends cards or puts up decorations on Christmas Eve, do they? And we weren't selling anything that you could give to someone as their actual present, unless you were a real cheapskate. Wrapping paper was probably our best line. And small novelties for livening up Christmas lunch. I wondered if I should buy some myself. We spent a lot of the time marking up stock for the sale next week.

At lunch Becky and I discussed our respective plans for Christmas. Becky and her mother, she told me, would be spending Christmas at her boyfriend's parents' place, but what she was really looking forward to was her friend's New Year party. I said I wasn't doing anything for New Year, but older people didn't so much. Becky said her parents had always gone out when they could. I didn't like to ask why her father was apparently no longer in the picture.

At four o'clock we had not had a customer for over an hour and Irene, who I suspected might have had another sherry since the one we had shared, and possibly another after that, declared that she didn't care what Area thought: it was time to call it a day.

I quickly hovered while Irene and Becky cashed up, then we were putting on coats, hats, scarves and gloves and wishing each other a merry Christmas. I shook hands with Irene, and when I turned to Becky to do the same she leaned forward and gave me a small kiss on the cheek. I must have looked embarrassed because she laughed. I thought it was a nice gesture though, a small token of support maybe.

Outside we gave one another child-like little waves as we walked off in different directions. I wondered what Irene was doing for Christmas, and for the first time it occurred to me that she had never said, at least in my hearing.

I was still feeling a little trepidation about Christmas as I got back to the flat. If I hadn't been about to drive, I would probably have had a drink to settle my nerves.

A card had been pushed under my door. It featured a somewhat risqué picture of a young lady with oversized breasts dressed in a Santa outfit a couple of sizes too small for her and, for some reason, sitting on top of an elf. It was from Ella. The writing inside was spidery and childish, which seemed odd, until I remembered that she still doesn't have full used of her right arm. I supposed it was in response to the one I sent her a week ago – with a traditional mountain scene, I think – but even so it was nice to get it. I put it on top of a bookcase, spreading the other cards out to make room for it. I wondered about having the picture on display, but figured that no one else, except perhaps Ella herself, was likely to see it. It also meant, I was pleased to see, that my total number of cards had reached double figures, which seems to me to be the absolute minimum you need to receive to ensure that you haven't become socially invisible, even if some are from people you haven't seen for years and don't expect to.

I had a quick cup of tea, re-checked my holdall to ensure that I hadn't forgotten anything (I packed mostly last night) and ensured that I had the bag of presents (mustn't forget that!) Then I decided to have another shower, though I'd had one before work: you can't always tell if you've got sweaty during the day, and you don't want the grandkids' first impression of Granddad to be that he smells! For the same reason I cleaned my teeth again as well. Then I inspected myself, took a deep breath and sent Lisa a message to say I was on my way.

Although I never admit it to third parties, it is always a bit of a relief when the Maserati starts. It occurred to me for the first time that its bright red paint was suitably festive, a match for

Santa's outfit! We were soon out in the traffic, which was heavier than normal, with SUVs full of families off to see their relatives, some with big piles of wrapped presents showing through the back window. I exchanged waves with some smiling children, and only one of them stuck her tongue out, which struck me as a reasonable result.

In the past I have got to Lisa's place in thirty minutes but today it took forty-five. It then took another fifteen minutes to park: the 1930s suburban terrace houses are large, full of character and very fashionable – no doubt a great investment for Lisa and Neil – but there's no off-street parking, unless you count the pavement as off-street, which a lot of people apparently do. I drove round until finally someone came out of a space ahead of me. With almost no rearward vision through the hood, I gingerly reversed the Maserati into the gap, expecting at any moment to hear the grind of the alloy wheels against the kerb or, worse, bumper against bumper. My manoeuvre succeeded at the second attempt, with no damage done. Someone who'd had to wait behind me for almost a minute tooted as he drove past. There are days when having a Fiat 500 would be a better option for me than a Maserati Biturbo Spyder. But not that many.

The parking space was almost two hundred yards from the house and, laden down with luggage and presents, I was feeling the strain and puffing a bit by the time I arrived and pressed the doorbell. I hoped I wasn't sweating. I could hear the bell resonate as though in a large void, then nothing, then steps coming rapidly down the stairs. I saw a silhouette through the frosted glass, then the door opened and I was face to face with my daughter. My first impression was that she looked a little drawn and had put on weight since I had last seen her – was that a bad thing to think? – but she still has that beautiful smile, which was aimed at me as she told me to come in.

"That's Grandpa," she was saying, apparently to her lower right leg, and then for the first time I noticed that clinging to that limb was a small girl with lank brown hair, looking uncertainly up at me through her father's dark eyes.

"Hello, Jasmine," I said with a big smile. "It's Grandpa!"

Jasmine hid.

"Don't be silly," said Lisa. "Sorry about that, Dad."

"It's fine," I laughed. "Christmas can be overwhelming for kids."

"Come in, come in!"

Lisa shuffled awkwardly backwards with Jasmine still clinging to her leg, and I carefully advanced into the hallway.

"Sorry you're sleeping in the lounge but, well, we only have three bedrooms."

"Understood."

"And you brought your sleeping bag?"

I brandished it from among my load.

"Great. You can put your stuff in our room *pro tem*. Er, Neil's gone out on a present run."

"And Alfie?"

"Oh, he's asleep upstairs. So if you can be quiet when you go past."

"Will do."

"Good. Anything else?"

"Does Dad get a hug?"

"He does. Sorry, distracted by madam here."

Lisa flung her arms around me. She smelt a little of cooking but there was also the unmistakable smell of Lisa. What parent doesn't like the unique scent of their child, whatever age they are? I was beginning to feel happier already.

We released each other. Jasmine was still looking warily up at me. Then she turned and fled. Lisa shrugged.

I went upstairs and quickly deposited my stuff in an inconspicuous corner of the main bedroom. I always think it is intrusive to linger too long in private spaces like that. I did notice that the bed was enormous and had an ornate but uncomfortable-looking headboard. I also noticed a photo of Lisa, Jasmine and Anne on the dresser, three generations smiling together, Jasmine with her teeth closed as children do. I didn't suppose there were any pictures of me and didn't try to find out. Well, maybe by the end of this visit there will be.

I could hear the baby's rhythmic breathing as I passed the door of the nursery and couldn't resist putting my head around the door and watching him for a few moments. The light wasn't good, but I could make out that he was starting to sprout some tufts of hair, and that they were probably blond, like his mother as a child. There was a peaceful but determined expression on his face that I liked too. Babies are an affirmation of life, aren't they?

I came downstairs. Lisa was in the kitchen preparing some food. I put my head round the door and asked if there was anything I could do to help. Lisa said she was fine and why didn't I go and make myself comfortable in the lounge; Neil would be back soon. She also offered me a beer with a knowing smile and, when I accepted, directed me to help myself from the fridge, which I did.

Terrible thing to admit, but I was sort of hoping Jasmine wouldn't be in the lounge. I'm not very good with small kids unless there is someone from their immediate family to translate for me. I mean, I was fine with Lisa obviously, but with other peoples' children I struggle. Some adults seem innately to be able to relate to all kids, and I envy and admire that.

Jasmine was indeed in the lounge, sitting on the sofa with her legs dangling in mid-air, eating a packet of crisps. She was paying rapt attention to some sort of grey cartoon dinosaur on the television screen. As she had run away from me once, I thought it best not to sit down next to her, and instead chose an armchair from which I was looking at the screen at a forty-five-degree angle and couldn't really see what was going on. I opened my can of beer as quietly as I could; Jasmine was so engrossed in the cartoon that she didn't seem to hear it, and I wasn't sure that she even knew I was there.

What should I say or do? I really wanted Jasmine to like me because, well, she is my granddaughter and also – and I know this sounds pathetic, but you can say anything to your own diary, can't you? – if Jasmine thinks Grandpa Alan is wonderful, then Grandpa Alan is going to get invited round more often, which he would really like. I imagine Anne is really good with her.

I was sure by now some grandfathers would have had Jasmine squealing with delight as they held her upside down and spun her around the room, but I was just sitting there awkwardly sipping a beer. I watched her when I could, trying not to stare. I liked the way her chubby little cheeks moved as she ate her crisps, the ingenuous amazement on her face as some new real-world-impossibility played out in 2D on the screen, the way her legs kicked against the front of the sofa when something exciting happened.

"Is that your favourite?" I ventured finally.

Jasmine shook her head but didn't look round. She stuffed another crisp into her mouth.

I tried again. "What is, then?"

She said something that I didn't catch.

"It's about a pony," Neil explained as he came into the room.

I must have looked surprised as I hadn't heard him come into the house. I got up and shook hands with him and exchanged pleasantries. He didn't look particularly thrilled to see me, but he has quite a blunt, down-to-earth manner about him, so you can't always, or ever, quite tell. Anne told me once that Lisa thought I didn't like him, which wasn't true. But what sort of father are you if you think someone *is* good enough for your daughter? The only thing I have against him is that he works in insurance, which in my experience is just a means of taking money off people and then finding all sorts of reasons not to give it back. Lisa says he works in 'reinsurance' which apparently is something different (I used to have a friend in the same line), but it's all the same to me. But it does seem to pay well, and I think his career is progressing nicely too.

For the moment, though, he wasn't paying any attention to me, because he had noticed that Jasmine was eating crisps, and that wasn't supposed to happen.

"Sweetheart," he called out in the direction of the kitchen, at the same time trying to remove the packet from his daughter's reluctant hands. He turned to me: "You didn't give her these, did you?" he asked, a little aggressively I thought.

I held my hands up. "Nothing to do with me. She was eating them when I came in."

Jasmine threw me a fierce look, as though I had somehow ratted on her. Lisa came into the room to join the inquest, drying her hands on a towel as she did so. "Oh, Jas," she said, "you know you can't have crisps before dinner!" She looked at me, and I thought there was an element of reproach in her expression, as though I should have known and done something about it. I felt embarrassed, though I couldn't think of a reason why I should.

The packet had finally been wrested from my granddaughter's grasp, but now she was screaming with rage. Her parents pushed her out of the room, closing the door behind them. For the next few minutes I was alone, except for the cartoon dinosaur on the screen. I couldn't hear what was going on in the kitchen above the sound of the television, and wasn't sure I wanted to.

Neil came back about ten minutes later, beer in hand. He threw himself onto the sofa with a sigh and closed his eyes. "Never have kids," he said.

"Bit late for that," I laughed. "And I can tell you it works out OK in the end."

"I hope so."

I felt a little disappointed that he hadn't taken the bait, the opportunity to say something nice about his wife and my daughter, but I supposed he was tired. Lisa tells me this is his busiest time of year at work. I was about to ask him about that when Lisa called him again. "You'll have to sort madam out," she shouted, "unless you want to breastfeed the baby."

Neil closed his eyes again for a second before replying. "OK. On my way."

"And she's been sick now."

Dinner was an ordinary affair, just the three of us, plus a baby monitor, but it was OK for all that. I was trying to be a sympathetic listener, and to make it clear that they must allow me to be useful and not just excess baggage. We had pizza and a bottle of wine, which seemed fine to me. Not Christmassy, but that could wait till tomorrow, and I could smell the turkey which was already cooking in the oven. I offered to do the dishes, but almost everything would go in the dishwasher, so there was no need.

We adjourned to the lounge with what was left of the bottle of wine, but quite soon I noticed how red Neil's eyes were, and Lisa's were actually closed, though she was still talking. At around ten o'clock they said they were all in, though I was welcome to watch TV as long as I liked. I went and fetched my bags, worked out how to convert the sofa into a bed, and wrote this diary entry. It's ten thirty on Christmas Eve and I expect in a few minutes to be fast asleep.

Friday 25 December

Christmas Day!

I see it says Friday, but of course Christmas isn't any particular day of the week, is it? It has its own peculiar characteristics. It started with a four-year-old scowling at me. I could feel her breath before I opened my eyes and saw her standing over me. She had in her hand a naked doll with which she appeared to be proposing to hit me over the head, had her mother not come forward and grasped both her arms at once. I assumed for a moment that Jasmine still blamed me for the crisp incident the previous evening, but it turned out she had moved on.

"You're obstructing the lounge and preventing presents being given out," Lisa explained with a chuckle.

"What time is it?" I asked, realising that I couldn't immediately locate my watch.

"Er, eight fifteen," Lisa replied, looking at a clock on the mantelpiece.

"Not that late, then," I ventured, a little grumpily I have to admit.

"No, but madam has been up since, er, just after Santa left."

My mind recalled Lisa at a similar age. I understood. "Sorry, sweetheart," I said, addressing Jasmine directly and giving her a big smile. "Give Grandpa five minutes and then we'll both see what Santa has brought you." Simultaneously Jasmine and I both looked up at Lisa for approval.

Five minutes later, having been joined by Neil, as well as by Alfie, somewhat oblivious to proceedings in his cot, we made a start. I had hurriedly remade the sofa, folded up my sleeping bag and put on yesterday's clothes, but I was conscious that I probably looked dishevelled and that the 'stuffiness' Lisa had alluded to when opening the window in all likelihood matched my breath. I wished I had woken earlier and made myself presentable in the bathroom.

But, of course, no one was looking at me. We started politely, taking it in turns to open gifts, but that was rapidly abandoned: it was the Jasmine show, and to a lesser extent the Neil-on-behalf-of-Alfie show. Jasmine had a huge tower of gifts, mostly wrapped in identical paper, that was taller than she was. She ripped at the paper with gusto and displayed a typical child's facial honesty, so that it was perfectly clear what she liked and what she didn't, though even her mother seemed to find this somewhat random, as though in an hour's time her preferences might be completely different. She soon had a great stash of dolls, crayons, dressing-up type stuff and various bits of merchandising from characters I didn't recognise, which I assumed were to do with children's films and TV. I felt oddly nervous when she got to my gifts – I could see the different wrapping paper – though I had got stuff from Disney's *Frozen* franchise, at Lisa's suggestion, and thought that was a safe bet. And I was almost irrationally delighted when she obviously did like them, and more so when her mother told her to thank Grandpa and a hint of a little shy smile was aimed in my direction. Jasmine quickly moved on of course, but four-year-olds aren't known for their attention spans, are they?

Neil meanwhile was opening presents for Alfie and brandishing or shaking each one in turn in front of his son's face; he was describing them all in a baby voice I hadn't previously heard him adopt, and which I suspected he wasn't fully conscious of. My grandson was admirably unimpressed by any of it. The needs of babies are so basic. Maybe we'd be better off if we stayed that way.

The adult exchange of gifts was a small sideshow. I had taken Lisa's advice on what to get Neil, as I always have to, and we politely acknowledged the books, toiletries and underwear we had given each other before reverting to the main event. I was quite pleased when it was finally over and we began stuffing our wrapping paper into the sack that Lisa had suddenly produced for the purpose.

I was finally able to get into the bathroom. I tried to be as quick as I could, because I think it's rude to monopolise the bathroom too long in someone else's house, but by the time I had figured out the shower, mopped up the floor where water had escaped through a gap in the screen, shaved (which I should have done first as the mirror was now steamed up), cleaned my teeth and applied deodorant, almost half an hour had elapsed.

As I came out, I heard Neil telling Lisa that he had overridden the clock on the hot water, which I hoped wasn't the result of my having used too much of the stuff.

"That's better," I said loudly, in case someone said something that I wasn't supposed to hear, and didn't want to hear. "I feel much more civilised now."

It was still only nine thirty. I looked out of the window. It was a crisp sunny day. Only snow was missing. I was beginning to feel Christmassy. Had I been offered a drink, I would have accepted, but I thought it was too early to ask. Instead, I went into the kitchen and made myself useful as toaster monitor as Lisa went off to feed the baby and Neil busied himself with trying to coax Jasmine into digesting some Coco Pops using, I noticed, the same spoon-as-divebomber motion and sound effects my generation used on our own kids. Bribery was also being used, with the promise of a visit to the swings if she ate up like a good girl. (I've never understood the evolutionary purpose of children being reluctant to eat: you'd think their growing bodies would be all for it.) In time-honoured fashion a compromise was reached, and the cereal abandoned after four mouthfuls, the remainder ending up in the bin and down the sink.

"Good girl," said Neil. "Go and get ready, then."

Jasmine ran off and reappeared a couple of minutes later in a purple quilted jacket decorated with cartoon characters, carrying a small pair of pink wellingtons. She seemed unsure as to which boot went on which foot and unexpectedly looked at me rather than her father. I was able to arrange the footwear in the right order and then crouched down so that she could steady herself with her hand on my shoulder while she earnestly concentrated on inserting her legs into the correct openings.

"Shall we show Grandpa where the swings are?" Neil suggested. Jasmine looked a little confused for a second but turned to me and slowly nodded. Grandpa couldn't have been happier if he'd won the lottery.

The walk to the swings took us past where I had parked the Maserati. To my relief it was still there and apparently undamaged. "That's Grandpa's car," I told Jasmine, who was walking in the middle, holding hands with both Neil and me so that we could periodically swing her into the air. Jasmine looked at the car and then at her father for guidance as to how she was supposed to respond.

"It's very old and very odd," Neil told Jasmine acerbically. My son-in-law doesn't get it at all. He likes German SUVs. And I let him marry my daughter.

"Just like Grandpa," I said before anyone else had the chance to.

The swings looked modern and well maintained. There was a group of teenage boys hanging around by the roundabout and I could have done without their presence and music, though to be fair to them one of their number who had been leaning against the side of the swings moved away as we approached. I wondered what their home lives were like if they were choosing to congregate in a park on Christmas Day.

Neil didn't seem to think anything of their presence. He and Jasmine had their roles well practised. He lifted her into the seat, then fastened it so she couldn't fall out. She held onto the chains, closed her eyes and prematurely started to swing her feet, while her father moved round behind her to begin pushing duties. I stood to one side and was able to have a rare one-to-one conversation with my son-in-law, who was able to respond, or otherwise, to Jasmine's shouted instructions at the same time.

"How's work?" I asked.

"Very busy. Difficult renewal season. It's a hard market."

"As in...?"

"High prices."

"That's good, isn't it?"

"Not necessarily. The high prices are caused by a shortage of capacity."

"I see," I said, though I didn't.

"Sorry about what happened to you," Neil said, as though he had rehearsed the phrase.

"All good things..."

"Are you enjoying your retirement?"

The question flustered me a little. "I haven't necessarily retired," I replied.

"I see. Lisa says you're working part time in a charity shop?"

The question sounded slightly dismissive, but I decided it wasn't intentional. Should I tell him? I wanted to confide in someone. "Actually my sins may have followed me there."

"How so?"

"They asked my old company for a reference."

"I see."

"But I'm going to appeal."

"No, because you'll go over the top and fall out."

"Sorry?"

"I was talking to madam. She wants me to push her higher."

"Oh." We both laughed.

"Serious shit, though," Neil told me. "Diversity and inclusion is the thing now. Even in the City."

"And I'm all for it," I replied vehemently. "And have been for the past forty years. Even when it wasn't fashionable!"

"Lisa says you were arrested once on a demo. Is that true?"

I was surprised that Lisa had mentioned that. I hoped she was proud rather than appalled. "It is," I confirmed. "Anti-fascist march in the 1980s. No charges were brought, but I missed a day's work and was pictured in the paper, so I had to explain to the company. Thirty-nine years with one employer and two brushes with the disciplinary process: one for opposing racism and the other for alleged 'racial insensitivity'. And my views haven't changed at all in the meantime!"

If I was expecting admiration, or even sympathy, I was disappointed. "It's a minefield," Neil told me, "but you have to know how to navigate it, Alan. Complete career-breaker otherwise. Best to keep your mouth shut and just go with whatever the policy is. Still, you have your pension fund."

So even my son-in-law thought I had been naive and stupid. I went to object but decided this wasn't the day for that. And maybe I knew he was right.

In any case I had lost his attention. "Your head's coming off? I don't think so, darling. But get off and Grandpa and I will take a look at it and glue it back on again at home. How's that?"

Jasmine stopped swinging her legs and slowed down, scuffing her wellingtons against the ground as she came to a halt. Neil examined her head while I earnestly agreed with his findings that it was still an integral part of her body. Then we set off home. One or more of the teenagers called out inaudible abuse as we left.

I was feeling very mellow and not a little sleepy by the time we finished lunch. The food was excellent: the traditional roast turkey with, as they say, all the trimmings. It appeared to be a joint effort between Lisa and Neil; I don't know if he has taught her to cook, because Anne and I never really did. Though what

Anne has taught her in recent years I wouldn't know of course. A sherry before lunch and more than my fair share of a bottle of wine during it (because Lisa and Neil felt the need to be sober around and when responsible for children in a way that my own generation didn't always do) had relaxed me and loosened my tongue a little. In that state I recall with some embarrassment becoming overly sincere and asking Lisa how her life was going, which was doubly stupid because Neil was present and, as with any parent supervising small children, Lisa wasn't able to give me her full attention.

Jasmine remained the centre of attention when she was in the room. Once again she didn't eat much and soon left the table to resume playing with her toys in the hallway, where Lisa could keep an eye on her by looking over my shoulder. Jasmine came into the dining area a few times to make some sort of announcement before running off again. She was also keen to show her new toys to Grandpa, who did his best to look impressed but didn't always understand what she was saying, and didn't want to upset her by repeatedly asking her parents to translate.

It was only with the dishwasher whirring away and both Jasmine and Alfie having afternoon naps that Lisa, Neil and I were able to repair to the lounge and attempt some semblance of an adult conversation. Then we found we were still talking about the kids, or what was on television or, briefly, about football. And then we all fell asleep.

I was awoken by the arrival of a sudden large weight in my lap, which turned out to be my granddaughter, losing her footing as she tried to show me another doll. I was pleased to realise that it was one of the *Frozen* dolls that I had bought her, though concerned at the wear and tear that it was already exhibiting, which suggested it wouldn't live to see Boxing Day.

I looked around and realised that Lisa and Neil were no longer in the room, and I wondered how long I had been asleep. I checked to ensure that I hadn't dribbled, and was relieved to find that I had not. Jasmine was now kneeling on the floor where she had arranged a group of dolls in something like a circle and was making up a story about them. She was still holding the *Frozen* doll (Elsa, I think, or was it Anna?), which was apparently speaking, to the other dolls and to me. I had the impression I was expected to join in, so I sat on the floor beside her, finding myself a cushion when I realised how hard the wood was. I picked up one of the other dolls which I thought might like to join in the conversation, but Jasmine clearly intended this to be a monologue and pushed it away with her free arm. Elsa/Anna was obviously very cross about something or other, and it didn't look like any of the others would be getting any tea.

I wasn't finding this very interesting, so after a couple of minutes, fortified by the alcohol still flowing through my veins, I suggested I should be a horse; Lisa always really liked that when she was little. Jasmine seemed familiar with the game and, with me on all fours, she climbed onto my back and we set off in a trot towards the bay window. Her feet dug into me a little as she spurred me on, and more than once her doll came into contact with the side of my head – I couldn't tell if deliberately or not – but I decide to put up with it, particularly when Jasmine started to squeal with delight. That drew her mother into the room. She initially looked surprised, then smiled, went away again and quickly returned with a phone to take our picture. "This will embarrass you, Dad" she said as the flash fired. Jasmine immediately wanted to see the results and seemed to approve. From my low vantage point and without my glasses I struggled to see it when it was briefly waved in front of me. "I'll send it to you," Lisa promised. "There you go. Done!"

It is a good picture, and doesn't embarrass me at all. I have a similar one of me and Lisa, except that is a bit blurred because in those days you had no way of telling until the prints came back weeks later, and taking a back-up was expensive. At least for once you can't see Anne's thumb in that one.

Jasmine had obviously decided this was the Grand National rather than a four-furlong sprint, so we went up and down for quite a while longer, though probably not as long as it seemed. I had forgotten that small children measure boredom completely differently from adults: their attention span can be ten seconds or less, but equally they will happily watch the same cartoon a hundred and thirty-seven times! Finally I hit on the bucking bronco ploy, pushing up on my arms and arching my back, hoping that Jasmine would gently slide off. But she seemed to think this was great fun and hung on tenaciously, and I couldn't go any further for fear of hurting her. I was almost resigned to spending the rest of Christmas Day like this when Neil unexpectedly came into the room, said in a no-nonsense way that Grandpa had had enough, gently lifted Jasmine off my back and deposited her on her feet next to me.

"Now thank Grandpa," he said. Jasmine looked up at him uncertainly, turned and planted a tiny, gentle kiss on my cheek. Then, before I could reciprocate, she ran through her father's legs and out of the room.

The rest of the day was a bit of an anti-climax in many ways, and I don't mean that unkindly. There was a stack of playing cards and other games that Lisa had thoughtfully set out, but we never got round to playing any of them. Until both children were in bed asleep – and even periodically afterwards – one or other of them always demanded the attention of at least one of their parents. I'm not complaining about that, because when you accept the hospitality of people with children you take them as you find them.

When Jasmine came in to say goodnight she had already lost some of the familiarity towards Grandpa that she had had only a couple of hours earlier: she didn't want to kiss him, and no one was going to force her to, least of all me. "She's tired," Lisa said, apparently reading my thoughts. I waved at my granddaughter and looked forward to more games with her tomorrow.

The three of us sat in front of the television for the rest of the evening. Much of the conversation continued to revolve around the children, which reminded me how much having them changes your life, even when they aren't physically present. The only interesting exchange was when Lisa was saying having a second child seemed to give a whole new dimension to the thing.

"Did you and Mum not consider having another child, Dad?" she asked suddenly. "I don't think we've ever discussed it."

I didn't think we had either. I noticed that Neil was looking at Lisa uncomfortably. I tried a joke. "We couldn't work out what it was that caused pregnancy. Fluke first time round."

"No, but seriously."

"You were so special that we thought we can't follow that."

"No, but seriously."

I was silent while I thought about it.

Lisa looked worried: "If you don't want to.. I only..."

I smiled at her. "No, it's not that. I'm honestly trying to give you an answer. I mean, we never decided *not* to have a second child. It didn't happen naturally, and I don't think we were comfortable with the idea of having to seek help."

Lisa nodded but said nothing.

"Would you have liked a sibling?" I asked to break the silence.

Lisa thought for a second: "I don't know. Sometimes I was a bit lonely."

"Were you?" I was genuinely surprised. "I never realised that. You had us and you had your friends."

"Even so."

"This is getting a bit heavy, isn't it?" Neil said with a smile. We both ignored him.

"Well, I'm sorry, sweetheart," I said. "I had no idea. Still," I ventured, as much as anything to alleviate my own feelings of guilt, "sometimes siblings can be playmates and sometimes they just fight."

Lisa's mood seemed to brighten. "Well, let's hope it's the latter with our two," she said. "Jasmine seems to be protective towards her little brother already."

Neil nodded in agreement and I readily joined in.

We watched a World War II film and an old 1970s Christmas comedy special, which seemed to leave Neil cold, but which Lisa and I enjoyed because we used to watch them together in the late nineties, when they were already museum pieces. More gets edited out each decade as views on what is acceptable change, though my memory wasn't good enough to work out what had been lost where.

Neil got up to go and check on Alfie. On his way back he went into the kitchen and called out to Lisa: "Shall I put a bottle of wine in the fridge for tomorrow?"

Lisa considered for a moment. "Probably not worth it for us. And Dad's driving."

I wondered for a moment where we were going. But that didn't make sense because my car only has two seats. Unless maybe Jasmine had seen Grandpa's Italian sports car and wanted a ride in it?

"Yeah, but your mum will drink it, in the evening."

"That's true. Go on."

I looked straight ahead, trying to maintain my poker face. Lisa and I hadn't specifically discussed how long I would be staying, and I knew I would be home before New Year, but I hadn't expected the bubble to burst so quickly, to be going back to the flat on Boxing Day. I really didn't want to either. But what could I say? That I think I can be in the same room as Anne with no awkwardness, even if she's with Howard, because I actually quite like the bloke? Which is mostly true, but not my call, is it? You don't outstay your welcome, not if you're hoping to be invited back.

So I would just need to make the most of what was left of Christmas. I decided to have one of the beers I had brought and was delighted when Neil said he would join me.

Saturday 26 December

I didn't sleep very well and from about six thirty onwards was wide awake. I was hoping to hear sounds of life in the house but there didn't seem to be any. At seven thirty I decided to go and use the bathroom and hoped that I wouldn't be waking everyone.

Back in the lounge I tidied up and packed my bags, then watched videos on my phone until I thought I heard a light switch flicked and the radio turned on in the kitchen.

Breakfast was much the same as yesterday, with me once more as toast monitor, though with less conversation. Jasmine still wasn't keen on a lot of Coco Pops, delivered by Stuka or otherwise, and the same mess resulted. I assumed, if Anne wasn't arriving until the afternoon or evening and they had been debating whether I would be drinking wine, that I was staying for lunch, but was on the lookout for any sign that I was expected to depart earlier.

I went into the lounge hoping that I would be able to play with my granddaughter again, and perhaps make enough of an impression that she would remember me next time she saw me, whenever that might be. My flanks were a little bruised from yesterday's rodeo, but I didn't mind at all.

Jasmine didn't appear though. At around ten Neil came in and told me she seemed a bit listless and her temperature was slightly elevated.

"Probably nothing. Just the excitement of yesterday," I suggested, thinking aloud but immediately realising how uncaring this sounds to the modern ear.

"Lisa's on the phone to the doctor," Neil replied coldly. "Not that they'll be open today, but it goes through to some sort of out-of-hours service. Usually anyway. I'm not sure about Christmas."

I didn't know either, so just tried to look sympathetic.

Lisa came in a few moments later looking grim-faced. "They said it's probably not serious, give it till lunchtime. Then we might have to consider going to A&E if it hasn't improved."

"Right," said Neil. "Well, she's asleep now."

"But I'd rather not wait. I'd never forgive myself... I think we should go now."

Neil didn't look convinced, but nor was he inclined to argue. I knew my opinion definitely wasn't wanted.

"Can you let yourself out, Dad?"

"Of course." Lisa came across and gave me a brief but tight hug. "Lovely to see you, Dad. Thanks for coming."

"Thanks for inviting me. I really enjoyed it."

I shook hands with Neil, and then he and Lisa were both off in practical mode, arranging the logistics of getting two adults and two small children to a hospital with enough stuff to last what might be a visit of several hours, or longer. I was sure that if they had wanted me to stay with the baby they would have said so, and although I thought I could have managed, I wasn't sure enough to volunteer. I opened the front door for them and was able to give Jasmine a big smile as her father carried her outside. Her little face, mostly hidden in the hood of her jacket, did look slightly flushed.

"Please keep me informed," I called out after them.

It seemed strange to be in the house alone. I went and fetched my stuff, set the burglar alarm as Neil had instructed, and then went through the front door and closed it behind me. It took two attempts to start the Maserati, which was clearly as reluctant as I was to be asked to move on Boxing Day.

The roads were empty, and although I made no effort to hurry, I was soon back at my garage. I put the car to bed and then walked slowly back to the apartment block with my baggage. None of the other flats seemed to be occupied, but I couldn't be absolutely sure about that.

My living space smelled stale and seemed bleak and uninviting, without human presence. I threw my stuff in the bedroom, made a cup of coffee and went and stood by the window. A few family groups were out for walks, some impossibly overdressed for the moderate temperature of a cloudy day, but they made a lot of good-humoured noise and seemed to be enjoying themselves. I wanted to wave at them.

I was impatient for a message from Lisa, which came sooner than I expected, via a text. It appeared that Jasmine hadn't even made it past triage. She was already feeling brighter and more energetic, and her temperature had dropped. So they were going home.

I replied that I was very pleased to hear it and to send Grandpa's love. And that it had been lovely to see them all.

Lisa replied 'Thanks xx.'

Boxing Day lunch was beans on toast.

I then had almost twelve hours to kill. That was how I felt. I kept looking at the clock, as though I were doing a particularly boring job and wanted to go home. I went for a walk. I watched TV. I tried but failed to read. I fell asleep but woke up a few minutes later. I had a few bottles of beer while watching nostalgic TV programmes, then switched to whisky, all in the hope of rekindling some sort of Christmas feeling, but it would not come. I hoped no one would see the light on in my flat and realise I was here, alone. I had a microwaved lasagne. I watched more TV and drank more whisky. I could hear the beat of music somewhere close, but not in the building, and assumed someone must be having a party. I thought about writing this diary but couldn't face it.

At ten thirty I went to bed.

Friday 1 January

Happy New Year! All sorts of things to tell you, whoever you are. A future me, I suppose.

I have a hangover, which I'm carrying like a badge of honour, as if I were fifteen rather than fifty-eight. I've been drinking plenty of water all day, and I think that has helped, though it probably needs a good night's sleep to knock it on the head once and for all.

I've decided (New Year's resolution?) to stop pedantically recording everything under the exact date that it happened, but rather just to make entries when I have anything interesting to say. So this is the first entry since Boxing Day.

The 27th to 30th December were pretty lean days, to be honest. I got used to my own company, as I always do, so I wasn't feeling emotionally out of sorts in the way I was on Boxing Day, but I can't remember very much about those days. I ate, slept, watched TV, read, went for walks, went for one drive. Not enough for four diary entries!

On Wednesday (30th) I bumped into Ella as I was coming out of my flat and she was coming up the stairs. She is still having problems with her right arm and was struggling with two bags, so I did my best to help her. We stopped briefly for a chat before she went into her flat. We exchanged Christmas stories.

"Yeah, I've been up north to see my family," Ella told me. "Love 'em to bits," she went on with a knowing roll of her eyes, "but in small doses, if you know what I mean."

I smiled and nodded, though I couldn't really relate to what she was saying.

"And," she continued in an almost conspiratorial whisper, "I don't think they really approve."

I nodded again. "I had a lovely Christmas with my daughter and family," I volunteered.

"That's lovely." Ella looked genuinely pleased for me. "How old are the kids."

"Jasmine is four and Alfie is still a baby."

"Cute?"

"Of course. Though I'm biased."

"Aw."

I blushed slightly, though I wasn't sure why.

"Anyway," said Ella, as though breaking a spell, "that's Christmas over for another year. Now New Year!"

"Indeed!" I replied, trying to sound enthusiastic.

"Talking of which, I'm having a party."

I experienced a very sudden feeling of simultaneous excitement and apprehension.

"So," Ella said with a pained grimace on her face, "apologies in advance for the noise if you happen to be in."

"Not sure yet. Probably," I stammered. "No problem. It's only once a year, isn't it? Thanks for letting me know."

Ella ended the conversation by getting out her door key and putting it in the lock. "See ya," she said.

As I walked down the stairs I was hoping she would say: "Just kidding. Ha, ha – the look on your face!" but all I heard was her flat door slamming shut.

Yesterday was nearly an awful day. I shudder now to think how close it came. From the moment I got up I had the sense of it as something I just had to get through. I've spent New Year on my own before, and I tried to convince myself that it was just like any other day, but it isn't: the outside world inevitably intrudes and you can hear the noise of countless other people enjoying themselves. And with a party right next door that was going to be very noisy and almost certainly go on long into the early hours, with people spilling out into the corridor as they got drunk, I was going to feel a bit as though I were under siege.

I could – definitely would – drink at least one bottle of wine to help pass the time, but it was a grim prospect.

In late afternoon, but before it got dark, I went out for a walk. It was cold and quite windy, and there weren't that many people about; the calm before the storm of partying, I supposed. I walked past the shop where I work and noticed properly for the first time how beautiful the white Christmas lights in the high road are. I wondered who puts them up and how much effort it involves.

A toddler was walking towards me with his mother, who seemed to be in her early twenties. She was paying him no attention as she jabbed at her phone screen rapidly with both thumbs. The little boy saw a small puddle on the pavement that he liked the look of and squealed with delight as he jumped into it. Then, as he was a couple of yards away from me, he saw an even larger puddle in a pothole in the road and decided that he liked the look of that even more. He darted towards it, only a few metres in front of a Transit van, which was coming along the carriageway at some speed. The van tried to swerve and instinctively I grabbed the boy and pulled him back onto the pavement. Spray from the van, as its tyres went over the pothole, splashed both of us.

The mother finally looked up from her screen. I expected to see fear and relief on her face. Maybe gratitude. Instead I saw pure anger.

"Leave him alone!" she shrieked.

I gently pushed the boy towards her, ensuring that I continued to shield him from the road.

"Get away from him, you paedo!"

I could have sunk to the ground there and then. A couple on the other side of the road turned and stared. I felt dirty and horrible. I cut short my walk and went home.

For the second time in two days I bumped into Ella, only this time she was coming down the stairs as I was going up.

"What's the matter with you?" she asked as soon as she saw me, and it was only then that I realised the sniffles I had been experiencing on my way home had turned into actual tears.

Two minutes later we were both sitting in my flat. I told her the story.

"That's just guilt," Ella pronounced. "The mother. She knows perfectly well she should have been keeping an eye out for the littl'un instead of staring at her phone. Doesn't want to admit it. So turns it on you."

"I'm sure you're right."

"I'm always right."

I sensed that Ella's patience wouldn't last long if I continued to feel sorry for myself. "Last month I was a racist, now I'm a paedo as well" I said with a laugh.

"I know," Ella said seriously. "If this continues, we'll need to seriously consider burning your flat down."

I laughed again.

"Now that I've cheered you up," Ella continued, "one other thing. I've been thinking – and I won't be in the least offended if you don't want to – but if you wanted to come to my party tonight…"

I rapidly weighed the advantage to my self-respect of playing it cool against the possibility that Ella might change her mind, and opted for safety. "That would be great!" I gushed.

"The thing is, Ella went on, it's a sort of theme party."

"Fine with me. What's the theme?"

"I don't know how broad-minded you are, Alan: I don't know you well enough. I'm going out on a bit of a limb here. It's a… fetish party."

"I see."

Ella tried to fold her arms before realising that it was still too painful. She adopted a folded-arms facial expression instead. "From the blank look on your face," she told me, "I'm getting the distinct impression you have no idea what that is. How old are you?"

"Fifty-eight."

"Right. Well, fetish, like leather or rubber? Kinky stuff?"

"I get it. Sort of fancy dress."

Ella laughed. "If you like."

"But I haven't got any..."

"I thought you were going to surprise me there, Alan, and confess to having a wardrobe full of latex. Well, I do have some stuff." She was now looking me up and down in exactly the same way she did when I first met her. "The only question is whether it will fit."

So, dear diary (and hopefully no one else), two hours later Alan Brierley was dressed as a schoolboy, for the first time since... well, since I left school, whenever exactly that was. And longer than that really, because I wasn't now dressed as a sixth-former but as someone rather younger, in long grey shorts, long grey socks, a white shirt, stripey school tie, bright blue blazer and a (not really matching) school cap so faded and battered that I assumed it was the genuine article. In fact, I don't think I ever dressed like that, even when I was a schoolboy; I'm not sure anybody ever did. Ella laughed when I pointed that out; she said that she was going in a nurse's outfit made entirely of PVC, and she's never seen one of those in a hospital either, so I would be in good company.

She had seemed curiously embarrassed, though, from the moment I knocked on her door at the allotted time. I hoped she wasn't having second thoughts about inviting me. I realised I hadn't seen the interior of her flat before, but it all looked quite normal: like my own flat, in fact, only the other way round, with brighter colours, more expensive and more tasteful furnishing and pictures, and a slight fruity smell which I guessed was shampoo or shower gel. Ella had a towel arranged turban-like on her head, so I assumed she had just showered; she was wearing a fairly shapeless onesie with tiger stripes.

She led me along the hall and stopped outside a closed door which, based on my own flat, I had worked out was the master bedroom. "Right," she said, seeming to blush slightly. "Broad-mindedness time again. This is my 'work room'. You can come in if you want, but if you prefer you can stay here and I'll bring stuff out for you to try on."

I said that the latter sounded like a faff, so I would come in if that was OK with her. Ella smiled but continued to look a little troubled as she unlocked the door and beckoned me in. The room was certainly different from the rest of the flat. It was a bedroom but it had no bed. On the right were a desk and a blackboard; something that looked a bit like a vaulting horse; and some sort of metal frame arranged in a cross formation. On the left were a range of wardrobes, one of which Ella had now opened. I didn't see inside for very long, but I did notice something that looked very much like a wetsuit. I also saw a mortar board and gown, beside which Ella appeared to have found what she was looking for.

"How about these?" she suggested. "Basic schoolboy. Comfortable and easy to get in and out of for a, er, beginner. And I've got a few sizes, so should fit, mix and match."

She handed me a stack of clothes. We both said nothing for a couple of seconds. It took me a while to realise that she wasn't intending to leave the room, a delay that she interpreted as reluctance.

"Look, if you'd rather not, Alan," she began. "I mean, it's fine if you just want to come as yourself. Really."

I shook my head. "No, I'll give it a go. When in Rome..."

Ella leaned back against the wardrobe. "You see, I do this all the time," she explained with a pained expression on her face. "And they know, and I know...but it's completely different when you have someone who isn't..."

Before she could finish her sentence, I was halfway out of my trousers (ensuring that my boxers were appropriately buttoned) in a determined bid to show willing. Within five minutes I had found a combination that fitted, and Ella stood back, hand on chin, to survey the ensemble. She concluded that my tie knot looked more family wedding than schoolboy - I tie a very good half Windsor if I say so myself - and came forward to mess it up appropriately, choking me slightly in the process.

After that we went into the living room and I helped Ella arrange the drink (including my own contribution which I'd been out to buy and hoped was suitably generous) and food, including some rather suggestive jelly and pate that we exchanged a smile over. We both seemed to have relaxed and, before I knew it, it was eight o'clock and Ella said she was off to get changed.

Five minutes later there was a lot of swearing coming from the master bedroom and she had not emerged. I knocked timidly on the door. "You OK in there?"

Silence for a moment. "No. This fucking arm. I can't get into this outfit."

"Oh dear. Anything else you can get into?"

"I want to wear this."

"I see. Perhaps when one of your friends arrives..."

"Too late. You'll have to help. Come in."

I cleared my throat, closed my eyes and opened the door.

Ella laughed as soon as she saw me. "Jesus, have you really got your eyes closed?"

I nodded.

"God, you're so sweet. Come here, then. Straight ahead."

I walked forward gingerly and bumped into something which turned out to be Ella's back.

"Right," she said. "All you need to do is gently lift my arm up."

I complied. My hand was on a very slippery surface, which I assumed was the PVC.

"A bit further. A bit further. Ouch. Ouch. No, keep going. It's got to be done." Finally there was a slithering sound and then Ella put her arm down. "Yes, success! Now if you can do me up at the back."

I fumbled for a moment.

"You can open your eyes now, you daft apeth!"

I obliged and quickly did up a couple of straps, apparently to Ella's satisfaction.

"Great!" She turned round. "What do you think?"

She had a small, starched cap on her head, and on her body a tight combination apron (complete with red cross) and dress, finished off lower down by black stockings and high-heeled black shoes.

"Excellent," I replied. "Though not very practical for the wards."

Ella laughed. "Time for your enema, Mr...Alan."

She came towards me, and as I backed away I hit my heel against something. It made a loud clanging sound. I turned and saw that it was the contraption I had seen delivered by the weedy men on my birthday, but I still couldn't figure out what it might be for. I felt a surge of pain in my foot, but it rapidly subsided.

"You OK?" asked Ella.

"I'm fine."

We were now in the doorway.

"I can't believe you closed your eyes," she told me. "I can't decide if you're a real gentleman or just a big child."

We both realised how I was dressed and laughed.

"There's my answer!" said Ella. "But thanks." She leaned forward and planted an affectionate, perfumed kiss on my cheek. I suspect I blushed.

We walked out into the hallway and Ella locked the door behind her. My expression may have given away the question I wanted to ask. "I'm not letting pissed-up people in there," she explained. "Some of that stuff costs a fortune."

The guests started to arrive around nine. Some seemed to have had no qualms about walking down the street (or maybe even travelling on public transport?) in various types of what I think is generically termed "bondagewear"; others, more discrete, arrived with cases and went off to Ella's bedroom to get changed. An ordinary looking couple, who had both arrived upright, emerged with the man on all fours, sporting nothing more than a pair of shorts and a lead around his neck, by which his partner, now clad in black latex, led him around the flat for the rest of the evening. I began to worry that someone I knew might come along. How embarrassing would that be, for both of us? A couple of people did look slightly familiar, but I concluded that I had perhaps seen them in the shop.

At around ten o'clock, when there were about twenty people at the party and the flat was pretty much full, Ella turned down the music and pointed to a sign she had put on the wall reading 'Consent, Consent, Consent' one word above the other. "Thanks for coming and have a great time," she announced sternly, "but you do not do anything to anyone without asking them first. Is that clear?"

There was a murmur of acceptance. Ella seemed to notice that some people were looking at me. "This is my friend and neighbour, Alan, everyone," she told them. "Er, he's basically vanilla."

I didn't know what that meant, but nodded to be helpful. A couple of people were eyeing me quite crossly, so I wondered if the description wasn't a compliment.

The rest of the evening was partly very normal and partly very strange. I got steadily drunker as it went on, but not embarrassingly so, I don't think. I couldn't remember the last time I'd been able to let my hair down like this – no worries about driving or getting home, or having to appear responsible. I could just eat and drink and talk to complete strangers about everything and anything. A small man of about my age with a lot of chains around his neck turned out to be an expert in the same 1980s software programs that I am! We must have discussed that for almost half an hour before his 'owner' came to get him. A very tall woman dressed head to toe in a black leather catsuit, and who said she was in a similar line of work to Ella, turned out to be a season ticket holder at West Ham, and we got through a couple of glasses of wine and several slices of quiche discussing their current defensive frailties and woeful underachievement for as long as either of us could remember, though I could remember much further back than she could, pointing out the cup victories of 1975 and 1980. She said she would have to ask her dad about those, which brought me up short a bit, because until then I hadn't seen her as someone with a family; which of course is ridiculous, as we all have, or have had, family at some point in our lives. I wondered what her parents thought of her career choice, but was still sober enough not to ask. She then changed the subject completely by asking if I was really "vanilla" as Ella had said, because, she explained, she would really like to cane me, and it appeared that Ella's room was free. That sobered me up even more; I managed to splutter something about appreciating the offer but being very squeamish about any sort of pain; and also opposed to all forms of violence as a general principle. That seemed to offend her unfortunately: she said it wasn't violence but a question of power transfer and sexual control. I said I was sure she was right, but I was afraid it still wasn't for me, at which point she just shrugged impatiently and went to talk to someone else.

But overall I really enjoyed the party. I exchanged glances with Ella a couple of times and thought she must be pleased I was mingling easily, that I wasn't sticking out like a sore thumb or following her around. By contrast there was a man who was indeed following her around, kissing her shoes at every opportunity, but she was giving the impression of being completely unaware of his presence.

At one point I found myself thinking that this was more fun than Christmas. I reproached myself for the thought and put it down to the drink. And then I reasoned that it wasn't a question of something being better than something else, but that pleasure and happiness came in different forms.

Midnight came round very quickly. As I had promised Ella I would, I opened the bottles of champagne in the kitchen, poured them into glasses and then distributed them on a tray while she turned on the TV to get Big Ben. A woman with dyed jet-black hair grabbed my ear and said the champagne was late and warm and what did I have to say for myself? I said she should try it first, which appeared to be about to enrage her until another woman standing next to her whispered into her ear and she immediately let go of me, put her hand over her mouth and said she was very sorry. As Big Ben bonged we all had a glass of champagne in our hand, apart from the man at the end of the lead who appeared to be intending to drink his out of a dog bowl.

For Auld Lang Syne Ella came and stood next to me, which I felt was a reward for something or other, then wished me a happy new year and planted a kiss on my cheek for the second time in a few hours. A lot of other people kissed me as well, both men and women now I think of it. I can remember someone kissing me full on the lips, but can no longer remember who.

After that it all gets a bit hazy. More drinking, some dancing I think, sitting in a chair on my own for a while, people-watching. Noticing that Ella was keeping a very keen eye on who was going in and out of her bedroom. The party must have wrapped up between three and four o'clock. I kissed some more people as they left. Ella said fuck it, leave everything as it is, we'll sort it tomorrow. I said I would come and help.

I don't really remember coming back to my flat. I must have crashed out as soon as I got into the bedroom. I woke up at around seven with a desperate need to pee, a very dry throat and the beginnings of a headache. Passing a mirror on the way to the bathroom, I was surprised to see lipstick on my face and a tie hanging limply around my neck, and I realised that I was still dressed as a schoolboy.

The next thing I knew it was ten o'clock. Light was streaming through the curtains. I propped myself up on one elbow and inhaled deeply. I still had a headache, but it appeared that the two pints of water I had belatedly drunk at seven had done their job, and the pain wasn't going to be of the write-off-the-day sort. My stomach was unhappy but not threatening to erupt any time soon. I got up and had a leisurely breakfast of cereal, tea and toast in front of the television, feeling quite at peace with the world, to the extent that I wondered if I was still slightly drunk. Then I went and had a shower and felt positively euphoric as the hot water rehydrated me from the outside.

I went back into the bedroom to get dressed and smiled as I saw the schoolboy outfit on the floor. I should wash it, I thought, though what about the blazer? It would be embarrassing to have to take it to the dry cleaners! I decided I would ask Ella first.

I remembered offering to help clear up today so went out into the landing and listened for signs of activity in Ella's flat. I thought I could hear clattering and the sound of a radio, so I gingerly knocked on the door. It was opened a few moments later and Ella appeared looking much as she had early the previous evening, with a towel on her head and the tiger-stripe onesie, with the addition of a pair of yellow rubber gloves.

I wondered if I had come at the wrong time. Ella followed my gaze to her hands and laughed. "Oh no," she explained. "These are just for cleaning up. Well," she winked at me, "most of the time anyway. Come in."

It was cold in the flat because almost all the windows had been opened, but that had achieved the desired effect of freshening the air, and there was now no more than a hint of the smell of beer and wine. And none of the clinging reek of cigarette smoke that there would have been in my younger days. The dishwasher was chugging already, but even so there was quite a lot still to do. Ella poured me a cup of coffee and then put me in charge of rubbish, which is also more complicated than it was in my youth when black sacks did for everything: now in the world of recycling (of which I entirely approve) I had one sack for cans and plastics, another for paper and card, a third for glass and a fourth for everything else that, much to the chagrin of the manufacturer, was "not yet" recyclable. It was a messy job and Ella offered me a pair of gloves to match her own, which I politely declined.

We found that, with the radio off, we could work in different parts of the flat and talk at the same time.

"You look very fresh," I told Ella. She did: even with no make-up her skin looked unblemished, without the tell-tale green tinge of too many drinks, or the red eyes.

"I'm fine," she shouted back. "Quite tame, really, wasn't it? And I'm used to it, to be honest. Perhaps I should get less used to it! You OK? Did you enjoy it?"

I said I was fine and that I thought it was a really good party. I thanked her again for inviting me, hoping that I didn't sound too much like a child, or too pathetic. Ella said it was her pleasure.

"Did anyone try to molest you?" she asked.

"Sadly not," I joked. "Oh, yes," I remembered. "The lady in the leather catsuit offered to cane me!"

Ella put her head round the bathroom doorway. "What, for nothing?" I nodded. "God, you're honoured, that's two hundred quid's worth normally, is that!"

"I think I offended her."

"I imagine you did. That's "Mistress Tamara". Well, actually, her name's Tracy, but don't tell her I told you that if you ever meet her again."

"Who are you?" I asked. "Mistress Ella?"

She shook her head. "No, you don't use your own name."

"So...?"

"I'm not telling you..."

"Fair enough."

"...because you'd look me up on the internet..."

I must have blushed slightly. She was right: curiosity is a strong emotion.

"... and I don't want you to."

"OK. Sorry if I..."

"But you can look up Mistress Tamara if you like. See what you were missing out on!"

"I'll do that," I said with a smile.

Ella had disappeared back into the bathroom. "Shit!" she shouted a few moments later. "Why won't anything come out of this?"

I threw another couple of cans into the sack and went to help her. She was holding a new bottle of bathroom spray cleaner. She handed it to me and I pinched, pulled and twisted the nozzle until it finally relented and moved into the 'open' position, then I gave the bottle back.

"Thanks," said Ella. "Sorry about that. I haven't done any cleaning for yonks, as you can probably tell. I usually have a guy who comes and does it for me."

"For nothing?" I asked, thinking about some of the men from last night.

Ella grinned. "Better than that. He pays me. A lot! But he's gone up to Scotland to stay with his wife's parents for New Year."

"Of course he has," was all I could think to say.

"But I shall be suitably disappointed with him when he returns. Neglecting his duties."

Ella started laughing at me, a deep throaty laugh. "Your face," she said. "You look so shocked."

But actually I was more confused than shocked. In front of me was a woman a generation younger than me, obviously with a very different outlook on life and very different experiences and sexual tastes from mine. She was dressed in a shapeless onesie and wearing no make-up. And yet I was enjoying her company more than I could remember enjoying anything for a very long time, and deeply worried that I might be falling in love with her.

Monday 18 January

A long interval between diary entries, which tells you all you need to know about my life at this time of year. Early January is an anti-climax at the best of times, with bad weather, the aftermath of Christmas and New Year and most people having no money, but more so this year for me without the benefit of full-time work to pass the time.

I have still been doing a couple of days a week at the shop, though in an atmosphere that can only be described as awkward – with Irene at least; Becky has been fine. I think we were all counting the days to the tribunal, which would at least settle things one way or the other. And that finally happened today.

I didn't sleep very well (I seem to write that a lot, don't I?) I gave up trying at about six thirty and got out of bed. I had a slow, if not really leisurely, breakfast and shower, as my mind was full of the questions I might be asked later in the day, and the answers I would give. I was doing very well in my own head, but I realised of course that the questions that catch you out are always the ones you aren't expecting.

Putting on a suit felt strangely awkward and unfamiliar, but I had decided that wearing one would be a good idea. Putting on a tie (for the first time since New Year's Eve, but in very different circumstances!) seemed even stranger, as though a shirt I had worn dozens of times were suddenly too tight.

Getting on the Tube reminded me that I didn't miss commuting. Travellers looked sad and weary and there was no eye contact. People played music too loudly and other people pretended they hadn't noticed.

I had been a little surprised when they let me know the address of the charity's headquarters, and I was even more surprised when I saw the building itself. It is a tall glass and steel structure overlooking the south bank of the Thames. Obviously the charity doesn't own the place, but it's an expensive area and most of the other tenants seemed to be financial firms; at least that's what I surmised from their names, written up on the board behind reception in the cathedral-like lobby area.

Ade had arrived before me and was sitting in a huge leather chair, flicking through a glossy magazine that he had presumably taken from the stack on the round glass table in front of him. He was wearing what appeared to me to be a green parka but was possibly something more fashionable, and under that a white t-shirt and jeans. He smiled and got up as I approached, and we shook hands.

"Thanks again for doing this," I told him. "I really appreciate it."

"Not at all, man," he replied. "Happy to help."

"I don't know how to make it up to you. Are you taking this as holiday?" I couldn't imagine that Kevin would be giving him the time off to help me.

Ade smiled. "I have a 'virus' today."

"I've been called a few things..." I replied and we both laughed.

Ade was altogether more business-like in the lift, and I could understand why his career was beginning to go places. Eniola had been advising him, he said, on what to say and what traps to look out for, and basically the idea was that the two of us needed to have our ducks in a row. I had thought of retaining Eniola when the charity had advised me that I was entitled to legal representation, even though, they said, the process wasn't intended to be adversarial; however, I had decided that I couldn't really afford it, not when all I stood to gain was retaining a non-paying part-time job.

The charity offices themselves were surprisingly smart and modern, though I supposed they could be paid for by a benefactor. There was a group of four young people talking and laughing loudly in the reception area: I noted that one of the men was wearing a beany hat, which struck me as a strange thing to wear in an office. One of the women had an Alice band in her hair and the other a pair of glasses on her head. The older woman at reception struggled with Ade's name and eventually invited him to write his own pass, which he did without comment.

We sat down again and waited ten minutes until the receptionist answered the phone and asked us to go through to the Biko meeting room, pointing at the corridor behind and to her left. All the rooms in that corridor appeared to be named after African luminaries, though I had to confess that I hadn't heard of a lot of them. Ade appeared to be finding peering at the small nameplates a little trying, but eventually we found the Biko room, knocked on the door and went in.

There was a large table in the room, on the other side of which three people were sitting, with their backs to a broad window. There were two women and one man. They were all middle-aged, and all white. I briefly made eye contact with Ade and suspected he was thinking the same thing. The man was sitting in the middle and appeared to be running the show. He had a large grey beard and a pair of thick-rimmed glasses perched halfway down his nose. The woman on his right could have been Irene's sister, and possibly was: she had short, iron-grey hair and was wearing a white blouse with a tall collar. The immediately notable thing about the other woman was that she had bright pink hair with black highlights. She also had long pendant earrings and was wearing a t-shirt with a fist on it and some words that I couldn't make out without my distance glasses. I had a curious inkling that she and Ade had taken an immediate dislike to each other, which I thought didn't bode well.

I won't rehearse all the introductory pleasantries. The man, with his cheek resting on his hand in a pose that suggested he was bored already and would rather be elsewhere, gave his name and advised that he was Chair of the charity's Conduct

Appeals Committee. His colleagues, he told us too quickly for me to catch, were Ms Something-or-Other and Dr Something-Else. We all nodded and exchanged weak smiles. Ade and Dr Something-Else continued to glower at each other.

"The initial finding of our HR function," the Chair told me, "was that our offer of voluntary employment to you, Mr Brierley, should be rescinded on the basis of non-compliance with the charity's policy on diversity and inclusion, which is important in any event, but particularly so for a charity that does its work in the developing world."

I nodded. "Yes," I agreed.

Dr Something-Else had folded her arms and was now staring disapprovingly in my direction. I resigned myself to winning two-one.

"This," the Chair continued, to the accompaniment of rustling paper as the panel all opened the lever-arch files in front of them, "as the result of taking up references from your previous employer, revealing that you had been dismissed following a racist incident."

"Bananagate," said Ade under his breath. He was now sitting back in his chair with his arms folded. I hoped the panel hadn't heard him. "He wasn't dismissed," he said more loudly.

The Chair took off his glasses and turned to Ade. "Er, Mr..." He looked down at his notes and decided not to attempt to pronounce Ade's surname. "Er, I believe you are here as a character witness?"

"I'm here as a witness of fact," Ade corrected him. Clearly Eniola had been coaching him.

"Right, well." The Chair moved uncomfortably in his seat. He did not appear sure how to handle Ade. "Not that what you have to say isn't important, of course it is," he offered kindly, "but if I could perhaps first explore Mr Brierley's own responses?"

"Go for it," said Ade.

"Thank you. Mr Brierley?"

I told them the whole story. Buying the fruit. Leaving one for Ade because he wasn't at his desk. Someone – not Ade – complaining to HR. My refusing to go on a course that I regarded as unwarranted and ageist. Eniola negotiating a compromise agreement on my behalf, paying up my pension so that I could leave.

"Mr, er.." Ms Something-or-Other seemed to share her colleague's difficulties with Ade's surname. "How did it make you feel when you found this banana on your desk?"

"I was surprised," Ade replied matter-of-factly.

"Did it strike you as a racist act."

A slight hesitation from Ade. "I thought it could be. Except that..."

"Yes?" Irene's sister was now trying to look sympathetic, something I couldn't see Ade falling for.

"Except that the people I work with aren't like that. So it would be someone I didn't know. Or if it was someone I knew, it wouldn't be racist. Not deliberately."

"Have you encountered racism in your life?" Dr Something-Else enquired, narrowing her eyes.

I thought for a moment Ade was going to ignore her completely. "Of course I have," he replied animatedly, "every day of my life. Still do."

I sat up in my chair.

"In what ways?"

"All sorts of things. Stereotypes. People assuming you must be good at sport. Jokes about black sexual prowess. People in the company congratulating themselves on employing me, showing off their liberal credentials, treating me like some sort of experiment."

"And Mr Brierley?"

Ade scratched the back of his head. "He was cool. He didn't employ me anyway. Yeah. I mean he's a bit 'old school', you know?"

"Old school?" Dr Something-Else looked like she thought she was getting somewhere.

Ade glanced quickly in my direction, then back at the panel.

Dr Something-Else looked down at her information pack. "Would that be a kinder way of saying that he suffers from unconscious biases?" She fixed me with a steely stare, then looked at Ade with an expression on her face that said she expected an answer.

Ade moved uncomfortably in his seat. "Yeah, possibly," he said quietly.

"Sorry, I didn't quite catch that."

Ade quickly recovered his composure. "Yeah, possibly. But nothing malicious. He's one of the good guys."

"I see. And do you think that our charity, or indeed your company, should employ someone who suffers from racial biases, unconscious or otherwise?"

"You can do training," Ade offered.

"Ah, yes." Dr Something-Else consulted her notes again. "But we've heard Mr Brierley was offered training and refused to take it."

"That was different," I interjected, unsure whether doing so was a breach of the rules or not. No one appeared to be trying to stop me. "I objected to the assumption that all people over a certain age are racist. It's ageist."

Irene's sister thought she should say something. "But your former colleague here says you suffer from unconscious biases," she began. "Do you think you do?"

I almost laughed. "Well," I reasoned, "if they're unconscious, by definition I wouldn't be aware of them, would I? But if I was aware of them, I would try to do something about them. Including training if that was helpful."

Ade unexpectedly reached out his arm and gave me a gentle punch on the shoulder. Dr Something-Else glowered at him again.

"Turning to the matter in hand, and conscious of the time," the Chair said, looking over my head at what I assumed must be a clock on the far side of the room, "what we can't get away from is that you, Mr Brierley, put a banana on Mr, er, (inaudible)'s desk. Is that not something that any neutral observer would regard as a lacking in cultural sensitivity and, frankly, a racist act? Like, I don't know, turning up in the office in blackface because after work you were intending to go to a fancy-dress party as a coal miner. You'd understand how it would look and not do it."

I realised how inadequate my earlier preparation in my own head had been. I considered thanking them all for their time and getting up and leaving. "I thought deciding who to share my fruit with on the basis of their race would be far worse," I said miserably. "That's all."

"Maybe Alan's a little naive," Ade suggested. "It's not a crime."

I allowed myself a small smile. That word again. The charge of naivety has pursued me throughout my adult life. I was accused of it by the company for my involvement with the anti-fascist protests all those years ago. My ex-wife cited it as one of the reasons why she could no longer put up with my presence. But I've always thought better that than to become a hard-baked cynic, no longer believing in anything. Perhaps that's naive in itself.

"The way I see it," Dr Something-Else interjected, "putting a banana on a BAME co-worker's desk is *prima facie* a racist act. It doesn't matter if it's intentional or not."

"No," Ade told her. "You're confusing it with the handball rule."

Dr Something-Else bridled in her seat. She appeared to be turning something over in her mind, and I wondered if it was whether she could accuse a black man of sexism.

"The thing is," Ade continued. "I'm the 'victim' here. So I think I should get to decide. I don't want or need you to tell me what I should find racist, OK? Because that's patronising and, you know, racist itself."

"I'm sure no one intended..." the Chair began emolliently, looking at each of his colleagues in turn.

But Ade wasn't listening. "I haven't seen a single black face since I came into this office," he continued with passion, "except photos on the wall and on nameplates on meeting-room doors, and one of your rooms, by the way, is named after someone my grandfather to this day regards as a terrorist. If I stick around until you go home and the cleaners arrive, I bet I'll see black faces then. You, lady," he turned to Dr Something-Else, "have been looking at me from the moment I came in as if I was some sort of sell-out because I'm supporting my white friend here. What gives you the right? Do you think black people like you? That they're grateful for what you condescend to do for them? I don't know why Alan even wants to work for you. You don't deserve him!" He sat back and folded his arms.

The Chair cleared his throat. "Is there anything else you would like to say to the panel, Mr Brierley?"

"Yes," I said, though I was under no illusion that anything I said was going to make any difference. "I worked for my previous company for thirty-nine years and had two brushes with the disciplinary procedures. One, back in the 1980s, when I was arrested while marching against the BNP, though I wasn't charged with anything. The company thought it was a breach of their rules anyway, and they couldn't understand why I was supporting what they thought was a far-left organisation. Because in those days, in our company, as in most others, racism *was* the accepted orthodoxy. My second run-in with HR you know about. And my opinions haven't changed one bit in the meantime."

It was my turn to be favoured with Ms Something-or-Other's kindly face. "I'm sure we all meant well back in the 1980s in our own way," she told me and her colleagues, "but I'm not sure we really understood the issues then the way we do now."

Ade and I had gone down several floors in the lift before either of us spoke.

"Well, that went well," I said, which broke the ice, and we both laughed.

"Sorry, man," Ade replied contritely. "But what do you want to work for these fuckers for, anyway? In a little shop? For nothing?"

I laughed again. The job wasn't much, I thought to myself. But it made a change from constantly being on my own with nothing to do, and I had started to look forward to it. Now I didn't suppose anyone would employ me. "Shall we have a commiseratory drink?" I suggested. Ade said he didn't think 'commiseratory' was a word, but he would be happy to join me.

Wednesday 27 January

I got the letter today. It wasn't a surprise given the way the hearing went, and also given that Irene contacted me last week to say that it would probably be better if I didn't come in until the panel had made its adjudication, which hadn't originally been the idea.

I would have to dig it out of the recycling and reassemble it to recall exactly what it said (petulant behaviour on my part I know, but I was upset at the tone of the thing) but basically it informed me that, based on the evidence presented to the panel and statements at the hearing, it had found no grounds not to uphold the original finding that employing me would be a breach of its diversity and inclusion policy, which was a core part of its values as an international charity.

I rang Irene to let her know, but it turned out that she had already been informed. The conversation was very brief: Irene said she was sorry and thanked me for the work I had done to date. I said could she say 'Hi' to Becky for me, and that I hoped I would still be welcome as a customer. Irene didn't answer that one but thanked me again and ended the call.

I knew that, as so often in life, I should pick myself up and dust myself down and just get on with it. But it proved easier said than done in the immediate aftermath of receiving the letter. It seems strange to write it, but I felt dirty.

Ideally, I wanted to talk to Lisa, but I thought it better not to bother her with my problems, at least until they felt less raw to me. I did send a message to Ade, who came back saying it wasn't a surprise, was it? And then, almost as if changing the subject, he added that Eniola had suggested I find myself a woman and then we could all go and have dinner together one evening. I replied saying that would be good, and that I would let him know.

I made a cup of coffee, ate too many biscuits, and spent a good hour just staring out of the window, watching people walk past but not really taking anything in, or caring whether anyone thought my continuous presence in the same spot was odd.

Finally, I texted Ella to see if she was available for coffee and a chat. She didn't reply, but a couple of minutes later there was a knock on the door, and when I opened it there she was, once again brandishing a packet of biscuits, this time hobnobs. That woman understands comfort eating. She came in and threw herself onto the sofa. "Christ, what a day I'm having!" she exclaimed.

I noticed that she was wearing a tweed jacket and matching skirt, a smart white blouse and an unusually sensible pair of flat black shoes. I was going to say something along the lines of 'Have you got a job interview?' when she pre-empted me.

"Oh this," she said. "Do you like it? It's my headmistress. Well, most of it. I thought I'd spare you the gown and mortar board!"

She chuckled and I laughed as well. "So, are you in a hurry?" I asked, hoping that she wasn't.

"Well, no. That's the thing," she replied incredulously. "I've just had a last-minute cancellation. Me? Can you believe it?"

I shook my head sympathetically.

"And, what's worse, it wasn't him that cancelled. It was his wife!"

"His wife?" I sat down as well.

"Yes. She came home unexpectedly and found him in the cupboard under the stairs," Ella told me flatly. I must have looked confused. "Where I had told him he had to go and sit for an hour every day. As punishment," she explained.

With difficulty I tried to put myself in his position. "Couldn't he have just said he was looking for something?" I asked.

"He was naked."

"Oh."

"But I agree: he should have thought of something."

"Sleepwalking?"

"Yes, that might have been worth a try, though it was the middle of the day. Instead, the idiot decided to be honest with her. And gave her my phone number. Apparently she 'knows people' and I haven't heard the last of this."

"Is that bad?" I asked earnestly.

"No, not really. Occupational hazard. Water off a duck's back. I'll see if Tracy/ Tamara wants him. She's having to help me out at the moment anyway, until my arm is sorted." Ella winked at me, and I found myself looking away like an awkward teenager. "Anyway," she continued, leaning back and resting her shoes against the legs of my table, "how are things with you?"

"Well, I can't follow that," I replied. "But not great. I got the letter from the charity today. I'm now officially the Grand Wizard of the Ku Klux Klan." I tried to smile but it didn't really work.

"Oh, that's a real bummer, Alan. I'm sorry."

"Yeah, well."

"You look so sad, mate. Do you want a one-armed hug? Come here then." We both stood up and she put her left arm around me and her head on my right shoulder. I reciprocated and took in the comforting warmth of her body and her expensive scent. I felt a little moistness in my eyes but was able to blink it away.

"Great," said Ella after thirty seconds or so, gently pushing me away and resuming her seat. "So, as in all things, you have to be practical: what you need now is a plan that tells them where they can stick their stupid job. Because you've got much better things to be doing with your time."

"Yes," I nodded. "Yes, I do."

"But first we need that cup of coffee before we both die of thirst."

I went to make the drinks, and when I came back I found that Ella had picked up a pad and pen from my desk and had found a pair of glasses from somewhere. "Right," she said, rattling the pen against her front teeth, "first item on the list."

"I'm not really sure," I replied.

"I can't believe you haven't thought about it. Come on, don't be shy. First item."

"Well, everyone always says travel, don't they?"

Ella looked at me seriously over the top of her glasses. "Well, you're not 'everyone' are you? Do you want to travel or do you not?"

"In theory..."

"Would travelling make you happier than not travelling."

I hadn't told her about the debacle of my Paris trip. "Not if I had to go on my own," I replied. I immediately felt embarrassed, in case Ella might think I was suggesting she should come with me, but she didn't seem to have inferred that.

"Right. So no travel until you've found a woman. We can come back to that later."

"Have you travelled much?" I asked.

"We aren't talking about me. Next. Any hobbies that you would like to make into an occupation?"

"No. Not really."

The same look again. "No, or not really?"

"No."

"Right. Voluntary work?" She wrote the words and then vigorously crossed them out. "Won't have you because you're an evil fascist."

"That's not funny."

"Sorry. Education?"

"Ah, yes." I sat up in my chair. "I started work at eighteen and I've often thought I would have liked to have done a degree. Not that it was ever an option."

"OK." Ella wrote that down as well. "What subject?"

"Well, even though I've worked in IT all my life, I sort of fell into it. I don't actually have a formal qualification in it."

"Is that what you want to do? On the same 'make you happier than not doing it' test as before?"

"No."

"So, something else."

Silence. Ella continued to stare at me as though she were expecting an answer. She cupped a hand to her ear to reinforce the point.

"English literature," I said finally, almost as though I were admitting something shameful.

"OK. Well, that's completely different. Why that?"

"I like reading books. I'd like to know more about them."

"Fair enough. Can you afford it?"

"I haven't looked into it. But I think probably yes, just about."

"Good. Mature student somewhere or Open University?"

"I can't see me in a class full of eighteen-year-olds, so O.U. I think."

Ella nodded. "Probably for the best. You'd be chased off any campus as an appalling Nazi anyway."

"That still isn't funny."

"Well, it sort of is. So to recap..."

"Does writing not hurt your bad arm?"

"No."

"Pity."

Ella stuck her tongue out at me.

"Actually..." I stopped. I could feel my face begin to flush and my heart rate increase. "No, it doesn't matter."

Ella took her glasses off. "What is it? Come on, don't be shy again. Look, it's another occupational hazard of mine that men tell me their secrets, and I can guarantee that whatever you are about to tell me isn't going to make the most shocking top one hundred!"

I laughed nervously. "Well, I'd quite like to have a go at writing something. Fiction."

Ella's expression wasn't encouraging. She put the pad and pen down on the table. I felt my face begin to flush again. "You and half the population," she said. "I mean, it's OK if you just want to do it for yourself, but you do realise the chances of getting published are tiny?"

"I was good at English at school," was all I could find to say, and I could hear how lame it sounded as soon as it was out in the air.

"And as your new coach/ adviser," Ella pronounced, "I would say that it is too solitary for you at the moment. I mean, by all means give it a go, if you've got enough other elements of your life that involve people, but at the moment I'd say it would make your head implode."

I didn't know how to respond to that, though I knew she was probably right. I had had the same unvoiced doubt in my own head; I had thought the charity-shop job was just enough to keep me sane, which was why I was more upset at losing it than it appeared to warrant. "Thank you, Doctor," I said with a smile.

"I know what I'm talking about, Alan. I've got a degree in psychology as it goes, but it's not just that: I understand people. You're looking surprised."

"No, nothing."

"You didn't think I'd have a degree?"

"I hadn't thought about it."

"Liar. Anyway, you're not the first. Moving on. Finding you a woman. How are we going to do that?"

"Who says I want one?"

"Huh! Everything about your entire being tells everyone that you want and need one, Alan!"

"I see." I hadn't realised it was that obvious. Or maybe I had.

"Have you had a partner since your divorce?"

"One. Margaret."

"For how long?"

"A few months. Shortly after I split up with Anne."

"What happened?"

"With Anne?"

"With Margaret."

"Oh, she was a much more intrepid traveller than I was. I guess she found me boring."

"No one for a while then."

I looked down at the floor. "I suppose not."

"Have you considered online dating?"

"I've considered it. Never done anything about it."

"Why is that?"

The reason was essentially a feeling, and it was difficult to put into words. "Lack of confidence. Gets worse the longer you leave it, I suppose. If the other two didn't want me, why would anyone else?"

Ella's expression was more tough love than sympathy. "Time to get back on that horse, fella."

"Maybe."

"Definitely. And here's a suggestion, though bear in mind that I won't take no for an answer: speed-dating."

I shook my head vigorously. "Definitely not. I can't think of anything more excruciating."

"Do it. Just to get some practice talking to women. You haven't got to go out with them. Or if you do, you haven't got to marry them. And how's this to boost your courage: for the first session at least I'll come with you."

That surprised me. "I'll think about it," I said.

"I'll arrange it," Ella replied.

I didn't protest any further.

"I need to go," Ella told me, levering herself up from her chair with one arm. "I've got someone online at twelve, and it's a completely different outfit."

I felt quite upbeat for the rest of the day. I looked into Open University courses but didn't book anything. I went over the conversation with Ella a number of times in my head and thought how valuable her friendship was becoming to me. Though later in the day I did wonder, hoping that the thought wasn't ungenerous, whether she had actually been looking for a companion to go speed-dating with.

Monday 1 February

I've been ignoring Ella's strictures about writing being too solitary for me at the moment because, although I took the point, it's not as solitary as doing nothing at all, which seems to have become the other alternative. There are only so many films you can watch, so many times you can sit through the same item on the TV news. I have been reading a lot, which is something I ordinarily love to do, but again there are limits, or there are for me at least. I found myself reading while leaving the television on with the sound down, as though the flickering image on the screen might convince my brain that I was not alone. Curiously, it sort of works.

But I wanted to be able to tell myself that I was achieving something. Before addressing the dreaded 'blank piece of paper' (screen these days of course) I persuaded myself that the reading I was doing and the internet searches I was making were somehow preparatory work for my novel. I have recently bought some bestsellers and read them to try to see if I could work out what the successful formula is. They were all of the 'accessible literary' type rather than thrillers (which I don't think I could write) or historical fiction (which would take too much research). It seemed that most of the authors were women, and much younger than me, but I decided not to be daunted by that. My findings were that my novel needed to be relatively short, feature a quirky main character, incorporate elements of dark humour but also a strong streak of whimsy, and conclude with either a poignant or an upbeat, life-affirming ending. Plot twists were also popular, so I determined to give that some thought as well.

Internet research was altogether more depressing. It appeared that as an Ordinary Joe your chances of getting published were about the same as those of being kicked to death by an alpaca. Millions of electronic manuscripts were being sent to publishers each year and being discarded unread. Apparently you needed a literary agent, but although some of their websites stated that they were prepared to consider submissions from the public, many of the accompanying photos were of terrifyingly imposing types in primary-coloured statement glasses, who might well have known Virginia Woolf personally, and didn't look like they suffered fools, or prematurely retired IT workers, gladly.

That put me off for a day, until I gave myself a talking-to. I told myself that while it was true that if I wrote a novel I would probably not get it published, if I didn't write one I *definitely* wouldn't get it published. Didn't Jesse Jackson once say something similar about running for president? Mind you, he was never elected, so perhaps not a good example.

On Saturday morning I sat down at the computer at eleven o'clock. I had a mug of coffee, supplemented by a further supply in the jug on the hotplate, and a generous supply of biscuits. I opened a new file in Microsoft Word. The page looked very white. The cursor blinked at me. I saved the file as "Novel-Draft1.docx". The cursor continued to blink at me.

I had decided not to work out the details of the plot first, because, it seemed to me, that would just be further procrastination, and, furthermore, I had heard interviewed authors saying that characters came to life and could surprise you with what they did; on that basis, I thought, pre-planning might be a waste of time. I had also read that first novels are usually semi-autobiographical, so I had decided to have a quirky fifty-eight-year-old man ('Adam' I had provisionally called him, both as a nod to my own name and to the idea that he represented everyone) as my main character, throw him at the world and see what it would do to him and he to it.

Not much, it appeared. I could get him out of bed and describe his everyday tasks; I could send him on a walk where he admired the wonders of nature, my descriptions of which I thought were spot on (and had been much praised in English composition at school), but I couldn't get him to actually *do* anything interesting. He couldn't be an IT worker, but what else did I know about? A writer himself perhaps, but that had been done to death. If he was happily married, that wasn't a story. If he was unhappily married or divorced, that brought back painful memories, and might invite a lawsuit from Anne if the thing were ever published! And alienate Lisa.

In that case, Adam had never married. I typed 'Adam had never married,' intending it as a plot note, but then decided it was actually a striking first line. Perhaps the rest of the novel could explore why not.

Why not indeed? I realised that I had got through three mugs of coffee and half a packet of plain chocolate digestives. Despite that, I was beginning to feel hungry and, looking at the clock, I realised it was lunchtime.

I had a leisurely egg and beans on toast in front of the TV, then fell asleep. When I woke up, I realised that I would probably need the saucepan again for dinner, so I washed up the breakfast and lunch dishes.

It was starting to get dark when I sat down again at the computer and took it out of 'sleep' mode. Why had Adam never married? What was his dark secret? Was he disfigured? If he was, an upbeat ending might be difficult. The woman who came to love him for his personality alone? I smiled: it sounded much too pious for a modern audience. His personality and sexual prowess, perhaps? Or maybe Adam was so attractive that he'd had countless women all his life and never felt the need to marry. But now he regretted it and was looking for love. That might have legs. I could probably write something from that starting-point as long as there weren't too many flashbacks to my hero's years as a serial philanderer: that might tax my powers of imagination too far.

I wrote: 'Adam had never married. But now he regretted it.'

I stared at that for a while. Everything I had read online, particularly the hints for would-be authors from literary agents, screamed that fiction writing was about showing not telling. And here I was violating that rule in the first line! I deleted the second sentence.

'Adam had never married.'

What next?

'Adam had never married. He didn't know why.'

I let out an involuntary laugh.

I was starting to feel thirsty. I went to make a cup of tea and cut myself a small slice of cake. I didn't want to get cream on the keyboard, so I sat down temporarily in front of the TV and realised it was about time for the football results. West Ham won away at Spurs. Seriously good news! I watched all the post-match interviews and punditry, and then realised that an hour had passed.

I went back to the computer. There was no prospect of me writing anything further that day. I decided I should sleep on it – I was sure that people often got unconscious inspiration that way - and then resume on Sunday.

I didn't write anything on Sunday.

Today I investigated Open University courses on English literature and creative writing – ideally, I thought, I would like to combine the two. I filled out the online expression-of-interest form and will look forward to seeing what I get back. I feel I just need a little assistance.

Ella WhatsApped me late this afternoon to say that we are going speed-dating this Friday. "No ifs, no buts" she said. She's not a woman to be argued with.

"OK," I replied, "what time?"

Friday 5 February

I don't know why, but in my mind's eye I had been expecting more glamorous surroundings. Of course, when I thought about it, it wasn't likely that a speed-dating company would have enough events to justify permanent premises, though they could at least hire a smart conference room in an upmarket hotel. Perhaps they do in other areas, but there aren't any upmarket hotels around here that I am aware of, so I guess the church hall has to do.

Such buildings all seem the same to me, period-piece remnants of post-war austerity. The hall tonight (which, for some reason, I've never been in before) ticked all the boxes: there was the obligatory closed serving hatch; bleak strip lights; functional Formica-topped tables whose metal legs scraped across the floor as they were moved into place; wooden chairs, each with a lump missing in a different place; scored and scarred linoleum; and the smell of old food, cleaning products and damp.

As we walked in, I looked at Ella to see if she was thinking the same, but she just stared blankly back at me before giving me the hint of a smile of encouragement. I made no comment, telling myself that she had gone to the trouble of organising this for both of us, so it would be churlish to complain.

Compared to the image she usually presented to the world, Ella had consciously toned herself down, I thought. Her make-up, particularly around the eyes, was subtler. And though her clothes – a sleeveless white top I hadn't seen before and smart designer jeans – didn't seek to hide her natural curves, they didn't flaunt them either. Her shoes were black with modest heels and looked fairly new. She was wearing her hair down, in which state it fell well below her shoulders, and it had clearly been recently washed. I had had to help her into her jacket, which is something I have become quite adept at.

I noted that Ella hadn't commented on my appearance, but on the other hand she hadn't told me to go home and get changed, so I guessed I looked at least OK. I had concentrated on looking presentable: showering, shampooing, deodorising and removing extraneous hairs wherever they might be found. Plus clean teeth and fresh breath. I was surprised to discover how old most of my clothes were and thought of buying something new, but I suspected that shopping on my own I would end up with items similar to those I already had. So I plumped for a checked smart-casual shirt, my own best jeans and a pair of brown shoes I cleaned with actual polish for the occasion. My coat, I realised, looked disappointingly anoraky, but it was the only one warm enough for a February evening, and I assumed I would be taking it off before I met anyone.

A woman was greeting everyone as they walked into the hall. She smiled at us as though it were our first day at school, and gave each of us a leaflet and a piece of paper with a unique number on it. She told us to sit wherever we liked for the moment. Her badge said she was Ros from Pinnacle Connections. We found a table near the back and sat down. It appeared that we were two of the last to arrive. Ella began to scan the room in a way I think she intended to be surreptitious, but as it involved craning her neck a couple of times it wasn't wholly successful. She exhaled and sat back, turned to me, winked and smiled. "No customers!" she whispered. "That's a relief."

I didn't know what to say to that, so I just smiled back. I made my own attempt at clandestinely reviewing my fellow speed-daters, both to see who I might be meeting later and to assess what the male competition was like. Almost everyone else seemed to be doing the same, making fleeting eye contact before looking away. It reminded me of the first-evening drinks on the singles' holidays I'd been on, usually a fairly dismal occasion, even if you went on to make good connections later in the trip.

It appeared that Ella and I were at opposite ends of the age spectrum in the room, and that Ella was the best looking of all the women, a fact that clearly wasn't lost on a number of the men. She was now sitting low in her chair, looking directly in front of her, but I suspected she was not unaware of the attention she was receiving. The other women ranged from the grandmotherly to the elegant to the power-dressing, with one or two small timid souls casting anxious glances towards the door. I told myself that first impressions were always misleading, and that once you got to know people, odd though it sounds, they did actually *look* different. I was encouraged, though, by the appearance of most of the men, who looked like a bunch of ageing lorry drivers searching for a housekeeper who also did sex on demand. I wanted to eavesdrop if one of them tried his 'banter' on Ella. Two of the men looked like serial killers; so it really was like my singles' holidays! None of the women was looking in my direction though, so I guessed that even in this company I was physically nothing special. But I knew that.

Ros had walked into the middle of the room and now began speaking. There had been no need to get our attention or call for silence. "Hi," she said. "Thanks for coming. Particularly the first-timers, but also some of our veterans I can see." A woman called out something and Ros laughed and thanked her by name. It hadn't occurred to me this might be something you needed to do several times. My spirits fell a little.

"So," Ros went on, "mainly for our new friends but also a polite reminder to our existing customers." She went through a recital of what you were not allowed to say, or ask, or indeed ask for, in order to ensure that everyone could enjoy themselves in a safe environment. There was some mirthless nervous laughter. "Now," Ros continued, "for the newbies, you won't all be meeting everyone. Based on the information you gave us on the online form, including your interests, likes, dislikes and ages of people you would like to meet, our computer algorithm, with some human assistance, has determined who should meet who. The piece of paper you have been given shows both your number and the numbers of the people you will be meeting, in which order, with brief notes about them. Please ensure you move on promptly at the end of the allotted time, even if you're sure you've just met the love of your life!" More nervous laughter.

"What online form?" I whispered to Ella.

"I did both of ours," she whispered back. "I made you more colourful. You'll thank me later."

The first person I was partnered with (if that's the right phrase) was called Sylvia (I think) and all I discovered in the five minutes we spent together was that she was a grandmother. She showed me pictures of her grandchildren, which I was politely complimentary about, and told me how well they were doing at school. I volunteered that I was a grandfather, and felt guilty for a moment that I didn't carry a photo of Jasmine and Alfie with me at all times, but I had the impression Sylvia didn't want to be interrupted, and received no response when I attempted to tell her something about myself. I tried a different tack, asking her about her own interests, but was met with a blank stare. So that was Sylvia, a grandmother.

The next one was called Elaine and informed me that she had a practical no-nonsense approach to these things. She was probably a couple of years younger than me, though dressed two decades younger, and had large, long triangular earrings that jangled as she spoke. She was wearing a perfume that was strong but not overpowering. I had the impression that I was being examined against a checklist and, once I had confirmed that I was no longer working and lived in a small flat, she began to glance to one side to see who might be coming along in a minute.

I took the opportunity to look across the room to see how Ella was getting on. She was sitting back with her arms folded and a slightly pained expression on her face, while a guy who must have been fifty, with long hair, a denim jacket and a shirt with one too many buttons undone, appeared to be trying to work his charm on her.

I liked my next partner. Her name was Debbie and she seemed a little shy and nervous, telling me that this was the first speed-dating event she had been to. I said that was something we already had in common, which seemed to make her smile briefly before she looked down at the table. She was quite petite, with curly dark hair, and I estimated that she was probably on the cusp of fifty. She said she worked for the NHS and was also interested in green issues. Trying not to sound too earnest, I said that preventing climate change was the most critical challenge of our age. Debbie nodded and gave a list of organisations and asked if I was a member of any of them. I had to admit that I was not, though I added (it sounded a little forced, even to me) that, now I at least temporarily had more time at my disposal, I should look at getting more actively involved. Debbie nodded again but looked disappointed, as though she thought I was just parroting what I imagined she wanted to hear.

She then asked if I had really been a champion break-dancer. At first I thought I had misheard, but Debbie showed me her copy of my profile, which I quickly read. "Someone making a joke at my expense," I told her good-humouredly, but she looked as though she thought the joke was on her. I knew I should quickly say something to dispel the ensuing awkwardness, but to my own intense annoyance I didn't have the wit to come up with the right words. I quickly glanced at Debbie's profile, which I hadn't previously read. Nothing jumped out except that she was a widow, and before I could decide whether that was something I could ask about, Ros was asking us all to move around again.

I briefly made eye contact with Ella and mouthed "break-dancer?" at her but she just cupped her hand to her ear and gazed innocently back at me.

I've actually completely forgotten some of the women I subsequently spoke to. I don't mean that dismissively, because they no doubt said the same about me. It's just a facet of the human brain, that each time something is repeated the impression it leaves lessens.

I do remember my last partner for the evening: she was called Lucy and had a shock of purple hair. She also asked about the break-dancing, and seemed disappointed that it wasn't true. She then enquired when I had left the priesthood, which caused me to glare in Ella's direction again, though this time it turned out Lucy had confused my profile with someone else's. I looked round to see if I could tell which of the other guys had previously been a man of the cloth, but it wasn't at all obvious. Lucy seemed attractive and vivacious, kept the conversation going and listened to what I was saying, and I was about to make an extra effort to sound interesting when I glanced at her profile and saw that she kept spiders. Not going to happen, sadly.

Ella seemed curiously reluctant to be in my company until we had left the building, so I didn't force the issue. I didn't think anyone who saw us together could possibly have assumed we were a couple, if that was what she was worrying about. I found myself next to Debbie in the orderly queue to exit the hall and took the opportunity to say that it had been a pleasure to meet her. From her expression I couldn't be sure that she remembered me at all, so, to jog her memory, I volunteered that I fully intended to start break-dancing lessons next week. She now looked both confused and embarrassed, but nodded politely and wished me a good night, which I returned.

Ella had waited for me a few yards from the hall. She was making little jumps on the spot to keep warm. The temperature had dropped considerably and there was now a mist in the air; you could clearly see your breath refracted in the stark light of the streetlamps.

"How did it go?" she asked as we started walking.

"OK," I said. "Good practice at least."

"No one in particular?"

"No," I said too quickly. "Well one possibly, but she didn't seem interested in me."

"You sound like a teenager."

I laughed. "Well, it is a bit like that, isn't it? Starting again. Anyway, she went off me when she found out I wasn't a champion break-dancer." I had decided to take Ella's joke in good part, for fear of offending her, though I wished she hadn't done it.

Ella threw back her head and laughed. "Did you like that? I was originally going to go for lion tamer."

I smiled gamely. "How about you?" I asked.

"Just here to keep you company, remember" she replied confidently. "You need to fill out the form now and see."

I told her I didn't know how that worked. She explained that you say who you would like to see again, and if they say the same, you're given each other's contact details.

"I see," I said slightly disconsolately. I would be putting in one then, and expecting none in reply. "And you can't ask them to reconsider?" I asked, demonstrating once more my regrettable habit of thinking aloud.

"Of course not," Ella replied indignantly, stopping so that she could look directly at me. "That's semi stalking. Have more self-respect, man!"

I nodded apologetically. "I expect the guy in the denim jacket will be putting you down on his list," I said in an attempt to deflect the focus away from me.

Ella stared at me through narrowed eyes. "God, did you see him? God's gift to women, fifty-five going on twenty-five. Kept calling me darling. My eyes are still stinging from his aftershave."

I laughed. "Well, you had a really inscrutable expression on your face; that's probably why he ploughed on."

We had arrived back at the flats and Ella let us into the block. "That's my 'you wouldn't believe what Tamara and I would do to you if we had you over her bench' expression," she told me in a half-whisper as we walked up the stairs.

"Well, I hadn't seen that expression before," I replied.

Ella was now opening her own door. "Lucky for you," she smiled. "Good night."

Sunday 7 February

Oh dear, Brierley. You've done it again.
How to set this all out neutrally? So:
Yesterday was a quiet day. I submitted my form online to Pinnacle Connections (Ella having finally sent me the login details) stating that I would be interested in seeing Debbie again. According to Ella, some men pretend to like all the women just to see which of the women liked them, then don't follow up. She says knowing things like that about men help spur her on when she's engaged in her professional activities. Sadly, after today, I don't suppose I will be getting to hear any more of Ella's opinions on anything.

I thought today would be as quiet as yesterday, but just before lunchtime Ella called me and said she was having problems with her computer and her usual man wasn't available. Did I think I would be able to help? I said my expertise was mainly in business software, but I'd take a look if she wanted.

I was surprised a couple of minutes later to find myself being led into her bedroom. The computer was mounted on a metal trolley, and attached to it was a small camera. Ella lowered herself onto the bed, being careful not to damage her bad arm, and picked up a remote control from the bedside cabinet.

"So," she explained. "I'm supposed to be online in two hours and this poxy thing is not working. Look," she jabbed impatiently several times at the remote, "the camera doesn't move, and even if I could do without that, I'm not getting a picture, so presumably at the other end they won't be either. And I've got a couple of guys one after the other paying serious money."

I cleared my throat. "Well," I said, "this isn't my area but a couple of possibilities spring to mind. I can't promise anything, because it could easily be something else entirely, and then you'll need your expert guy."

Ella sounded a little disappointed in me. "OK," she said. "Whatever you can do."

"If I can't fix it, can you use your phone instead?" I asked, once more thinking aloud.

Ella looked offended. "No," she said simply. "No, I can't. Not in this price bracket."

"Understood," I replied sheepishly. "Just give me a minute."

I wheeled the trolley into the kitchen and put the laptop on the table. To my delight my first hunch turned out to be correct: Ella must have accepted the default security settings on a new update of MacOS, which included not allowing access for cameras. I just needed to change the setting, close and reopen the app Ella was using (I didn't look too closely at that) and a clear image of the kitchen wall appeared on the screen. I didn't think that fix would make the remote-control work, but for some reason it did, and I tried not to look surprised.

"All done," I told Ella, who had been standing a couple of feet behind me all the time with her arms folded. I did my best not to sound too smug.

"Well done you!" she replied, coming forward to look at the screen and briefly ruffling my hair with the flat of her hand as she did so. "That's brilliant. I'm seriously impressed! You've got the job."

"My pleasure," I beamed.

"Well," said Ella, looking up at the clock. "That must be worth lunch at least. Nothing fancy, I'm afraid, I'm just doing scrambled eggs on toast. OK with you?"

I said it was, and a few minutes later the laptop and camera were back in the bedroom, and Ella and I were sitting opposite each other at her kitchen table with plates of food in front of us. Somewhat incongruously, given the food, and the time of day, we each had a large glass of white wine, with the remainder of the bottle standing open between us.

Ella helped herself to a top-up. "Long afternoon ahead," she observed.

"Dutch courage," I said, for something to say.

Ella looked a little put out. "Well, no, it's not a nerves thing," she told me. "I'm the one calling the shots, don't forget. They're just paying."

"Understood."

"But," she went on, looking at her own reflection in the wineglass, "it's a kind of artificial situation, if you get me."

I nodded. "Anyway," I said, finding that I wanted to change the subject, "have you heard back from the speed-dating?"

"Nothing to hear," Ella replied. "I didn't like anybody, did I? What's your news?"

"Nothing," I answered, trying to sound nonchalant about the fact. "But I only liked the one anyway."

"Which one was it?"

"You probably didn't notice..."

"I probably did. Which one?"

"The third one. Petite, curly hair."

"Looked like a tree-hugger."

"She has some environmental interests."

"Told you. I'm a good judge of these things. The last one had much better boobs. Are you not a boob man, Alan?"

I shifted uncomfortably in my seat. "Well, it's not all physical, is it? Certainly not at my age."

Ella snorted. "This is me you're telling this to. One of England's foremost experts on the male psyche."

"Not this male's psyche."

"Perhaps you're secretly gay."

"I am not gay," I replied slightly testily. "Not that there's anything wrong with that," we both said in unison. We laughed. "Anyway," I said ruefully, "the last one keeps spiders."

"Really?" Ella said, looking up at the clock. "Yuk! Anyway, I should probably be getting on. One hour till showtime and I'm stood here in a tracksuit with no slap on!"

Ella re-filled her glass and then stood up. She walked round behind me, lifted up my plate and deposited it on the counter behind me. She put her hands on my shoulders and leaned forward. I could smell the wine on her breath. "Thanks ever so much for fixing my computer," she said. "Saved the day." She leaned further forward so that I could see her face. "And you do know I'm just teasing with the other stuff? This woman doesn't want you, her loss. You'll do fine."

And then I could feel Ella's lips on my skin, and instinctively I just turned my head until my lips met hers and for a split second I enjoyed their moisture and warmth.

Ella recoiled. "What the fuck are you doing?"

"Sorry, I thought you..."

Ella was now wiping her mouth with the back of her hand. "I was just giving you a friendly peck on the cheek!"

I started to feel dizzy. "I'm sorry," I said. "I think I should probably leave."

"Yes, you better had."

And so I did.

Monday 8 February

I didn't really want to get out of bed this morning, even though I couldn't sleep. I kept thinking about yesterday.

You had made a new friend, Alan – and how often does that happen if you live on your own and are in your late fifties? – and then you had to ruin it by doing something as stupid as that. Now you're a sex pest as well as a racist! Without ever intending to be either. But old enough to know better, so don't feel sorry for yourself.

I watched TV and nibbled at food, read a bit and waited for the day to be over. Emails I received were all commercial ones and no one phoned.

I heard Ella's door open a few times and footsteps going up and down the stairs and along the hallway. I wondered if I should talk to her, or text her, or put a note through her door. Or buy her a gift to apologise. But would that look weird and compound the problem? I won't avoid her for ever - eventually we will bump into each other anyway - but I have decided it is probably best to leave it for a few days at least.

"Sometimes I despair of you," Anne used to say. Sometimes I despair of myself.

Sunday 14 February

Nothing worth writing in my diary since last Monday, and I feared today was going to be another empty day. I popped out earlier to buy the Sunday Times – at the second attempt actually, because the first time I heard footsteps and retreated into my flat in case they were Ella's – and thought reading the paper would pretty much be my day.

I had in fact nodded off reading the sport section when the phone rang. It was Lisa.

"Lovely to hear your voice, sweetheart," I told her, and it was. "Is everything OK?"

"Yes, fine," she replied. "Neil's taken Jas out for a walk and Alfie's asleep, so for once I have a few minutes for a chat."

"That's great," I said, though I was so keen to talk to her that for a moment my mind went blank and I couldn't think of anything to say.

"How's my favourite granddaughter?" I asked eventually.

Lisa exhaled. "Oh, you know. Energetic!"

I laughed. "I bet!"

"Don't you want to know about your favourite grandson?" Lisa asked after another short pause.

"Of course I do, darling. And my favourite daughter. And my favourite son-in-law."

"We're all fine, Dad. Alfie's definitely developing a little personality of his own. I think he's going to be very different from his sister, much quieter."

"They're the ones to watch!"

"Indeed. Neil is still working all hours. But that's what you have to do to get on these days. How about yourself?"

I couldn't say 'absolutely nothing' so I had to tell her the only thing I did have to talk about. "Your old dad went speed-dating!"

"Shut up, Dad! You did what?"

"It was the woman next door's idea. I think she just wanted someone to go with."

"Who's this mysterious woman next door? Tell me more!"

"Oh, no," I could feel myself blushing. "It's nothing like that. She's only about forty. And if she was interested in me – and she isn't – she wouldn't be asking me to go speed-dating with other people, would she?"

"I don't know. Maybe trying to make you jealous. Or find out what your type is. What does she do for a living? Is she rich?"

Now I was definitely blushing. "I'm not sure exactly. She works from home, something online I think."

"Hmm. Sounds mysterious. Though I never really understood what you did."

"Well, there you go." I was relieved to change the subject, though I found that Lisa's use of the past tense continued to bother me.

"Talking of work," Lisa cleared her throat. "That's part of the reason for the call, actually. I've decided to go back to work part time. The money would be useful, and to be honest with you I would quite like a change of surroundings once in a while: different people, adult conversation, a bit of an intellectual challenge."

"Well, that's understandable," I replied. "Good for you, darling. That's great. You know I always support whatever you want to do."

Lisa exhaled. "I was hoping you'd say that. It's only two days a week to start with and Mum says she'll be happy to have the kids. Only thing is, one day a fortnight she can't. We were a bit stumped because Neil's folks live miles away, but then Mum said 'why not ask your father?'"

I hadn't been expecting that. I was surprised both by the question and by Anne's apparent faith in me. For a split second I froze.

"Hello, Dad. Are you still there?"

I collected myself. "Yes, still here. Let me think about that for a moment." The expectation at the other end of the line was palpable; I couldn't sound hesitant. "No, of course I will," I said firmly. "I'd be delighted."

"Are you sure?"

"Yes, absolutely."

"You don't sound it."

"Well, there's only one little thing."

"Yes?" The slight waver in Lisa's voice suggested she thought I was about to disappoint her. I wanted to avoid that at all costs.

"Well, I'm a little out of practice at looking after small children," I explained. "Is there any sort of, er, training that I could get?"

"Ha, ha. Mum said you might say that. She said why don't you look after them between you a couple of times? That way the kids will get more used to you too before you have them on your own."

I hadn't expected that either. "Yes, that's fine with me, if it's OK with her, and I suppose it must be if she's suggesting it."

"Yes, though you'll have to promise the same as her that there'll be no saucepan throwing. Our set is brand new and cost a fortune."

I laughed. "Your mum and I were never saucepan throwers."

"I know."

"But if we change our mind, we'll bring our own."

"Thanks."

"And go out in the garden."

"Of course. Anyway, to go back to romance, seeing as it's Valentine's Day, not that that figures much in my life these days with two small kids – lucky if I get a card – are any of these speed-dating women going to get the benefit of your sense of humour? Any interest? I don't know how it works."

"No one so far," I said quietly.

"You didn't like any of them?"

I was becoming quite uncomfortable and hoped Lisa couldn't hear that. "No, I did like one..."

"But she didn't like you. Ah, poor Dad. Well, there's always next time. Plenty more fish in the sea, as you used to say to me."

"Did I? I thought I was more sensitive than that."

"When Dave the biker dumped me."

"God, I'd forgotten about him. Well, he was a complete troglodyte, wasn't he? Our Hoover had more brain cells than he did!"

Lisa gave a full-throated, relaxed laugh. It was a wonderful sound to hear. "Fathers and daughters, eh?"

"Yep, it's all in the genes. Wait till Alfie starts having girlfriends."

"Some time before I have to worry about that. He can't even talk yet, let alone chat up girls. So," Lisa was suddenly more serious, "is this Thursday too early? For the kids? With Mum?"

"No, that's fine," I replied. I'll cancel my lunch date with the Clooneys."

"He can come round when I am here."

"I'll let him know."

"Thanks, Dad."

"Love you."

"Love you too."

"Oh, and good luck with the job," I began to say, but Lisa had rung off.

Thursday 18 February

Anne and I would both say, I think, that we had a 'civilised' divorce. The passage of years in our marriage saw an increase in mutual irritation and a growth in expressions of disappointment (mainly on Anne's part, to be truthful) but not much in the way of actual shouting. I know some people feel that shouting is good: get it off your chest, they say, get it out in the open, but I don't think it would have worked in our case, ignoring the psychological damage it might have done to Lisa. I suppose some people would say that I gave up too easily, that I should have 'fought for my marriage', but to be frank, I think it came to a natural end. Moving towards middle-age had removed the basic compatibility we had enjoyed in the first years of our relationship, leaving both of us wondering what we were doing sharing a house with this stranger, who no longer even looked like the person we had fallen in love with twenty years earlier. We stayed together while Lisa was at school, then split up during her first year at university. The news didn't surprise her in the least; it turned out that the facade we had been presenting hadn't fooled her at all. Which left me wondering whether we shouldn't have credited Lisa with greater intelligence and sensibility, and gone our separate ways earlier. Who knows?

Before today, I calculated as I drove over to Lisa's place this morning, Anne and I hadn't spent more than an hour at a time in each other's company in over ten years. I was a little apprehensive, to tell the truth, but figured that the practical task of looking after two small children would occupy us both fully, not leaving time for much else, least of all reopening old wounds. The important thing was to appear to be natural, I told myself, while understanding that there was no longer any intimacy between us.

"God, are you still driving that old thing?" Anne asked, peering past me as she opened the front door. Unaccountably I had been able to park right outside.

"'That old thing' is a thoroughbred Italian sportscar," I reminded her, narrowing my eyes in indignation but smiling at the same time.

Anne smiled as well, then turned her cheek towards me, inviting me to plant a polite peck on it, which I duly did.

Our exchange of pleasantries was cut short by Jasmine who, in what is clearly her party-piece, came running along the hallway and wrapped herself round her grandmother's leg. For a moment she looked up at me warily – I tried to console myself that eight weeks is a huge expanse of time when you're four – but then a smile of recognition spread across her face and she detached herself and buried her head against my outer thigh. She squealed as I picked her up and followed Anne into the house. Trying to be playful, I narrowly avoided banging my granddaughter's head against the doorframe as we entered the kitchen, but she didn't seem to mind.

The kitchen was in a state of some disorder. Jasmine had a set of toys on the floor next to an open cupboard door, and as soon as I put her down she went back to them, sitting with her knees in the air while she tried to decide what to do next. Alfie was lying in his cot on the other side of the kitchen table. The washing machine was humming in the background and giving off a sickly warm smell, which mingled with the aroma of coffee from the machine on the worktop. Anne offered me a cup and poured it for me.

There was a moment of awkwardness, when neither of us knew what to say. We both realised that Jasmine had noticed and was looking up at us.

"Baby needs changing," Anne told me matter-of-factly.

"OK," I replied. "I'll do it." I was aware of a small elephant in the room. "But you'll need to supervise me the first time."

I couldn't remember ever having changed one of Lisa's nappies; nor could I now remember why I hadn't.

Anne let out an almost inaudible sigh, which I thought she was entitled to. She told me to roll up my sleeves and I obeyed. Then any hopes that this might be a two-person effort evaporated as Anne leaned back against the worktop and folded her arms. But, to be fair to her, her instructions were clear and easy to follow. By the time I had finished, I had the impression that this wasn't going to be too difficult for me, once I had more practice. Basically, it required a certain dexterity to ensure that you didn't drop the baby on the floor (bad idea) while trying to remove the old nappy or fit the new one, and there was an art to getting the thing tight enough but not too tight, which took me a couple of attempts. Then it was about reducing to an absolute minimum the amount of shit you got on yourself. The biggest downside, though, was the excruciating smell, which nothing had prepared me for, and had me asking Anne whether a visit to the doctor might be in order. I noticed a certain glint in her eye as she laughed and told me it was nothing out of the ordinary. To my mind it certainly had no place in a room used to cook food, and it clearly disturbed Jasmine, who crossly picked up some of her toys and scuttled off into the hallway.

Alfie looked appreciative anyway, smiling up at me as he wriggled from side to side, and I could feel a bond starting to grow between us. He wasn't sufficiently appreciative, though, not to screw up his wrinkled little face only a couple of minutes later, start straining, and once again fill the air with noxious fumes.

"What happens now?" I asked Anne ingenuously.

The glint was back. "Same again, fella."

There was too much nappy-changing, so that I vowed to look up at what age potty training was achieved when I got home, but it didn't ruin the day. To be fair to her (which I seem to be saying a lot), Anne hadn't planned the day as some sort of long-delayed revenge, and I spent as much time playing in a pretend castle with Jasmine as I did trying to get fluids into one end of my grandson and remove them from the other. I relearned how to deal with a sudden, unprovoked tantrum, and also learned that modern kids sometimes are so enthralled by their screens that they don't want you there at all. I wasn't sure that I approved of that.

Above all, I found it very tiring; by three o'clock in the afternoon I was flagging and looking forward to going home, and hoping that neither showed. Then a miracle occurred: both of our charges were asleep at once, leaving Anne and me alone in the kitchen with no noise to disturb us except the rhythmic breathing and gurgling noises issuing from two baby monitors.

We rewarded ourselves with a cup of tea.

"This is less weird than I thought it might be," Anne told me artlessly.

"Yes," I agreed. "Thanks for suggesting me to Lisa, by the way. Seriously. And for agreeing to do this today. I wouldn't have been able to cope without some guidance."

"Easy to get out of practice," Anne replied generously. I didn't try to correct her. "And things change anyway. Kids change. Looking after Jas now isn't like looking after Lisa when she was her age."

"I suppose not," I said. The thought hadn't occurred to me previously. "Do you remember Lisa as a toddler?" I asked, immediately realising it was a daft question to put to someone's mother. "In those little corduroy dungarees she used to have. I thought she was the cutest child I had ever seen."

Anne smiled. "Not that you were biased or anything."

I grinned. "Yes, but even objectively she was a cutie. Everyone said so."

"To us."

"True."

"And she could be a stroppy madam too. As can her daughter."

"I haven't seen too much of that."

"You will. The little one seems more placid though."

"Should we have had another one?" I asked, thinking aloud yet again before I could stop myself. I sometimes think my mouth should have a twenty-second delay, like they use on phone-ins in case someone swears.

"Ouf!" Anne exhaled deeply. "What a question to ask after all these years!"

Something inside me wanted to know the answer. "Something Lisa mentioned at Christmas," I explained. "And I've had more time recently to think about things, and wondered whether it would have made a difference."

"To us?"

"Yes."

"No."

"Well, in a funny way that's a comfort."

There was a brief pause while Anne listened to murmurings on the baby monitors to determine whether there was anything that required attention. I had a guilty realisation that I had been oblivious to them and that I would need to pay more attention. "Fine," Anne pronounced. "Probably just dreaming. So, what happened to your job then, mister? Lisa said you were sacked for racism or something. That doesn't sound like you at all."

I explained as briefly as I could. I left out my sacking from the shop and the tribunal because I thought it only complicated matters.

"That's terrible," Anne sympathised. "You should sue them."

I explained why I couldn't, the deal that Eniola had got for me.

"That's good," Anne agreed. "Getting your pension paid up like that. And don't worry: I won't be coming after it. A deal's a deal: I got the house, you got the VHS tapes."

I had to smile at that. "And my Italian supercar."

"And that old banger of yours. But, going back, did you not tell them you were big in the Anti-BNP protests?"

I grinned sheepishly. "I don't know about 'big'! But it doesn't interest them. Ancient history. Either they've never heard of it, or they think it's all changed and that we didn't really get it in those days. But we did get it. And one difference to today was that we were doing it because we thought we were right, not because we thought it was a good career move. But I suppose that just makes me sound bitter."

Anne punched me gently on the arm. "Still a little bit of the old fire there, Alan," she told me. "That's a good thing. The guy who got arrested for his principles. That was part of what attracted me to you, even if politics were never really my thing. Did you know that?"

I had to think for a moment. "Sort of," I replied. "I knew it hadn't done me any harm in your eyes."

"Aah. Then what happened to you, Alan Brierley?"

I was going to ask her what she meant, but in truth I knew exactly what she meant. "Well, I don't know," I sighed. "Responsibilities, disappointments at work, compromises you have to make. And I was never a figurehead, was I? And I didn't *set out* to be arrested: I just was there, and *was* arrested. Maybe you saw something in me that was never really there."

"Maybe. But I don't think so. You settled for too little."

I felt the old anger rising inside my head, but decided not to be goaded, not to go down that well-trodden road again. I was going to keep calm, at least outwardly. "Not everyone can be out front, leading," I said.

"You had it in you."

"But I didn't, Anne. I was never 'a contender'. And if I'd faked it, I wouldn't have been happy."

Anne looked surprised. "Were you happy, then?"

I wasn't sure how candid I wanted to be. "Well, it's a relative thing, isn't it?" I replied. "I was happier than I would have been if I'd been pretending to be someone I wasn't."

Anne didn't seem to like the answer. "You know, even when things got bad between us, Alan," she told me, "I never hated you. I just saw wasted potential and wanted to shake you!"

I didn't want it to get back to Lisa that Anne and I had had a shouting match, so I held my tongue and counted to five in my head before replying: "You did the right thing: you left and found the person you were really looking for. A successful man with his own company."

To my relief, Anne either didn't pick up on the implication of my words or decided to ignore it. "You should find someone else, too, Alan," she said in a soft voice. "Don't you get lonely?"

"No. Well, occasionally."

"Lisa says you tried speed-dating."

"God, does she tell you everything I tell her?"

"I don't know. And there's a mysterious younger woman next door."

"Now you're just teasing me. The pair of you."

"Well?"

"I went speed-dating once. Two weeks ago."

"And?"

"One I quite liked. But didn't like me."

"How do you know?"

"You have to say. And she didn't."

"Oh. And the woman next door?"

"We're on friendly terms." I didn't want to say 'were'. "She wanted to go, but not on her own."

"Good looking?"

"Fairly."

"Career?"

"She's a dominatrix."

"Very funny. OK, I'll change the subject. Anyway, I need to check on Alfie. No, stay there, it's fine."

Anne got up and went out of the room, leaving me alone to collect my thoughts. But I didn't think it would be healthy to brood for too long. After a couple of minutes I left the kitchen and tiptoed up the stairs and along the landing. I could hear Anne talking soothingly to Alfie, but instead of joining her I stopped outside the open door to Jasmine's bedroom. The curtains were drawn, but there was a small amount of soft illumination from a child light plugged into a socket in the far wall, and an elongated shadow emanating from the doorway. I recalled similarly watching Alfie at Christmas. My granddaughter was lying on her back, making slight whooshing noises as she breathed. Her face was a picture of innocence and her flawless skin betrayed not the slightest sign that anything was worrying her, or ever had. I wondered how long it could stay like that. For her sake, I hoped it would be forever.

Monday 22 February

Two things to note today (Alan, you are in danger of getting a life!)

My second dry-run with Anne and the kids. My first solo is this Thursday, which I'm a bit apprehensive about. Anne was helpful again and the kids were no trouble really, just a bit of grief getting food into them, and Anne trying the old ploy of warning Jasmine that she won't grow if she doesn't eat, the same ruse we used on Lisa and that my parents used on me.

It's great how adaptable and non-judgmental small children are. Jasmine doesn't seem to think it's strange at all that Granny and Grandpa don't live together, but why would she? Maybe in a couple of years she will ask. I hope for their own and the kids' sake that her parents stay together, and I think they're a good match; but people change, so who knows?

But fair play to Anne today: she patiently told me everything I needed to know and gave me some lists of things to remember to do, and the order in which to do them, lists that I have brought home with me to read through and memorise, because I don't imagine you can get a checklist out to consult when, say, a four-year-old is having a potty crisis or a baby is projectile-vomiting. Anne also steadfastly shook her head and refused to overrule me when Jas didn't want to do as I was telling her and had turned her big sad eyes towards her grandmother.

Thursday is the big one: how the kids will react to me on my own.

On the way home I stopped at the supermarket to stock up on food. I found a parking bay with a space each side – bodywork repairs cost a fortune on the Maserati – and then some clown in a huge German SUV came and parked next to me, even though there were loads of empty spaces.

"Don't see many of those," he said as he almost limbo-danced out of his door to avoid hitting it against the side of mine. "Still, I imagine they rust away."

"Only if you let them," I said for lack of a more cutting riposte.

There weren't too many people in the supermarket, and I quickly filled up my trolley with the modest amount of food that will fit into my fridge-freezer. I was tutting over the woeful lack of choice in the bread section in early evening when I spotted her. Wheeling a trolley like mine down the aisle that intersected the one I was in, thoughtfully adjusting her glasses while she consulted a list of some sort, was Debbie from speed-dating.

I momentarily froze. Should I make a point of speaking to her (of course, you should, Alan, you're a mature man, not some sort of bashful teenager) or try consciously to avoid her (she had shown no interest in wanting to see me again after all, and it might be that people who go speed-dating don't want it to be known publicly)? In the end I did neither and ended up, I'm embarrassed to admit, just shadowing her around the store, trying to look nonchalant and avoid eye contact until I could come up with a plan. Suddenly she made a dash for the tills, and I had a choice of completing my shopping, in which case there was a good chance I would never see her again, or going after her. I could feel myself begin to sweat, and I was even a little breathless, as I picked up pace and headed for the checkouts. There I had a large stroke of luck: all the tills had queues, which meant that I could stand behind Debbie without it appearing weird.

I breathed deeply. "Oh, hi there," I said in my best surprised voice. Debbie turned round but didn't appear to recognise me. She was wearing a grey hoodie and a pair of dark blue jeans; an assemblage that suited her, I thought. "Alan," I said. "We met a couple of weeks back, admittedly very briefly, at, er," I looked round to see if anyone was in earshot, "'Pinnacle Connections'." I whispered the last bit.

Debbie looked a little discomfited. She shifted from foot to foot and scratched the back of her neck.

"Oh, yes," she said, collecting herself. "I remember. How did you get on?"

"So-so," I replied, conscious that I wasn't really answering the question.

"Oh, well. Maybe try again."

"Yes. And you?" I tried desperately, but probably unsuccessfully, not to sound too interested.

"Well, funnily enough I'm meeting someone for a drink later. Wish me luck!"

"Of course," I said airily. The queue in front of us was moving, so that at any second Debbie would be starting to unload her trolley onto the conveyor-belt and the opportunity would be lost. I had a picture of myself as Anne apparently saw me, a man who had 'settled', who in effect had given up. "The thing is," I said, hearing the nervousness in my own voice, "I know you didn't select me, but I wonder if you would reconsider. I don't think I make very good first impressions, to be honest, so speed-dating probably isn't for me."

Debbie looked startled. The cashier turned her head towards us, and I began to worry that she might call security. "Sorry," I started to say, "I didn't mean to...I'll go and join another queue." I started to back up but collided with another trolley that I hadn't heard arrive behind me. Now I didn't know what to do.

"Well, give me your number," Debbie said quietly; she wasn't smiling but she didn't look hostile either. "I'm seeing this guy tonight, but you know, maybe if...perhaps I'll call you."

I found a scrap of paper in my wallet and jotted down the number then handed it over.

"Thanks," said Debbie.

The cashier cleared her throat loudly, drawing Debbie's attention to the long expanse of empty conveyor-belt, which Debbie now started frantically to fill from her trolley.

When I got to the car, I realised I didn't even have any milk, so I went back into the store and got the remainder of the items I needed. I knew I had to be realistic with myself and that Debbie almost certainly wouldn't call. But at least potentially, in pursuing something I wanted, I was back in the game. And that, I told myself, must be a positive.

I wondered which of the guys it was that Debbie was meeting tonight. Was it bad of me secretly to hope that her date didn't go too well?

Thursday 25 February

Jasmine's contention, as far as I could understand it, was that ducks and spaceships were one and the same. She had been pursuing this thesis now for the past thirty minutes or so as we stood at the edge of the lake in Lisa and Neil's local park, throwing small cubes of bread more or less successfully towards the group of water birds/ intergalactic transports gliding to and fro in front of us.

It was a crisp, sunny winter's day. Jasmine was wearing the same quilted purple coat and pink wellies she had sported on our visit to the swings on Christmas Day, together with a white woolly bobble hat that was slightly too big for her, and matching gloves. As a result she looked impossibly cute, and had drawn smiles from almost everyone we passed on the way to the park, jumping up and down as I tried desperately to hold on to her hand without losing control of the pram. I had got a bit carried away in my attempts to ensure that Alfie wasn't cold, and had ended up mummifying him with the exception of a small opening for his face; but he seemed happy enough, to the extent that he definitely wasn't crying and definitely was breathing, though the glories of nature I was describing to him, the iridescent frost on the trees, the stark freshness of the air (even in London suburbia), the majestic life-force of the gliding ducks, seemed to pass him by completely.

"You need to throw the bread *to* the ducks, not *at* them," I told Jasmine, as for the second time one of the squares hit a bird in the beak. She turned and grinned at me, but I just shook my head in response: I had determined not to be one of those indulgent grandparents who let their grandchildren do whatever they like. You can't tell what is going on in a four-year-old's head, but I do know they are not immune from the sort of viciousness found in the rest of humanity. Or maybe she just thought she was shooting down spaceships. "Play nicely and be gentle with the ducks," I admonished her.

"Why?"

"Because you should always be nice to everyone and everything."

"Why?"

"Because then they'll be nice to you."

Jasmine seemed to accept that. Her next handful of bread went carefully into the water, unfortunately causing something of a feeding frenzy between rival ducks that startled her, and caused her to burst into tears. I bent down to comfort her, wipe her eyes and blow her nose, conscious all the time not to let the pram out of my sight. I envied my mother's generation who had been able to leave unattended prams outside shops and elsewhere without a moment's anxiety, and wondered what had happened to us that that was no longer possible.

I suggested we move on. Ideally, I would have had a push-chair for Jasmine, but that didn't seem practical with a pram as well. I wondered why you could buy double push-chairs and double prams but not, as far as I was aware, a hybrid of the two. Perhaps I had spotted a gap in the market and should put my inventor's cap on as soon as I got back to the flat.

Jasmine had made a swift recovery. "They go 'kerpow'," she told me, stamping her feet in an indentation in the concrete that happily today was not full of water.

"Do they," I said, "that's nice for them." I was conscious that for Alfie's sake we shouldn't be out in the cold too long – even allowing for my over-enthusiastic swaddling skills – but I had been keen that we should at least leave the house, so that Jasmine would tell her mother where we had been, and my daughter would be impressed by my organisational skills.

As it was now mid-afternoon, in truth my organisational skills had got off to a slow start. I had been quite worried first thing and during the drive to Lisa's, wondering what might go wrong that I hadn't prepared for, and what Lisa would think if I had to contact her. She had certainly given the impression that she had full confidence in me, but she had also ensured that I had her number (which is strange as I have rung it enough times!) so I suppose she must have had some misgivings. Jasmine looked very sad and worried when Lisa said goodbye to her, but I hoped that was because she missed Mummy rather than because she didn't want to be with Grandpa.

For my first solo, Lisa had left me children who had already been fed, clothed and washed, so for the immediate future all I had to do was keep them entertained and alive, which I hoped wouldn't be beyond me. I moved us all into the living room. I was happy to play the horse game again (as I had on Christmas Day and also last week under Anne's watchful eye) but Jasmine seemed to sense that something was different. She sat on the floor and picked up an iPad, and seemed reluctant to give it to me when I told her that I would need to unlock it for her; but eventually she did. When I gave it back, I was amazed how quickly she found the game she wanted and started playing it, her face immediately a picture of rapt concentration.

A couple of times last week Anne politely pointed out that I was ignoring Alfie or, more accurately, treating him as an object that needed to be serviced until it started walking and talking and became more interesting. None of that would happen, she reminded me, unless he was given mental and physical stimulation, mostly by his parents, but we could do our bit as well. Suitably chastened, I had asked Lisa for some books to read to him; she had given me a couple, but they all had about four words to a page and, even holding up each page so that my grandson could see the illustrations – brightly coloured and slightly baffled-looking lions and giraffes for the most part as I remember – I was going to run out of reading material in less than an hour. I had also brought with me this month's *Classic Car*, on the offchance of having some time to myself if both kids were asleep at once, and thought I would test the theory that babies are only really interested in your voice, not what you are saying. Alfie watched me attentively, gurgled and smiled as I read him a road-test of a Ferrari Daytona. Not a Maserati, sadly, but close enough. If his first words are "4.4 litre normally-aspirated V12" I guess it will be traced back to Grandpa, but that's a risk I am willing to take.

I was clearly making friends with Alfie, but unfortunately Jasmine was now being a bit of a pain. She had looked crossly at me and theatrically covered her ears as soon as I started reading aloud. Realising that with her hands on her ears she couldn't play with the iPad, she had shuffled across to the far end of the room and hidden herself behind an armchair. I could hear the pinging of the game she was playing but not a sound from my granddaughter herself.

"You OK, Jas?" I asked in a playful tone, smiling at Alfie to let him know I hadn't yet finished impressing him with the finer points of Pininfarina's styling prowess.

"Where's Mummy?" came a slightly grumpy, slightly plaintive tone from the far end of the room.

I had been expecting but also dreading this. "Mummy's at work," I replied softly. "Mummy now works on Mondays and Thursdays, doesn't she?"

"Why?"

"Because she wants to earn money to buy nice things for you and Alfie, and your dad."

"Why?"

"Because she loves you."

A short pause. "Where's Grandma?"

"She's also at work. Only today. You'll see her again on Monday."

Jasmine crawled out from behind the armchair. "When's Monday?"

I realised four days to wait for anything might seem like an age to a toddler. "Very soon," I said brightly.

Jasmine looked happy with that. "Do you work, Grandpa?"

That threw me a bit. "Not at the moment," I replied with a smile. "I did, for about forty years, which is ten times the number of years you've been alive!"

Jasmine looked back at me blankly. I should have known that multiplication wasn't a concept her brain would be able to grasp. "Why?" she said.

"Why what, darling? Why haven't I got a job?" Because I'm an evil racist that no one will employ and that you should be ashamed of being related to. "Well, I'm just taking a break while I look for something else, Jas. Which means that I get to spend time with you, and Alfie, which is great, isn't it?"

Jasmine gave a four-year-old's best impression of a polite smile, but ended up looking bewildered.

I had to laugh. "Well, it's great for me anyway!" I insisted. I looked at the clock: it was still only around ten o'clock. It was going to be a long day.

Knowing that you aren't supposed to bribe children, I had instead presented the trip to the park and feeding the ducks as a reward for cooperation, i.e. eating some food, at lunchtime, but I supposed that it came to the same thing. Similarly, relieved that Jasmine's encounter with the ducks hadn't given rise to any serious injuries on either side, I offered the further reward of an ice cream, having noticed a stationary van in the distance doing a good trade despite the cold weather. Jasmine knew exactly what she wanted: a large multi-fruit concoction that I hoped wouldn't make her sick later, and which I didn't have the energy to try to scale back. In fact, a large proportion of it ended up on her chin or on the kitchen towel I had presciently tucked in at her neck to protect her coat. I bought a smaller vanilla cone for myself as well, an action Jasmine appeared to approve of, and we sat side by side on a low wall, eating in silence apart from Jasmine's unselfconscious slurping. The last time I could remember eating an ice cream had been in Paris, lonely and alone, not a good memory. The time before that might have been a decade ago. Well, it was something I would look forward to doing more of now, with the alibi of a four-year-old companion.

My phone rang. It startled me because I wasn't expecting a call, and made me realise how rarely I received them. I didn't recognise the number, but as the network wasn't flagging it as possible spam, I decided to take it.

"Hello," said a quiet woman's voice. "I hope this isn't an inconvenient moment. It's, er, Debbie, remember? You said... Hello?"

"Oh, hi!" I said expansively, trying to make up for the awkward start to the call and prevent her ringing off. "How are you?" I could feel my heart speed up.

"Fine. It sounds like you're outside somewhere."

"Yes, I'm in a park with my grandkids."

"Oh, OK. Well, if it's not convenient..."

"It's completely convenient," I replied instantly. "The worst thing that can happen in the next few minutes is for ice cream to end up on clean clothes." I glared at Jasmine who grinned mischievously back at me.

Debbie laughed. "OK, well I guess I have that to come."

I laughed too. I hoped having grandkids didn't make me sound old.

"You OK?"

"Yes, fine."

"So," I said quietly, feeling that my throat was a little dry, "would it be possible to meet up sometime?" I closed my eyes to hear the response. I immediately realised that was a bad idea when I was supposed to be supervising children who could do anything at any moment, and quickly reopened them.

"Yes, let's do that."
"Saturday perhaps?"
"I can do that."
"Great. What would you like to do?"
"Just go for a meal? Then we can have a good chat."
"Perfect."

We made our arrangements and ended the call. I sat for a moment staring into space and breathing in the fresh air.

"Smiley Grandpa!" said Jasmine, who now sported a prosthetic chin made of various flavours of fruit ice cream. "Can I have another one?"

Saturday 27 February

Dinner with Debbie.

I felt quite nervous all day (this really is becoming a theme, Alan. Do other people get like this?)

Debbie had suggested the venue, which saved me one job. To be honest, I haven't eaten out much since I moved here, so I would probably have gone online or walked up and down the high road to find somewhere that looked nice. I did google the place Debbie had suggested and it looked very nice, definitely more fashionable than anywhere I would have chosen, and quite expensive. But not catering exclusively for vegetarians, and I had decided not to pretend to be one and potentially embarrass myself by not knowing what to order.

Looking in the mirror yesterday, I saw tufts of hair growing over my ears and debated whether to get a haircut, but I worried that I might look like I was trying too hard. In the end I settled for just pushing the hair back, which seemed a good temporary fix. Today I started getting ready in mid-afternoon, showering with expensive shower gel (a gift I think), washing my hair and applying anti-perspirant liberally. I had a wet shave, thankfully not nicking myself, then applied a small amount of aftershave, being careful not to overdo it like the man Ella met at speed-dating.

That was the easy bit. Clothes were more difficult. Three weeks ago I would have asked Ella's advice, but I still haven't seen her to talk to. I would really like to try to mend my bridges with her, but I could hardly start the process today by asking her to advise me on how to transfer my unwanted attentions to the next unlucky victim!

So I ended up in the same clothing quandary I had before speed-dating. I looked in the wardrobe to determine what possible combinations were available to me, and immediately wished I had undertaken this earlier in the week and then used the opportunity to wash some of the shirts and freshen them up. My least bad sartorial option turned out to be my 'best' casual shirt, a subtly striped Austin Reed number, still presentable though probably a decade old now; some chinos which had a little bit of fraying around the front left pocket, hopefully not apparent at a distance; and my faithful, slightly scuffed (even after cleaning) brown shoes. Did I need a jacket? I thought so. Only one choice then, the old tweed job with elbow patches that Anne always thought made me look like a schoolteacher from the 1950s. Well, it would have to do, and I could always take it off once we started eating.

I was pleased that I could walk to the restaurant, which meant I didn't have to worry about parking, and also that I would be able to drink a little to calm myself and loosen my inhibitions, while taking care that I didn't get drunk and embarrass myself.

I had decided I should arrive first, but preferably not too early. Unfortunately, I didn't time it quite right, because as I came level with the front window of the restaurant, the door to a very smart, new-looking Tesla parked right outside opened, and Debbie stepped out onto the kerb.

"Hi," she said, with an unassuming smile, "perfect timing!"

I smiled back and agreed, and we shook hands, which seemed quite formal. I opened the restaurant door for her, then followed her to reception, from where we were led to our table by a smiling young waiter who called us 'guys'. We made small talk for the first few minutes, both of us so keen not to let the conversation flag that we didn't really say anything at all, and when the waiter returned we hadn't even begun consulting the large menus. He suggested he take the drink order and come back in a few minutes. Debbie ordered a soda water and I asked for a Belgian bottled beer, worried that requesting a draft bitter might give the wrong impression, even assuming a place like this served it in the first place.

"I walked here," I said by way of explanation of my choice, which immediately seemed clumsy, as though I were suggesting Debbie couldn't have a drink later if she wanted one.

"Go ahead," Debbie replied. "I won't – I've got the car in case I get called out." She opened her bag and brandished a pager in my direction.

"Oh, yes," I said, trying to earn points for having listened to Debbie the first time we had met, "you told me you worked for the NHS."

"Yes, well – might as well get it over with. I'm a doctor."

"Well, that's great," I said inanely. Debbie appeared to be expecting a follow-up question. "Specialising in..?" I enquired.

"I'm a consultant anaesthetist. I put people to sleep. Hopefully not you this evening." There were little crow's feet around her eyes when she laughed, and there was a warmth to her expression that I liked.

"Well, that's great," I repeated even more inanely, feeling a rising sense of panic and trying not to let it become audible. What on earth, I asked myself, did I have to offer that would be of any conceivable interest to this obviously successful, well-off professional woman? She just hadn't been giving off that vibe at speed-dating, and I had got the wrong idea. I imagined she would be leaving as soon as she politely could, or maybe pretend to have been paged to get away.

"And what about you?" Debbie asked while tearing off part of a bread roll and thrusting it into some sort of green dip.

I had rehearsed this, but I still knew it was going to sound dull and unimpressive. "For a very long time, until a couple of months back, I worked in software development," I told her. "I'm taking a break while I try to decide what to do next, if anything."

"You should help us out," suggested Debbie, who had now harpooned a black olive. "Our IT is terrible."

I nodded. "It's all out of date," I explained. "Ancient versions of Windows with lots of security problems."

Debbie didn't look very interested. "So, you're not going to do the break-dancing full time then?" she asked.

I laughed, but was very flattered that she had remembered. "Only as a last resort," I replied. "I don't think my back is up to it anymore."

"You should get it checked out. We have some really good orthopaedic surgeons. Rarely kill anyone."

I laughed nervously. "Just age probably."

"How old are you?"

"Fifty-eight."

"Bit of a gap then," Debbie said, as though thinking aloud. "I suppose we need to study these menus before the man comes back."

We silently perused the choice of food until the waiter reappeared with our drinks and took our order. Debbie ordered something that I didn't quite hear and I, thinking that maybe there were degrees of offensiveness for vegetarians, decided not to go with the beef steak but instead to opt for the swordfish, which was the next best thing, even though it might make me look as though I were stuck in the 1980s. Once we had ordered, Debbie got up to go to the ladies. As she walked away, I realised that in my nervousness I hadn't really taken in her appearance. She was wearing a nice but simple black dress with matching bag, little baton gold earrings and modestly heeled black shoes. Her hair hung naturally but looked recently washed. All of which suggested to me, now that I had the Dutch courage of a little alcohol inside me, that she had thought having dinner with me was at least worth some effort, though my own attire now looked even more inadequate than it had earlier.

I noticed that most of the other clientele in the restaurant were much younger than us, of a variety of ethnicities, and for the most part casually if probably expensively dressed. One group near the door kept looking in my direction and I wondered if they might be junior doctors or nurses curious about the consultant's private life. They looked towards Debbie as she returned but she did not acknowledge them.

I had a few seconds to decide where to try to take the conversation next. Normally, I thought, you would ask about family, but I did know that she was a widow, so was that wise?

"You were telling me about your interest in green issues," I said as she sat down, hoping that didn't sound hopelessly earnest. "Great car by the way."

"Thanks," she replied. "I've only had it for a couple of months. And it's only as green as the method used to produce the electricity of course."

"That's true," I agreed. "They're really quick as well, aren't they?"

Debbie looked surprised by the question. "Well, I'm probably a bit too old for all that. And I've seen a lot of fast drivers in A&E at work, so..."

"Of course, no I didn't mean..."

"You like cars, then?" It sounded like an accusation.

"Well, yes. Within reason."

"What do you have?"

I cleared my throat. "I have a late 1980s Maserati Biturbo Spyder," I said, noting that I sounded half proud, half embarrassed.

"That doesn't sound very green." Debbie was smiling.

I shrugged. "Well, it hardly does any miles and it already exists. So I figure keeping it is greener than scrapping it and having another one made, which is where most of the CO2 is produced apparently."

Debbie didn't look happy with my response, which now sounded smartarse to me as well. "Maybe," was all she said.

I was saved by the arrival of our food. I still couldn't work out what Debbie had ordered: it looked like some sort of pasta shells with a creamy sauce, but I didn't want to reveal my ignorance by asking. My swordfish, coming as it did with chips and grilled tomato, looked very unsophisticated by comparison, as though I would soon be ordering black forest gateau to follow. I looked at the people on the other tables as much as I could without giving the impression that I wasn't interested in my companion; as far as I could tell, no one else was having the swordfish.

We politely asked each other if we were enjoying the food, which we were, but it was clear that this amounted to trying to make conversation and that the date (was it even that?) wasn't going well. I was just confirming Debbie's initial view of me, which had been that she didn't want to see me again. I couldn't think of any other uncontroversial topic to breach the growing silence, so family it would have to be.

"Do you have any kids?" I asked brightly, just as Debbie put a forkful of food into her mouth. She held her free hand up to denote that I would need to wait a while for her reply. I muttered 'Sorry' quietly.

"Yes," she said finally. "One of each. David has graduated but is currently working as a ski instructor while he decides what he wants to do with his life. Do you ski?"

I admitted miserably that I never had.

"And Becky has finished her Masters and is in a similar limbo, working in a charity shop while she polishes her c.v. and plots world domination. But at least I get to see her, for now." Debbie gave an indulgent parental smile and I reciprocated. "And you were saying you're a grandfather?"

I decided to attribute the sound of surprise in her voice to my youthful looks rather than to incredulity that anyone would ever have agreed to have sex with me. I explained about Lisa, and about Jasmine and Alfie, and that I was now looking after my grandkids once a fortnight.

"Rather you than me," Debbie said to my disappointment. "I have to confess I found it a bit of a chore at that age. Much preferred it when they grew up and I could have a sensible conversation with them."

"I get that," I replied. "But it's also nice to be with a child who is seeing things in the world for the first time. Their perspective challenges things you've long since taken for granted."

Debbie's expression suggested that I had at last said something interesting, but when she asked me for an example, I couldn't immediately think of one. "The downside at that age is all the tantrums," she said acerbically. "And all the poo." We both laughed. I tried but failed to think of a suitable rejoinder, and we lapsed into silence.

We had almost finished our food, and when I glanced at the clock, I saw that we had only been in the restaurant for an hour and ten minutes. Debbie declined desert but agreed to have coffee, perhaps feeling, like me, that we needed to make ninety minutes for the sake of basic courtesy. In the event, the bill was slow in coming, so a hundred and three minutes had elapsed by the time we put on our coats and headed to the door. In the meantime, Debbie had mostly talked about her work, something I had encouraged by asking supplementary questions like someone desperately shovelling coals onto a fire to keep it going. We shook hands outside and thanked each other for a lovely evening, theatrically commenting on how cold it was so that there was an excuse not to linger.

I was home much earlier than I had expected to be, and slightly inebriated (I'd had a second beer in the restaurant in the hope that it might stimulate my conversation) so I got a further beer out of the fridge and sat down in front of the TV for the rest of the evening. I tried to be positive: at least I was back in the game, whatever that game was, for the first time in many years. More negatively, though, it seemed to me that the date had foundered not because of some basic temperamental incompatibility between us, but because my life, and by association I, were fundamentally less interesting than most other people someone like Debbie would expect to meet. What could I do about that at the age of fifty-eight? I was also surprised at how different Debbie had seemed tonight compared to our first encounter, vastly more confident, though why wouldn't she be, in her professional and financial position? I wondered if I had misread her at speed-dating, or perhaps that evening she had been just feeling awkward and out of her element. Why had I actually preferred the notion that she might be timid? I'm no alpha male, so had I just been setting my sights lower in the expectation that anyone more self-assured would reject me?

On the walk home I realised I had gained no further insight into how Debbie had come to be a widow, if indeed that was correct on the speed-dating form. I also wondered whether Debbie's daughter had put her up to the speed-dating. And then it finally occurred to me to ask myself – I blamed the weather for freezing my brain – how many girls there were called Becky with master's degrees working in local charity shops. That I would doubtless never see mother or daughter again saved me from the truly cringeworthy prospect of Debbie innocently introducing me to an embarrassed-looking young woman, and a conversation after my departure beginning: "Mum, you know the old boy I told you about, who worked briefly in my shop before being sacked...?"

Sunday 28 February

Feeling more cheerful now than I was first thing this morning.

I wasn't expecting to have much to do today, so when I woke up I looked at the clock, turned over and tried to go back to sleep again. I gave up around 8:45 – I was starting to get a headache, which is usually a sign of too much sleep – and had a leisurely breakfast while watching the Sunday morning politics programmes on TV. It was the usual combination of trip-up questions and evasive answers, so I was none the wiser at the end. I wondered if I should go into politics as 'the man who always tells the truth', but I doubt that's a good strategy if you want anyone to vote for you.

I went out to buy the Sunday Times. As I arrived back on my landing, I heard the chain being removed from the door opposite, but in my haste to get back in the flat before Ella came out I fumbled and then dropped the keys. I was bending down to pick them up when I heard the door behind me open and then approaching footsteps. I pretended not to have noticed, and quickly put the key into my lock, experiencing a feeling of relief when it turned.

"Are you avoiding me?"

I turned round. Ella was wearing a shiny black catsuit and was heavily made up; in heeled boots she towered over me.

"No," I stammered. "Well, yes."

"Yes?"

"Well, I don't know. I thought..."

"I've got forty-five minutes. Put the kettle on," Ella instructed me, pushing me into my own flat in front of her.

I didn't argue. I dropped the paper on the sofa as I passed it, and quickly scanned the room to ensure that it was presentable for a guest, then went into the kitchen. When I came back with the drinks and biscuits, Ella had her boots on my coffee table and was reading the culture section. I put the mugs down. Ella said 'thanks' but continued to read in silence, her head hidden behind the paper. I went and opened the window slightly, having detected a slight stuffiness in the air that I thought would be apparent to Ella too.

"I don't know what to say," I began honestly.

Ella peered at me over the top of the paper. "You're forgiven," she said.

"Thanks."

"As long as you write out one hundred times: 'I must not try to kiss mistress'." She wasn't smiling.

"Oh."

"You'll do that?" She disappeared behind the paper again.

"Well, I hadn't..."

Ella put the supplement down with a slap. "I'm kidding," she said, leaning forward, "unless you want to, of course, if that's secretly your thing."

"It's not," I laughed nervously.

"Well, something must be. No one's completely vanilla in my experience. One day I'll get it out of you."

I tried to think. I wondered if I dared ask Anne if my lack of sexual adventurousness was one of the many things that had contributed to our divorce. I succeeded only in going red.

"Take my next client who is arriving in," Ella checked her phone, "thirty-four minutes. Respectable, successful professional man, whose wife thinks he has gone out to play golf, but who is making a detour on the way back so that I can put him over my lap and spank his naughty little bottom. From the bewildered look on your face, I would say that wasn't your thing either, but I'll keep trying to work it out."

"So your arm's better now," was all I could think to say.

Ella looked at me quizzically. "Very practical thought," she said. "Yes, it's getting there, thanks. It's been three months, mind. Taking it gently, not back doing the big stuff yet."

I decided not to ask what the big stuff was, or whether it would be audible from my flat. I hoped not.

"So now I've forgiven you," Ella continued, "back to the main effort, which is to find you a woman."

"I had a date last night," I blurted out, realising I sounded like a teenager.

"Tell me more."

"The woman from speed-dating."

"The tree-hugger? I thought she didn't like you."

"She didn't. Well, she didn't dislike me as such. But anyway, I bumped into her in the supermarket."

"Good for you. And?"

I gave a thumbs-down sign.

Ella looked disappointed in me. "Oh, why's that?" she asked.

I sighed. "It turns out she's a successful professional woman, a consultant anaesthetist." I stumbled over the pronunciation, which made Ella smile.

"So?" she said, with her head on one side.

I decided to confide in her; it couldn't hurt, and might help me work out where I was going wrong. "So, basically I bored her to death," I explained. "Nothing I could tell her about me could compete with her life, or was even at all interesting. I ended up trying to talk about subjects where I hoped I could at least express intelligent opinions, and then it just came across as though I was starting arguments with her."

Ella laughed sympathetically. "Sounds like a bit of a disaster," she agreed. "Still, nothing ventured. Might be good practice for the next one."

"I suppose so."

"Definitely. And – no offence to you – but if this woman's got all the answers in life, what's she doing at speed-dating in the first place?"

I almost commented on the irony of the remark before I realised that Ella was serious, and that she still maintaining that she had gone to speed-dating only to keep me company. "She might ring you today or in the week," she offered brightly.

"She won't."

"But if she did?"

I shook my head. "I would be very pleased. I've been on my own too long, I know that." It was cathartic to be able to open up to someone, but I didn't want to sound too abject.

"Understood," said Ella. "Well, all is not lost. Maybe I'll help you with some date preparation: how to be scintillating and make an impression."

"Turn up in that outfit," I smiled, thinking it was OK to venture a joke.

"Talking of which," Ella told me, "it's so tight that I'm not sure I can get out of this sofa of yours. Can you give me a hand?"

I did so carefully, and as I hauled her up I was surprised to detect the unmistakable smell of alcohol on her breath. I assumed it was from last night.

A few minutes after Ella had left, I heard footsteps coming up the stairs. I should have minded my own business and continued to read the paper, but curiosity got the better of me and I went and listened at my door, without opening it. What was incongruous was the ordinariness of the conversation, as though Ella were an office receptionist. "Hi," she was saying. "Great to see you again. Come in. How did your round go this morning? Would you like a drink before we start?" Then her door closed and I heard nothing further.

Sunday 7 March

Bittersweet is an overused, possibly clichéd word, but I think it might be quite apt for today.

As I said when I was in Paris, I don't like graveyards. I wouldn't say I am exactly phobic, but in a way I wish they did not exist. I much prefer to have memories of people as they were, rather than sit in front of a sad little stone in the middle of a field and pretend they are there because the physical remains of their body (even more tenuously in cases of cremation) are a few feet away. My own will states that my ashes will be scattered, and I am happy with that, and I'll then remain in the memories of a few people until they too die.

But once a year, usually on the nearest Sunday to their wedding anniversary, I make the trek to my parents' grave in the municipal cemetery. In the old days, Anne would come with me and select some nice flowers to leave in the little container. Left to my own devices these days I usually take some chrysanthemums, which are easy to cut and come in a pleasing variety of colours, I think. We never insisted that Lisa should come along, and sometimes she did but mostly she didn't, though she got on very well with her grandparents, my dad in particular, who, I suspect, had always wanted a daughter. Since she moved away, she hasn't come at all, which is why I was amazed, when I spoke to her in the week (the ostensible purpose of the call being to confirm that I was available for duty again next Thursday) and casually mentioned it, to hear her say that she had been thinking about it and would like to join me. I immediately said I would be delighted to have her company or the family's, the more the merrier, but she said, no, it would just be her, which surprised me even more. But also pleased me, to be truthful, because, much as I like the kids, and Neil, the only way really to find out how someone is getting on is to talk to them one to one and face to face, which very rarely happens with my daughter and me.

I looked forward to Lisa's visit for the rest of the week. We had arranged to meet at the cemetery, because parking is easier there, but just in case she ended up coming back to the flat, I tried to tidy and freshen it up, in the hope that it wouldn't feel too much like the domain of a solitary male. I worried a little about us running into Ella, for all sorts of complicated reasons.

I bought my flowers at the supermarket this morning, so they would be as fresh as possible. Walking into the store I abruptly halted when I thought I spied Debbie's silhouette in the distance. I didn't know what I would say to her, so I quickly picked out the best bunch of chrysanthemums that were on display and bought it at the self-service till.

I had arranged to meet Lisa at three o'clock. I can walk to the cemetery, but as well as the flowers I had shears, a cloth, a brush and a small watering can, none of which I would want to take with me in the unlikely (but hoped for) event of my daughter having time afterwards to go for some food, or even just a drink; so I took the Maserati. It started second time, which is quite good in early March, and with light traffic I got to the cemetery and parked about ten minutes before the allotted time. To be fair to the council, I thought - as I waited for Lisa and desperately hoped I would not receive a phone call to say that she was having to cry off - the cemetery, which extends over the brow of a hill into the distance, is far from the grim forbidding place it could be: it is very well tended, there is floral colour in all directions and a set of sensible rules is enforced to preserve some sense of decorum. So, if you're someone who wants your eternal slumbers to be accompanied by your favourite Status Quo track played endlessly on repeat, this isn't the place for you.

Lisa arrived about fifteen minutes after me. I watched her pilot the tall SUV into the car park, manoeuvring it around another vehicle that was leaving, with the look of serious concentration on her face that she has had ever since she was small. It still surprises me that my little girl can drive a car, though of course she has had a licence for well over a decade now.

She climbed out then walked round to the passenger's side and carefully retrieved her own flowers from the footwell. I went over to her; she looked at me almost shyly, I thought, then gave me a one-armed hug which allowed me to plant a little kiss on her hair.

We walked along the path to the grave side by side, and I was surprised and pleased that Lisa clearly remembered where it was and was not following me. "I just bought flowers," Lisa told me, gesticulating towards my plastic bag, "because Mum assured me you would have everything else."

We both smiled. "Are those chrysanthemums?" she asked. "I'm rubbish with flowers."

"Spot on."

"Mum said that as well. She said get something different." Lisa brandished her bouquet at me. I think they were tulips, in various bright colours.

We arrived at the grave. "Well, I think we should use your flowers, give Mum and Dad a change," I said brightly. Lisa blinked and said nothing, and I realised she might have thought I was pointing out that she hadn't been for a while. But sometimes you do more damage by trying to dig yourself out of a hole, so I let it go.

"Hi Nan and Granddad," Lisa said to the stone.

Our teamwork was impressive: we calculated the right length for the flowers, she held them while I cut them, then I let her arrange them artistically while I went to get some water from the tap nearby.

"What do you think?" she asked when I returned.

"Beautiful," I said. And they were: just the right colours and shapes in the right combination. "Except that there isn't one in the middle hole."

Lisa nodded. "I've left that for one of your chrysanths."

"That's a lovely thought, sweetheart," I told her, and I shed a tear and had to wipe it away with my hand. I carefully cut what I thought was the best dark crimson chrysanthemum and placed it gently in the centre of the arrangement. I delicately added the water, ensuring that it did not overflow and drown Lisa's efforts, and I brushed and wiped the stone while Lisa pulled out a few blades of grass that were beginning to cover the edges. Then we both stood back and had a few moments to admire our work, and for our private thoughts. I put my arm round my daughter and was delighted when she reciprocated.

After I don't know how long, maybe a couple of minutes, maybe less, Lisa shivered and turned to look at me. "You good?" she asked.

"Fine," I replied, and I honestly was. I had been staring at the stone, but I think about my parents every day, still have conversations with them in my head, so visiting the grave isn't especially emotional for me. Except for the thought that one day I too will be gone, and that I need to achieve something in the meantime, even if it's only something as simple as being at peace with myself, knowing that I have done what I could.

"Bye, Nan and Granddad," Lisa said, giving them a little wave. "Love you."

We started to walk back to the cars. I wanted to ask something, and yet for the first few seconds I couldn't; my mouth went dry.

"Have you eaten?" I asked finally. "I thought maybe we could go and get something to eat." I steeled myself for disappointment.

Lisa stopped and looked at her watch. "The thing is, Neil's got the kids, and he's been working really hard recently..."

I wanted to say that it wouldn't kill him, just this once; that I knew he was a great dad, but that he sometimes played golf at the weekends while Lisa was at home with the kids; but I knew better than that. I wanted to say, please, just this once, just a cup of tea and a cake. But I didn't need to.

"Oh, sod it," Lisa said. "Why not? Is that pizza place still in the high street?"

"Not the one you remember. But there are two others."

"Come on then," Lisa said, and she put her arm round mine.

And then a curious thing. As we resumed our walk towards the car park, I saw a solitary dark-haired woman in the middle distance, bending down to put flowers against a small gravestone that glinted in the early spring sun. And although my eyesight isn't as keen as it once was, by the arch of her body, even by the way she moved, I was convinced it was Ella.

"Are you OK," Lisa asked me. "I suddenly lost your attention there."

"Sorry, sweetheart, I was just thinking for a moment."

Lisa grabbed my arm more tightly. "I haven't been in the Maserati for years," she said playfully. "Let's take that."

"You called it 'the Maserati'," I said delightedly.

"So?"

"Not 'your old banger'!"

"You're so easy to wind up, Dad!"

"Roof down?"

"In March?"

"Live a little."

"Doesn't it fall to bits if you move it?"

"Only sometimes."

"Give it a go then."

"OK."

I felt so happy.

The restaurant was busy, so busy in fact that the only table they could find for us was by the door, which meant a shock of cold air every time anyone came in or left. I am always surprised these days that all half decent restaurants are full right through the afternoon and evening, which shows nothing really except how infrequently I have eaten out in recent years. Lisa, by contrast, was pleasantly surprised that we managed to get in at all.

"What used to be here?" she asked as she wriggled to get out of her coat, not helped by the fact that the chair of the person behind her, at the next table, was much too close.

"A bank," I told her. "Closed like most of the others. We've only got one left now."

Lisa only shrugged. "Who uses bank branches these days?"

"People older than me, I suppose. Still," I said, looking around me, "it looks like the new owners have retained the licence to print money!"

It wasn't a very good joke, and now Lisa looked worried. "Why, is it very expensive?" she asked, picking up the huge menu in front of her to study the prices.

"Not that expensive," I reassured her, "and anyway this is Dad's treat, so have whatever you like."

"You sure?"

"Completely sure."

We ordered some drinks and then got down to the serious business of menu-studying. Yet I was conscious that I didn't want to sit in complete silence for too long. I didn't want to interrupt Lisa's food deliberations, but as soon as she put the menu down I jumped in. "So, tell me about the new job. How's it going?"

Lisa looked out of the window, then back at me. She put her elbow on the table and propped her chin up on her fist; it's a mannerism I have always liked: when she was a pre-teen it told you she wanted to be serious.

"No, it's good," she said. "I mean it's only finance, which is a posh word for accounts, but it gets the grey cells working."

"Well, good for you," I told her. "You inherited your brains from your mother, so it would be a shame not to do anything with them. Unlike your dad, who isn't a qualified anything."

Lisa peered at me as though my modesty was unconvincing. "Well, I've always thought you were something of an expert in...actually I'm not exactly sure what it is." She grinned and blushed as though sharing a slightly embarrassing confidence. "Mum doesn't seem to know either."

"Legacy computer systems and old programming languages," I told her. "There's the future!"

"Don't knock it, Dad. People like that will always be in demand. It'll see you out... I mean, if you want to..."

It was my turn to look out of the window, though all I really took in was my reflection. "Yeah, well. Sitting it out for the moment. Anyway, never mind me: I'm much more interested in you."

I was interrupted by the waiter, who arrived with our drinks and now, a little impatiently I thought, asked to take our food order. I motioned at Lisa to go first and noted how specific and detailed her order was, like Americans ordering a sandwich. Then it was my turn, and I could see that my daughter had a big grin on her face. "I think I can guess!" she said.

I was torn between ordering something else in order not to be dull and predictable, or sticking with my original choice, which my saliva glands were already preparing to welcome. "I'll have the calzone," I told the waiter.

"I knew it!" Lisa banged the table with the flat of her hand. "Same for the last twenty years," she told the obviously uninterested waiter, who curled up his mouth in the slightest of smiles, folded the menus and walked away.

"I like calzone," I protested. "If I came here every day, I would try different things, but it's a rare treat so I have what I like best."

I sounded more pathetic than I had intended to, and now Lisa was looking at me as though I was trying to tell her something. "Just teasing, Dad," she said.

"I know, darling. So, with your new job: are they nice people?"

"Seem to be. I haven't been out with them socially, and can't see me having the time to do that any time soon. Some of them are quite old anyway, so I don't know how often..."

"Like, over forty?"

Lisa shook her head earnestly. "No, proper ancient. Over fifty!"

"And still alive?"

"Apparently. Just about."

We laughed, clinked our glasses and said 'cheers'.

Lisa's phone beeped. She looked at it, appeared to be irritated by what she saw, tutted, and put it down again.

"Problem?" I asked tentatively.

"Not really," Lisa replied crossly. "Neil telling me Alfie won't go to sleep. What does he want me to do about it? It happens all the time; I don't contact him at work!"

"I see," I said, trying to sound sympathetic without being undiplomatic, knowing that when people criticise their spouses they aren't inviting you to join in.

Lisa leaned forward as though she wanted to share a confidence. "Did you ever wish you didn't have children?" she asked.

"Ouf!" I exhaled. I sat back and gestured towards Lisa with both hands. "Look at you. Of course I don't."

"No, not now. But when I was little: did you ever wish you hadn't had me?"

"No," I said, looking her straight in the eye. "I mean, I can't pretend there weren't times when you were being a pain, as all small children can be, when I didn't wish you'd go away temporarily, I mean just out of the room, but I never wished we hadn't had you. And the older I get, the more the thought of it terrifies me, to be honest."

Lisa smiled but sniffed, opened her bag and got out a tissue, with which she furtively dabbed under her eyes before blowing her nose. I noted she still does that two-handed, as we taught her to when she was a toddler. "I worry I'm not a very good mother," she said quietly.

"You're a great mother," I insisted. "And it's one of those paradoxes, isn't it? It's only the good ones that worry about it. The bad ones don't care."

"It just doesn't come naturally to me."

"That's a myth, sweetheart. Everyone learns as they go along."

"That's what Mum says."

"And I always agree with everything your mother says."

Lisa laughed, which was good to hear.

"Well, on this occasion, anyway," I said. "But seriously, I feel sorry for your generation, with the weight of expectation on you when you have kids. I could sound like a grumpy old man here..."

Our eyes met and we both smiled.

"...but parenthood seems to have become fetishised over the last twenty years, so people imagine there is some sort of idealised state of nature in which other families are living, in complete harmony and knowing exactly what to do in all circumstances from day one. And anything less than that is a failure. And it just isn't true."

"Maybe once they're a bit older, and the tedium of nappies and potties and sick is behind us..."

"Well, there are challenges at every age. But don't wish their childhood away. One of the worst things for parents is how quickly children grow up."

"So, why do we do this? Are we all masochists or something?"

"I think we're wired to want it. Although you can be unhappy, and occasionally very unhappy, with children, I don't think most of us can ever be completely happy without them. It's basic genetics."

"You've been thinking about this, Dad."

"Well, I'm getting on a bit, and I've had quite a lot of time to reflect recently."

Lisa didn't seem to want to pursue that. "I sometimes wish Neil would do more. I mean, he is a great dad, and I know he works long hours, and doesn't have any choice in that if he wants to get on, and I want him to get on, so then I think I'm being an unreasonable bitch."

"You're probably right."

"Dad!"

"As soon as you got out of the car today, I thought to myself 'there's an unreasonable bitch if ever I saw one'."

Lisa looked at me with a rueful smile. "You don't change, do you?"

"No, but the thing is, unless you're a fictitious family on social media, you can't have everything. You have to decide what you want most, and there are compromises involved. Kids, when they grow up, remember whether their childhood was happy, not whether their family had a bigger telly than the neighbours. And for kids, being happy doesn't mean having parents who spend every waking hour obsessing over them either. Parents should be allowed to have other things in their lives. And kids should be allowed some personal space."

"Should I be writing this down?"

"Now *you're* making fun of *me*. These are just things I've gathered from experience, not from having been a brilliant example: I'm only too aware of that. I look at what Neil does with the kids, and I think 'why didn't I do more? Did I really need to spend so much time at work?' It was a bit different because your mum originally wanted me to earn money while she stayed at home. But if I had my time again..."

"None of us gets more than one shot at it," Lisa interrupted me. "You were fine. You're still my favourite dad."

I saw the waiter coming out of the kitchen, carrying two plates, one of which appeared to be an enormous calzone. I thought once we started eating the moment would be lost.

"It's really lovely to be able to talk to you like this," I said, "just the two of us. And I'm enjoying looking after the kids. I was beginning to worry in the last few years that I was losing you from my life."

Lisa looked at me and shook her head, but her expression suggested that what I had said wasn't totally unexpected, or my concerns imaginary.

"No," she said with a sigh, "it was never that. Just so busy in recent years with marriage and then the kids. And, you know, it's been a bit complicated over the years with you and Mum not being together anymore, and wondering if I would be expected to take sides, which I obviously didn't want to do.

"I'm sorry," was all I could think to say.

"Not needed," she replied quietly. The waiter arrived at our table. "Right," Lisa said more brightly, "now that we've established that neither of us is the worst parent ever, I'm going to spend my last half hour of freedom stuffing myself full of pizza."

Monday 8 March

Well, OK: I'm a dreadful nosey old person with too much time on his hands.

This morning, it being a nice, sunny day, though disappointingly cold for the start of spring, and having nothing better to do, I let my curiosity get the better of me and walked back to the cemetery.

I briefly returned to my parents' grave to make sure that the flowers were still there, Lisa's tulips and my lone chrysanthemum, but I knew that wasn't the real purpose of my visit. Almost furtively, looking around me to ensure I wasn't being watched, I moved to the row where I thought I had seen Ella yesterday, and started examining the headstones as though I were just a mildly interested passer-by. Because of the distance from my parents' grave, I couldn't be absolutely sure where Ella had been standing, or one hundred percent that it was even her, but my best guess found me in front of a small grey, marble stone which looked quite new. The grave belonged to Amelia Eloise Clark, and the few days' difference between the dates of birth and death, three years ago, were enough to reduce me to tears. Some pink and white flowers had been carefully arranged in the holder behind the stone. And on the stone itself was a small, smiling teddy bear, sensibly protected against the elements by a transparent plastic wrapper, and with it a small card with a handwritten "To my little miracle. All my love forever. Mummy" and enough kisses to fill the space completely, front and back.

I wiped my eyes, collected myself and stood back. I realised I didn't know Ella's surname, but I was pretty sure I did recognise her handwriting.

How did she cope with something like that? I searched my memory to see if this new knowledge explained anything about

Monday 8 March

Ella or her behaviour, but I wasn't sure that it did. I wanted to find her and hug her, but of course I can't.

Wednesday 10 March

I haven't encountered Ella and haven't contacted her. I'm worried that I won't be able to act naturally. Having already almost ruined our friendship once, I don't want to risk it again. I am at least bright enough to realise that I can't ever ask her about her daughter.

How, then, to be supportive? Just, I suppose, be generally kind and understanding. That isn't a bad mantra for any situation, is it?

I do hope, though, that one day she may feel able to confide in me, if she wants to. I remember telling Lisa on Sunday that the idea of never having had her terrified me, and it is absolutely true.

This morning I went out for a walk to clear my head. I found myself idly looking into estate agents' windows. I realised that it hadn't occurred to me for a very long time to consider whether I should buy a house. When I first started living alone, after Anne and I split up, it seemed sensible to get a flat because of financial uncertainty, the limited amount of free time I had while I was working and, perhaps most importantly, the nagging feeling that in a building on my own, without the sound of other humans, I might become very lonely after a lifetime of sharing accommodation.

But now? Maybe the upkeep of a house and, more appealingly, tending a garden in the summer months, are exactly what I need to fill my time and give me a project with some sense of satisfaction. Maybe. I decided not to go into the estate agent today, but to do some research online first. Could I get a house with the proceeds of this flat, plus the tax-free lump sum from my pension? I might need to move further from London, but that would be OK as long as I could still get round to Lisa's. I could keep in touch with Ella and invite her round.

I kept walking, still preoccupied with my own thoughts, and the penny did not drop until the last minute that I was walking past the charity shop I worked at. I glanced through the window and made immediate eye contact with Becky, who was rearranging a display in the window. She looked startled to see me, but immediately began waving frantically, disappeared from view and then reappeared at the door.

"Come in," she beckoned.

I hesitated and remained standing awkwardly on the pavement.

"It's all right," she reassured me, as though talking to a child with night terrors, "Irene's not around."

I walked gingerly through the door. I assumed we would be alone, but I saw there was a bald-headed man in his sixties standing at the till. We exchanged polite smiles.

"That's Trevor," Becky told me in a whisper, "not all that bright, to be honest, but he means well, and he's, er..."

"Not a Nazi like me?"

"Exactly. Sorry about the tribunal."

"Expected."

"I suppose. Anyway," Becky folded her arms and held me with an exaggerated, indignant stare. "What do you have to say for yourself, young man? What are your intentions towards my mother?"

I thought about pretending not to have made the connection, but decided that wasn't going to be convincing. I laughed nervously and cleared my throat. "So you worked it out," I heard myself say lamely.

"Well, you didn't need to be Sherlock Holmes. Almost as soon as she started talking about you. And then having exactly the same name."

"That would be a clue," I agreed.

We both smiled.

"Well?" Becky asked. "Did you fall down a big hole or something?"

"No," I replied. How candid did I want to be? I decided I had nothing to lose. "To be honest, Becky, I thought I bored your mother to death. Everything she was telling me about her life was far more interesting than anything I could think of. So I couldn't imagine she would want me to contact her again."

Becky nodded sympathetically. "She does that, I'm afraid. When she first meets people. I've told her it puts people off. It's very competitive in her profession, and she doesn't know when to switch off."

"I see," I said, though I now felt completely confused. "So you're saying I should contact her?"

"If you want to."

"Does *she* want to? I mean, I appreciate your trying to help, and don't take this the wrong way, but it could get really embarrassing if she's already made up her mind about me. It could look like harassment."

"Go for it," Becky advised with a thumbs-up. "Mum's really down-to-earth when you peel away the professional veneer. I mean, Dad was a bus driver."

"Really?"

"Well, no, he was an ENT consultant actually. But he might have been a bus driver, if ,er..."

"He'd driven buses."

"Exactly. So you'll call her?"

"OK. Maybe the three of us could go out," I suggested brightly.

Becky gave me the look of disgust reserved to children contemplating anything even vaguely relating to their parents' sex lives. "Too weird," she said bluntly.

I laughed. "OK," I said, "I'll call her, I promise."

Becky smiled and gave me as thumbs-up. "Great," she said. "My work is done. Off you go then."

Sunday 14 March

Like a shy, awkward teenager not sure if he dares ask the pretty, cool girl out for a date, I have been avoiding calling Debbie until today. Every day I have intended to, and every day I have picked up the phone and put it down again. Did Becky really know what her mother wanted, I asked myself, or was she just flying a kite of her own (though even that, I supposed, would be quite flattering in its way?) What if Debbie had met someone else in the meantime? Or I rang at exactly the wrong moment when she was busy at work, and got an angry or abrupt response? And how would I explain not having called earlier? Did I have to explain that? In today's society, was making the next move still up to the man? I really had no idea.

I think I was a bit distracted on Thursday when I was looking after the kids, and saw on Jasmine's little face an uncomprehending disappointment at Grandpa not being much fun today, an emotion I vowed not to be the cause of again. I did ask Alfie for his opinion when the two of us were alone, but he only smacked his lips and gurgled in response. He has a lot to learn about women.

By Friday I thought I couldn't put off contacting Ella much longer, so I WhatsApped her and invited her round for coffee, then steered the conversation round to my quandary over Debbie. Ella was characteristically, but helpfully, unsympathetic. She said the woman still sounded like a bit of a fancy pants to her, but if I was interested then I should stop dithering and get on with it. If I needed an incentive, how about some sort of forfeit? She had a glint in her eye about that, so I politely declined, but she would in any case have been disappointed because I did call Debbie today. To preserve chronology, though, I'll come to that in a moment.

My phone rang just after lunch and I wondered initially if it might be Debbie, or even Becky having lost patience with me. But when I looked at the screen it turned out to be Sunil.

"Hi, mate," I said. "Great to hear from you. How are you?"

"All fine, all fine," he replied with that understated laugh of his. "And how about you, my friend? Got bored and gone back to work yet?"

I explained as briefly as I could about the charity shop, how my sins had followed me, and about the tribunal, trying not to sound too despondent about it.

"That's crazy," Sunil replied. "You know what: the older I get, the more prejudiced I become against white liberals!"

I had to laugh at that. "I know what you mean," I told Sunil, "except that until they suddenly expelled me from the club at the end of last year I *was* one, for decades."

"They're patronising people," Sunil insisted. "I don't like them, and I don't need them."

"Well, that's certainly true," I agreed. "With your success."

"And what were you doing working in a charity shop anyway? What were you doing with your brain? Don't you need a bigger challenge?"

I didn't know how to answer that. I waited for Sunil to go on.

"I should apologise," he said. "I said I would call you in a couple of weeks to arrange lunch and that was four months ago."

"Well, you're a busy man."

"I am, but in business you should keep your promises. You told me that about a week after I started."

"Did I?" I laughed.

"You did. So anyway, how are you fixed for lunch on Wednesday? I have something I would like to run past you."

"That would be great," I said immediately, feeling no need to pretend to have to consult my diary. "I'll look forward to it."

As soon as I had come off the phone with Sunil, I wanted to call Debbie. Confidence is a slippery, elusive thing, isn't it? I immediately rang her number; unfortunately, it went to voicemail. For some reason, with my new-found resolve, that possibility hadn't occurred to me, and as a result I left a slightly awkward message. With my mood a little dampened, I went to make myself a cup of tea and sat in silence in my armchair waiting for the liquid to cool. I didn't stay disheartened for long though: it seemed to me that there was a good chance that Sunil was going to offer me some sort of work, and even if he eventually didn't, or it was a role I didn't want, then I could at least spend three days optimistically expecting something good.

The phone rang. It was Debbie. She sounded friendly, if a little business-like, and said that she had been called into work and was in the car on the way there. There was a lot of background noise, and I wasn't sure she would be able to hear me very well, so I decided it would be better to dispense with any small talk and come directly to the point. Without saying much about our 'date' two weeks ago, which I now thought – based on what Becky had told me - might have been as painful for her mother as it had for me, I simply said that it would be nice to meet up with her again. To my relief, she agreed without obvious hesitation, then suggested that I accompany her to see a play at the National Theatre this Friday, for which she had a spare ticket. As I had with Sunil, I immediately agreed. We arranged when and where to meet and then rang off.

The rest of the day wasn't very exciting, but it didn't need to be.

Wednesday 17 March

It has become a partly endearing, partly annoying ritual of my lunches with Sunil over the years (even when we were working together) that he insists on going to Indian restaurants so that he can complain about the inauthenticity of the food and inform me, usually within the first five minutes, that the waiters are actually Bangladeshi rather than Indian.

More going through my wardrobe and agonising over how to dress for the occasion. I didn't want to look too much as though I thought this might be a job interview, but on the other hand, in a world of smart, and not-so-smart, casual, Sunil still does smart smart. His suits look expensive, his shirts are crisp and white, and he may well be the last regular buyer of silk ties in London. I can't compete with that but did decide to put on a suit, together with a shirt that was all white but for a thin, blue vertical pinstripe. My inability to eat in Indian restaurants without getting the food on my clothes was a cause of exasperation to my ex-wife throughout our marriage, and in this case I had always had to admit that she had a point. So I decided that, rather than cover my tie in the restaurant (which I always think makes adults look like babies) or remove it at the table (an invitation to any companion to get out a splash guard), I would simply dispense with it.

Sunil was already seated when I arrived. Without getting up, he was shaking hands and exchanging smiles with a couple of middle-aged Asian men who were passing by on the way to their table. As soon as they had gone, he saw me and gave me a friendly wave. Before I had properly sat down, the manager came over to greet us and take our order. I also noticed the people Sunil had been shaking hands with craning their necks to see who I was. I've noticed the ever-increasing deference with which Sunil is treated in Indian restaurants in recent years;

I don't know if it's a 'community' thing, or whether I should ask, or whether I shouldn't.

"Bengalis," Sunil told me on cue, as soon as the manager had left us. "From Bangladesh." He then told me that this was a new branch but actually owned by the same family as another restaurant we had gone to several times over the years. "They like my business," he went on, as though revealing a confidence. I wasn't sure if he meant his custom or his actual business, so I just nodded politely and told him how pleased I was to see him, which was true.

Our drinks arrived rapidly, as I had now come to expect. Sunil doesn't drink at lunchtime, but I didn't think he would object if I did, given that I had no further plans for the day, so I had ordered a bottle of beer. We clinked glasses.

"Cheers!" we both said simultaneously. "Lovely to see you," I added. The waiter was hovering to see if we were ready to order our food, but Sunil waved him away.

"So what are you doing with all your free time?" Sunil asked amiably. It was a question that made me uncomfortable though, one that retirees (of which I may or may not be one) get a lot, I have noticed, as though they need constantly to justify their life.

"This and that," I replied breezily. "Investigating whether to do an English degree, which is something I have always wanted to get into. Spending more time with my daughter and grandkids, which is great."

Sunil nodded politely but didn't look convinced. He gestured at the menu, which I picked up and started to consult in silence. My curry-house selections are every bit as predictable as my pizzas; as I perused the various dishes I could see Lisa in my mind's eye shaking her head in embarrassment. The waiter returned and I ordered: lamb rogan josh (I mean, at least it isn't chicken tikka masala!), pilau rice, Bombay potatoes and mutter paneer. The waiter beamed back indulgently and appeared to be avoiding catching Sunil's eye. My companion did what he always does, which was to ask for something that was not on the menu. The waiter looked confused and, as though it were a matter of urgency, went to fetch the manager who, in turn smiling ingratiatingly at Sunil and scowling at the waiter, said that of course it was no problem at all.

I'm never sure if I pronounce the names of Sunil's wife and kids correctly, so I decided not to try. "Family all OK?" I asked brightly.

Sunil thought about it and nodded slowly. "My mother is in and out of hospital," he replied. "I tell her some of these doctors are clowns, we should try somewhere else. They're not cheap either."

I muttered that I was sorry to hear it, then asked about his kids.

"Oh, they're OK," he said. "Though I tell them, and I tell their mother: they need to concentrate more at school."

I smiled. "My grandkids aren't old enough for school yet," I said, "Jasmine's a bright little thing but I've no idea how that will translate to the school environment."

Sunil didn't look very interested in my family. "So," he said, "you strike me as a man who could do with a new challenge."

"Well, possibly," I replied, "though I'm certainly not missing…"

Sunil cut me short. "Now, you know my company is the market leader for new technology solutions in the financial services business software space," he told me.

I nodded, though I wasn't sure I did know that: his company has certainly done well from a standing start in a relatively short period of time, but others are bigger and two or three have reputations that are at least as good, I think.

"But," Sunil went on, "the board worries that we have too many of our eggs in one basket. What if we're overinvested in AI and blockchain and it doesn't turn out to be the holy grail we thought it was? So these white boy bankers tell me we should diversify without straying too far from what we know.

And I'm thinking, let's set up a legacy software division, headed up by my old friend, Alan Brierley." He sat back in his chair and gestured at me with his right hand.

I hadn't been expecting that. I didn't speak, and I suspect my face failed to register anything except surprise. Sunil looked non-plussed and forced a smile, though it lacked warmth. "Well, to be honest, I was expecting more enthusiasm," he said with a short staccato laugh.

"No," I replied, holding both hands up as though I were trying to deflect some invisible incoming object, "it's just that I wasn't expecting that."

"Well, what were you expecting?"

"Something more modest."

"Modest?" You could hear the disdain in Sunil's voice. "In this business, if you think modest you're going to be toast."

I had managed to recover my composure. "OK," I said, "tell me more."

Sunil grinned. "That's more like it. So we start with you and a couple of programmers, initially offering legacy system support to our existing clients, which is a gap in our offering anyway, and then build out from there to new clients, with cross-selling between our divisions in both directions. Aiming to keep it lean, so by year five you'll probably have twenty staff and say a dozen clients."

Year five? I had recently got used to thinking one day at a time. "And how long would I need to commit to this? I asked."

Sunil shrugged. "Six or seven years. Succession plan by year five. Still means you can retire at sixty-five, and a lot more comfortably than you can now, Alan. Good basic, bonus, shares and options. Buy a big house instead of a small flat. Invest. Travel when you retire without worrying about the cost."

"Does sound interesting," I replied, trying not wholly successfully to conceal my continuing apprehension. "Can I have some time to think about it?"

Sunil nodded. "If you wish. Our HR will send you a proposal by Friday. We'll need a response by Monday though."

"Are you talking to anyone else?"

Sunil shook his head. "The board wants someone who can start immediately. And who doesn't have a non-compete."

That told me that I probably hadn't been the first choice, but I wasn't in the least surprised or offended by that. I smiled at the thought. Sunil did not reciprocate.

The food arrived, and there was a short hiatus in the conversation while dishes were distributed around the table. Wanting to change the subject, and conscious that our relationship would change if I became his employee and that this might therefore be the last time I would be able to talk to Sunil as a friend, I brought up the manner of my departure from what, after so many years, I still referred to simply as 'work'. "So I asked Ade if he had experienced racism at the firm," I told Sunil, "expecting him to say no, but he didn't. He said he had, frequently. Did you ever get that?"

"Of course, all the time," Sunil replied forcefully.

"You see, that surprises me as well. So what did you do?"

"I pretended to be oblivious to it. And worked round it."

"Sorry about that."

"Well, it turned out OK, didn't it? And anyway, racism is everywhere, isn't it? White people don't have a monopoly on it. Take the guys I was talking to when you arrived: if we joined them at their table, I guarantee you they would be wishing you would go away and leave us alone. And earlier, when I was complaining about 'white boy bankers'? If I'd said 'Jewish bankers' you'd have raised an eyebrow, but I say white and you feel you have to give me the polite neutral expression of the white liberal, but it's just the same. It's a game we all play. And I still think that black guy in your office was probably trying to get rid of you."

"Well, we won't agree on that last point," I replied with a laugh. "You haven't met him and he's a good lad."

Sunil only shrugged. "Take this job," he said. "It's a great opportunity."

Thursday 18 March

I had a terrible night, tossing and turning, after Sunil's offer yesterday. Sometimes there are questions you would prefer that you hadn't been asked.

Of course, it's potentially a very good job. Only potentially, because the IT market is very competitive and Sunil's company isn't yet at the stage where it can afford to make any major mistakes and survive. But although I am comfortable enough with my paid-up pension, and can probably afford to buy a small house outside London, wouldn't it be better actually to be wealthy, so that for the first time in my life I don't have to be careful with money? I'm not being asked to invest in the company, so I can't actually lose, at least not financially. And with spare cash I could be generous to Lisa and the grandkids, which would make me very happy.

I went over the possible scenarios in my head time and time again.

Scenario one: I take the job and make a success of it. Pretty positive: I have more money and gain some sorely needed self-esteem. Downsides are the stress, regular insomnia like tonight's and loss of opportunity to do other things. Possible estrangement from my family again.

Scenario two: I take the job and don't make a success of it. More likely, I think, if I'm brutally honest with myself. What do I know about managing twenty people or cultivating new clients? Of course, I could hire assistants and seek help from Sunil and others, but at that level (I imagine) it's still a pretty lonely place. I'm sure they would get rid of me long before I could ruin the company, or even the division, but if that happened what would it do to my mental state? Wouldn't not trying be better than failing?

Scenario three: I don't take the job. I have enough to live on, minimal stress and can spend more time with the grandkids. But would I forever have a nagging feeling that I should have given the job a go, that I was mentally weak and feeble and had, as the saying goes, 'bottled it'? Wouldn't it reinforce the view of my ex-wife that I was not an achiever, a view that had led her to lose patience with me and transfer her affections to the business-owning Howard? Not that she would ever be likely to find out, but I would feel her contempt inside my head. And how would it affect my relationship with Debbie, or any other woman who might come into my life? I was pretty sure that dinner with Debbie the other Saturday would have gone differently if I had felt that I was closer to being on an equal footing with her, and as divisional head of a software company I would have been. In basic terms, weren't all women more attracted to successful men? Or was that just an outdated, and possibly misogynistic fear of successful women on my part? Relationships shouldn't be a competition, should they?

Too many questions circulating in my head. At around five o'clock I gave up trying to sleep and went and stood by the bedroom curtains, peering out into the road. There wasn't much to see except the yellow glow of the streetlamps and the occasional car or van driving by. I wondered where they could possibly be going at this time of the morning. I really wanted to have someone I could confide in, someone who had no particular interest in the outcome. Lisa wouldn't really do (even if she qualified on that basis), because she would tell her mother. Ella was the obvious candidate, and I would try to sound her out tomorrow. Though, if I knew her, she would take me through a set of logical steps which would lead to the conclusion that I should not take the job: did I need the money (no); on the balance of probability would taking the job make me any happier (also no)? Then she might be offended if I took the job anyway. Because, I thought, as I vacantly watched the brake lights of a bus illuminate as it slowed on the approach to a sheltered stop, the issue wasn't really either money or happiness, but how much I cared whether society would or wouldn't consider me a success.

Friday 19 March

Not quite the evening I expected.

I had arranged to meet Debbie at a restaurant on the South Bank at six o'clock to get some food before the play started at seven thirty. Something we have in common, I thought, is that we don't like sitting in a theatre for hours with our stomachs rumbling and then having to try to find somewhere to eat at ten p.m.

I walked into the restaurant punctually and spotted Debbie sitting at the bar talking to another couple. I crossed the room and she greeted me and then introduced me to Bob and Sheila who, I assumed, she had either bumped into or maybe just met. To be polite (and not appear tight-fisted in front of Debbie) I offered them a drink and was a little surprised when they both accepted, as did Debbie. I could only half listen to their conversation as I tried to get the bartender's attention then gave my order and paid for it, but it appeared to be about a foreign country, though which one I couldn't tell.

"Have you been to Dunedin?" Bob asked me as I handed out the drinks.

"No," I replied. "I've only been to Scotland once."

"We were talking about New Zealand," Sheila informed me.

I took a sip of the beer I had ordered. "Sorry, no. I've never been there at all."

"It's a great country," Bob said enthusiastically. "Plenty of time for travel now you've retired."

I nodded politely, and wondered how long Debbie had been waiting if she'd had time to discuss my life with these people.

"Shall we go to our table?" Debbie asked, looking anxiously up at the clock on the wall.

"Good idea," I replied. I smiled at Bob and Sheila. "Nice to have met you."

But as the waiter conducted us to our table, it appeared that Bob and Sheila were following us. And when we sat down at our table, they did the same. Sheila appeared to be trying to communicate something to Debbie, who in turn was trying not to laugh.

Bob beamed at me. "We all work together," he told me, as though he could clearly read my thoughts.

"This is our little hospital theatre club," Debbie said, simultaneously re-arranging the cutlery in front of her. "We do this about three or four times a year."

"There's usually four of us these days," Sheila said, "only Richard's gone to New Zealand."

"Which is why we were talking about it," Debbie explained quietly.

"I'm with you now," I said amiably. "Sorry about that – I don't think I'm usually that slow on the uptake!"

"No problem," said Bob. "Easy mistake to make. We'll try not to start talking shop and boring you to tears."

"So what countries have you visited, Alan?" Sheila asked, as though consciously trying to get me into the conversation. "Not New Zealand obviously, but…"

I was sure it was a perfectly well-intentioned question, but I now felt as though I were being interviewed. I gave the list, to the extent that I could remember it, and had to concede that it sounded like the history of a sunburnt British holidaymaker rather than of an intrepid traveller. From what I could see out of the corner of my eye, Debbie did not react at all.

Bob felt the need to change the subject. "And you like Shakespeare, I hope?"

I said I did, though admitted that it was the first time I had seen one of his plays at the National. I added that I was thinking of doing an OU English degree. Sheila nodded encouragingly. I didn't say that the idea might be scuppered by a job offer I had just had, as I had a strong sense that, although I would be interested in knowing what Debbie thought about it, I didn't want to discuss it in front of the others.

The waiter appeared at my right shoulder and began to give us the list of specials.

The play was *As You Like It,* but I was dismayed to find that I didn't. I couldn't fully follow the plot, which didn't help – if I'd had more warning, I would have bought a copy and read through it – but the production had also been set in revolutionary Cuba for some reason and some of the male parts were played by women and vice versa. I had rehearsed in my head something neutral to say about it during the interval, but needn't have worried: Debbie, Bob and Sheila largely talked about work, frequently apologising for doing so, but doing it anyway. Sheila apparently was a paediatrician while Bob seemed to be more of an administrator, though it was possible he had previously been a practising doctor.

The auditorium had been full for the first half, but the audience had noticeably thinned a little for the second, which wasn't any more enjoyable. I wondered if I was mistaken in thinking that English literature was for me, and whether I shouldn't after all stick to software, which I was at least comfortable with. Which was a further argument for accepting Sunil's job offer.

We made non-committal small talk as we left the theatre, zipping up fleeces in the cold night air. It turned out that Bob and Sheila were taking a different Tube line, so we said our farewells at the station with polite handshakes, saying that it was nice to meet each other and that we hoped to do this again.

The Tube was packed, and Debbie and I did not have much chance for conversation. Thinking that we might go our separate ways at the end of the journey, I said that it was very nice to see her again and thanked her for inviting me. With two stops to go, I also said that I had been offered a new job; I was no longer sure if I was trying to get her opinion or just desperately trying to appear more interesting. Debbie said that sounded exciting but that she couldn't really hear me very well: tell her again in a minute.

As we followed the crowd up the stairs and through the turnstiles, I once again started to talk about the job offer. Debbie cut me short and asked whether I would mind walking her home: she said you couldn't be too careful round here at this time of night. I said of course that would be no problem. It turned out that her house was only about three streets away from the station which, once we had negotiated the traffic, again left us with very little opportunity to talk. Debbie stopped in front of exactly the sort of grand, expensive Victorian terrace I had imagined she might have, and started rummaging in her bag for her keys. And then, to my complete surprise, she invited me to come in.

The house was tastefully decorated in a not-trying-too-hard way. There wasn't any of the awful all-wood or all-white minimalism you get in a lot of houses these days (I'm mainly going on things I've seen in magazines and estate agents' windows for that assessment) and a lot of original features such as the fireplace and the picture rails beneath the high ceiling had been emphasised. It looked well-judged to me, like a home, somewhere you could sit or lie in front of the television without feeling you were committing sacrilege. The main room had a burgundy carpet and two quite old, matching, green leather sofas, which gave the impression of having originally been expensive. I sat down on one, moving a discarded cardigan to one side, as Debbie went into the kitchen to make coffee. I imagined, though I hadn't previously given it any thought, that this must be the house she had shared with her husband. I could see photos on the mantelpiece, and one appeared to feature a woman, a man, a younger man, presumably David, and a teenaged girl, presumably Becky. I didn't like to get up and take a closer look in case Debbie suddenly came back and caught me. Would she think it was normal curiosity or intrusion? I didn't know her well enough to judge.

She came back with two mugs of coffee then left the room again and returned smiling and bearing a bottle of wine and two glasses. I nodded as she held up the bottle in my direction, and with an approving look on her face she filled up both glasses and handed one to me. She sat down on the other sofa with her feet tucked under her.

"Cheers," we said simultaneously as we reached across and clinked glasses.

"So what did you think of the play?" Debbie asked.

I had been trying to rehearse what to say in my head. I didn't think I could be honest given that Debbie had invited me. "I thought it was good," I began, "though I wish I had read it or at least a synopsis beforehand, so I would have had a better idea of the plot."

Debbie appeared to be thinking about that. "I don't think it's a particularly difficult plot to follow," she said seriously, "I mean, it's one of the comedies, but I just thought it was a weird production."

I relaxed. "Well so did I, to be honest, but I just thought I haven't been to the theatre much in recent years, so maybe…I was just trying to keep an open mind," I explained. "In Shakespeare's day all the women were played by boys or men, weren't they?"

Debbie didn't answer that point and didn't look impressed. "You should have the courage of your convictions, Alan," she told me.

"I'm not sure that's always sensible," I replied, thinking aloud.

Debbie said nothing but looked at me curiously, as though expecting me to expand on my thought. When I didn't, she topped up her glass, looked at mine, and saw with disappointment that it was still three-quarters full. "Drink up," she said, "I don't want to drink all of this myself." I gulped a couple of mouthfuls and Debbie filled my glass almost to the brim then put the bottle down again.

"So anyway," she asked. "What's this fancy new job you've been offered."

"Oh, yes." I sat up before realising that I had done so. "Head of Legacy Software Division."

"Is that good?" Debbie sounded genuinely interested. "I mean, it sounds important."

"Well, yes it's a good job, doing what I'm probably best at."

"Good money?"

"Potentially very."

"Slam dunk, then. Go for it! Must be better than working in a charity shop. Though, I don't want to put a dampener on it, won't you have the same, er, difficulty with references?"

"About that," I said. "Do I need to explain what happened when I left my job?"

Debbie shook her head. "Becky did. It didn't sound too terrible the way she told it. Just maybe a little…"

"Naïve? That's what everyone says."

"I was thinking more 'stubborn'. No, that's a bit rude' isn't it?" She smiled. "What's a better word?"

"'Stubborn' will probably do," I smiled back. "Anyway with this new job offer, the guy who runs it is a former assistant and current friend of mine. And he's Asian. So if he says I'm not a racist, I guess they will go with that."

Debbie pushed her hair back behind her ears. "I'm not sure it should work like that."

"Neither am I, but I think it does."

"Best to grab it then. If it's a good job and you might not get another opportunity."

I nodded. We sat in silence for a few seconds. I wondered if I knew Debbie well enough to use her as a sounding board. I wanted to, but there was the definite risk that she would think less of me as a result. I was painfully aware, though, that I'd had the written job proposal since this morning and was no closer to working out how I should respond.

"The thing is," I said finally, trying to make eye contact with Debbie but finding that she was looking down at her glass, "I'm not sure."

"I see," Debbie said slowly. Are you looking for... advice?"

"I'm not even sure of that," I replied.

Debbie smiled politely, but I noticed that she glanced furtively at the clock on the mantelpiece. Tonight, I thought, had been a big improvement on our first date. The last thing I needed to do now in front of this successful woman was to appear indecisive or, worse, just plain needy. "No, I'll work it out," I said more confidently. "First-world problems!"

Debbie nodded. "Excuse me," she said with a closed-lipped smile, getting out of her seat and carefully placing her glass on the coffee-table. I moved my legs to allow her to pass and she left the room.

I looked at the clock and, surprised at how late it was, checked with my watch. A couple of minutes passed. I didn't know why Debbie had left the room – I assumed to visit the toilet – but I felt it was hardly appropriate to listen out to try to confirm that! I wondered why I was still here. Had I not been picking up on hints to leave? I can be unobservant, but I didn't think so. Would it be rude if I left now? Did Debbie want me to stay longer? Did she want me to stay the night? Christ, did she want sex?! I felt butterflies in my stomach at the prospect. It had been a long time since... maybe it was like riding a bike. No, that was definitely the wrong image. But what were the rules on sex for the over-fifties? I had no idea. Did I want it? Well, yes, in the abstract. But right here, right now, with Debbie? I wasn't sure I was ready. Could I ask for a rain check? Time to prepare myself? Unlikely to go down well, I thought.

Debbie came back into the room, unselfconsciously sat down again and picked up her glass.

"Do you want me to go?" I asked. "I'm conscious of the…"

Debbie patted the top of my leg but appeared to stifle a yawn at the same time. "You're fine," she said. "It's Saturday tomorrow, I'm not working."

But now we needed something to talk about: a silence of more than a few seconds would be a killer.

"Do they not do operations at the weekend?" I asked lamely.

Debbie didn't look very interested in the question. "Usually only emergencies," she replied. "In the NHS anyway, and I don't do any private work, being a leftie."

I smiled and went to utter a further inanity, but Debbie interrupted me. "Do you want to stay, Alan?" she asked. She saw my eyes glance at the furniture. "No, not on the sofa. Come on," she continued impatiently, "we're grown-ups; we don't have to dance around this like teenagers."

"The thing is," I said thinking aloud once more, "I haven't got a…" I stopped and felt my face turn crimson.

Debbie looked as though she thought she couldn't have heard properly. "That won't be necessary," she said.

"Understood," I said, trying not to look even more embarrassed.

Debbie patted my leg again. "So if you'd like to go and 'freshen up'. Cloakroom is just down the corridor."

I did as I was told. The cloakroom was claustrophobic and had a roaring fan. As far as I could tell, my breath was OK, but to be sure I rubbed a small amount of toothpaste against my teeth then rinsed my mouth. I was undoubtedly sweating, but there wasn't much I could do about that. I peed more than I expected to, something I put down to nerves. I tried to wash my privates, but bits of toilet paper came off and stuck to me and I had carefully to pick them off one by one. I was probably in the cloakroom no longer than five minutes, but it was far longer than I intended.

"Sorry about that," I said as I walked back down the hall, but there was no reply. When I entered the sitting room, I immediately saw that Debbie was now slumped diagonally across the sofa, fast asleep. Her mouth was open and faint rhythmic snoring sounds were issuing from it.

I tiptoed out to the hall where I found a blanket in the cupboard. I slowly, gently pushed Debbie into a fully horizontal position, carefully arranged the blanket over her, watched her for a few seconds, took the cups and glasses out to the kitchen and then, as quietly as I could, let myself out of the house.

Saturday 20 March

I lay in bed this morning thinking about last night. I was sure I had done the right thing, but couldn't be certain Debbie would see it the same way. Would she be insulted?

Happily, it turned out she wasn't. She texted around eleven. I was relieved that she wasn't making an apology or asking for one. "Not sure what happened there," the text began. "Would you like to come round for lunch. 1pm?"

I immediately replied yes, had a shower, smartened myself up and set off early enough to arrive promptly at the agreed time, having stopped off at the off-licence on the way to buy a bottle of wine. Being no expert, I selected one which was, I hoped, expensive enough to suggest good taste.

Debbie answered the door with a wide smile on her face. She was wearing a tight-fitting polo-necked jumper which showed off the curves of her body to best advantage. As we walked along the hall, I realised I could not smell cooking. I had been expecting lunch and then (probably, hopefully) sex in that order, but Debbie obviously had other ideas. She took my hand and led me up the stairs. We arrived at a large master bedroom with an imposing, square, iron-framed bed positioned against the back wall.

"You don't need to…?" Debbie asked without letting go of my hand, "or if you do, don't be half an hour this time!" Something seemed to occur to her. "It's not Viagra, is it? I mean, it would be OK…"

I gave an embarrassed laugh. "No," I said, though I was indeed worried after all this time that I might not be able to perform. Or that I would have the opposite problem. I tried to divert attention towards Debbie. "And you aren't intending to fall asleep again?" I asked.

"What, during? Oh dear, are you that bad?"

We tried to kiss, but broke off until we had both stopped laughing. Then, completely unselfconsciously, we undressed and got into bed.

The earth didn't move, but it was good. I had not realised how starved I had become of the smell and touch and warmth of another human body. I sensed that Debbie was feeling the same, though I wondered how it would feel to have sex for the first time after you had lost someone rather than, in my case, broken up with them. Would the pleasure in any way be tinged with guilt?

"Always sex first, then food," Debbie told me as we stood in the kitchen. "Nothing worse than people bolting food because they're impatient to do something else. And who wants to have sex with indigestion?"

A comforting waft of warm cooking was coming at me from the fan oven. A spicy, herbal, slightly sweet vegetable smell. Debbie had declined my offer to assist with food preparation because, she told me, in true *Blue Peter* fashion she had one she'd done earlier, in this case some sort of vegetarian casserole. So, to appear that I was doing something, I had opened my bottle of wine and poured it into two glasses. Apparently, the casserole was going to be a while, so we took our glasses and went into the sitting room.

We talked about all sorts of things: families, work, politics, her activism on climate issues, all without any awkward pauses or resorting to inanity in the cause of keeping the conversation flowing. I started to relax. I thought I at least had a foot in the door; I had become inured to failure, expected it, but now it seemed it didn't have to be inevitable after all.

"Have you made your mind up on that job offer yet?" Debbie asked. "Sorry if I sounded a bit dismissive on that last night. I didn't mean to."

"I'll probably take it," I replied. "Why wouldn't I?"

Debbie said nothing for a few seconds. "I mean," she said hesitantly, "you know, as I keep saying, we aren't teenagers anymore. I hope I'm not speaking out of turn, but you do know you haven't got to do anything to impress the girl? I wouldn't look at you at all differently if you decide not to do it. To me, strength is deciding what you want to do in life, what makes you happy, and pursuing that. It doesn't have to be climbing Everest. Doing what other people expect, or might be impressed by, is the *weak* option."

"Thanks," I replied. "I agree with all that." A slight pause, but I didn't feel an immediate need to fill it. "It's complicated, though, isn't it?" I went on. "How many people actually spend their lives doing what they really want to do?"

Debbie put her glass down. "I do pretty much. I mostly enjoy my job and I'm very good at it. I don't like NHS internal politics, but I'm not aiming to be chief executive of the trust, so I avoid that as much as I can. My lovely daughter tells me I sometimes sound like a power bitch – so supportive of her – but I think that's just thirty years of holding my own in a man's world."

"I get that," I agreed.

"What, you're saying I sometimes sound like a power bitch?" Debbie fixed me with an exaggeratedly wide-eyed stare, which worried me for a moment, but she couldn't keep a straight face for more than a couple of seconds. We both laughed.

"I sort of find myself wishing that I hadn't been offered this job," I heard myself say.

"Well, then, that strongly suggests you don't want it, doesn't it?"

I thought about that for a moment. "The thing is, I like computers and software, and I don't like sitting at home with nothing to do. What I would really like," I continued, aware that I was actually working out what I wanted as I spoke, "is to do it two or three days a week on a consultancy basis, but without the hassle of management."

"Well, there you are," Debbie said with an air of triumph in her voice. "So pursue that. Tell him that's what you want to do, see what he says."

"I don't think he'll go for it."

"Nothing ventured… and if he doesn't, well, then you're back to your binary choice, nothing lost."

"True," I said slowly. "I could do that." I wondered, though, if I could then accept the full-time job if Sunil knew that I was less than whole-hearted about it. I decided not to test Debbie's impatience by wondering aloud. "Thanks," I said. "That's been helpful."

The afternoon and evening passed very quickly, and I made a conscious effort to try to pick up on signals as to whether I was expected to stay the night or not. I decided the answer was not; and when around ten thirty I ventured that it was probably about time I went, Debbie did not demur. I didn't think she would take to someone who was clingy early on, or ever, for that matter. But I still felt elated on the way home; I didn't think that was all afterglow, though it had undoubtedly been an embarrassingly long time since I had last had sex. It dampened my mood a little when I began to think about how I should behave in the coming days, how to ensure that the relationship developed steadily, how to avoid inadvertently being pushy and driving her away in the process. And I would need to do that myself, without anyone else's advice, however well intended, if only to prove to myself that I could.

The air seemed fresher than usual as I made my way back to the flat. I opened the external door then, almost as a reflex action, checked my phone to see if there was a message from Debbie. There wasn't, but that was fine. I bounded up the stairs two at a time. I had the key in my door-lock when, out of the corner of my eye, I noticed something on the floor outside Ella's flat. I turned and saw that it was a pair of legs, clothed in a recognisable pair of jeans. The legs ended at the wooden threshold, but were attached to the rest of a body that, through the open door, was prostrate on the hall carpet.

I ran across. "Ella, are you OK?" I asked stupidly. She didn't answer, so I quickly knelt down beside her. To my immediate relief, I could see and hear that she was definitely breathing, the loud rhythmic breaths of sleep, warm and smelling unmistakably, and strongly, of alcohol. I shook her by the shoulders, hoping that I wasn't hurting her. Her body felt limp, but I persevered, and she stirred, tried to wriggle away, then opened her eyes and attempted to focus on my face.

"What do you want?" she asked.

"Ella, are you OK?"

"Fine. Just having a bit of a sleep."

"Half on your hall carpet, half in the corridor?"

"Seems comfortable enough." She closed her eyes and tried to turn over.

"You can't stay there."

Ella screwed up her face crossly. "No one except you is going to see me."

"I'm not going to argue with you, Ella. You'll agree with me in the morning."

She offered no resistance as I pulled her into a sitting position then helped her to stand up. I supported her almost as a dead weight as we walked down her hallway and into her bedroom. I noticed that the camera was still rigged up facing the bed. I moved the duvet to one side as far as I could reach with my free arm, let Ella drop backwards onto the mattress, lifted her legs and rotated her until she was lying straight. Then I fumbled at removing her shoes, unsure as to whether the straps I encountered were for show or needed to be undone, and gently replaced the duvet. I went into the kitchen, found a large glass and filled it with water, then went back into the bedroom and set it on the bedside cabinet. Ella was sleeping soundly. I watched her for a few seconds, trying to decide if I should stay. But I didn't think she was so drunk that there was a risk of alcohol poisoning or choking; and how would it look if she woke up in the morning with no memory of what had happened tonight and found the old neighbour who had tried to kiss her asleep on the floor by her bed? I checked that the camera was not switched on, and then quietly left.

Sunday 21 March

I slept better than I thought I would, though it wasn't a particularly restful sleep as my unconscious mind grappled with all the things that were going on in my life. As it tends to do, it turned them into unhelpful, garish abstractions that made no sense as soon as I awoke, leaving nothing behind except a strong, disquieting unease.

I gave up trying to sleep at eight, and after breakfast and my morning shower I spent some time marshalling my thoughts, rereading the draft employment contract that had been sent to me, and making some notes on what I was going to say to Sunil. I was afraid I might still be persuaded to give the job a try, that there was still a small part of me that wanted it. But mostly I was looking at my phone, hoping for a call or message from Ella and, when that didn't come, impatiently watching the clock, willing it to get to a time when it would be reasonable for me to contact her.

At nine thirty I sent her a text. "Are you OK?" I asked simply. The reply came fifteen minutes later: "Yes. Why wouldn't I be??"

My fingers hovered over the keys for ten minutes after that, trying to decide how best to respond. Should I just let it go and pretend that it hadn't happened? If it was a one-off, then that would definitely be the right thing. But was it? Ten minutes later, aware that I was likely to get short shrift, I found myself knocking quietly, and with some apprehension, on Ella's door.

She opened the door a few seconds later. Her face looked wary but was otherwise expressionless. She was wearing a dressing gown and had a towel around her head. There was no make-up on her face, which looked blotchy and puffy, and there was a shiny, pellucid aspect to her skin.

"I don't want a lecture," was all she said.

She turned round but left the door open, so I assumed she was inviting me in. I closed the door behind me and followed her into the kitchen. She sat down at the table and put her hands around a mug of coffee that was already there. "Help yourself," she said, gesturing at the coffee machine. I poured a cup, though I didn't particularly want one, and leaned against the counter.

"So you're OK," I asked.

"I've felt better."

"Do you remember what happened last night?"

Ella shrugged. "I fell over."

"In the doorway?"

"As good a place as any."

"Yes, but Ella…"

"I said no lectures. Have you never drunk too much in your life, Mr Saintly?"

"Yes, of course I have."

"Well, there you are. I had a video call with a client I had to cut short because he was pissing me off, so I thought I needed a drink after that. And then I had another, and was getting the taste for it, and then it was a long, boring evening on my own, so I kept going. And I must have been a bit unsteady on my pins as I went out, and I must have fallen over."

"Fair enough," I said, "as long as you're OK now."

Ella nodded slowly. "Well, a bit of a headache," she said, "and I'm worried I might have damaged this arm again." She winced as she tried to move it.

"I hope not," I replied sympathetically. "Well, if there's anything I can do…"

"You can do my sessions for me today if you want."

I laughed nervously. "I don't think I'm exactly what your clients are after."

"Well, if you change your mind. There's a middle-aged plumber who likes me to stand on his cock in stilettos."

I pretended to think about it. "No, still not tempted."

Ella tried to laugh but it appeared to be making her headache worse.

"Why don't you take the day off?" I asked.

"Money," she replied. "Bills."

I didn't know what to say to that. I drank my coffee and put the cup in the sink. "Well, if you need me," I began.

"Sure."

I turned and headed for the door. Just as I reached it, Ella called out, "How about we go to a pub for a drink and a bite to eat?"

I immediately thought of Debbie and felt guilty. But that wasn't reasonable, I told myself: Ella and I were just friends. I couldn't offend her by letting her hear any hesitation in my voice. "Great idea," I replied. Tonight?"

The idea seemed to make Ella's headache worse. "Tomorrow," she said. "Tomorrow would be better."

"Tomorrow it is," I replied brightly.

Monday 22 March

I was surprised how surprised Sunil sounded, and even more surprised how pissed off he seemed to be. I tried to explain again: my age, financial needs, work-life balance.

"I don't get this at all," he said testily. "It doesn't make any sense. This is the best job offer you've ever had, will ever have, by a very large margin, Alan." I tried to explain that I understood that, that I really appreciated the offer but wanted to prioritise other aspects of my life, but he wasn't listening. "I can't do this on the phone," he snapped. "Come and see me. I'll transfer you to Jane."

After a delay of a few seconds, presumably while he told her what the situation was, I found myself talking to Sunil's secretary, a chirpy sparrow of a girl, who appeared to be having trouble finding any time in his calendar when he might be able to meet me. "Four o'clock," she said finally. "No, hang on. I might have to move...yes, let's say four o'clock: I'll reach out to you again if there's any problem."

"Fine," I said after a pause long enough to establish that Jane wasn't going to ask me if that was convenient for me, "I'll see you this afternoon." I felt slightly numb for a few minutes after the call ended, and just sat in the chair looking at the blank screen of my phone. But then that feeling subsided, and I was left with a much more serene sensation. I was in control: I would go to Sunil's office this afternoon, be polite, courteous and even friendly, but not allow myself to be bulldozed into doing something that I didn't want to do.

Sunil's company's offices weren't as large or as grand as I had expected them to be. And I was also surprised to realise that I hadn't been there before. The doors were smoked glass, there was a large, three-dimensional model of the company logo attached to the wall behind reception, all of the staff looked young, and surprisingly, given the boss's sartorial tastes, none wore suits, still less ties. But the overall effect was still more Croydon than Silicon Valley, though I didn't have the eye to be able to work out exactly why that was. Perhaps because the impression was created that expense *had* been spared. It occurred to me that any new company must have to balance the desire to project confidence against the need to avoid ruinous expenditure, but that they hadn't quite got it right here.

I sat flicking through an old copy of *What Car?* that had appealed to me over the *FT* and *Economist* with which it shared table space in reception. A smiling young woman approached, introduced herself as Jane and said that Sunil was ready to see me. I glanced at the clock on the wall and saw that it was about twelve minutes after four. She led me along corridors making small talk that I mostly didn't hear, then abruptly stopped at the open door to a large office and, in a gesture that reminded me of a flight attendant doing a safety briefing, directed me into the room.

Sunil got up from behind a large desk and came over and affably gave me a powerful handshake. As ever, he was immaculately dressed, and his expression momentarily suggested he was disappointed by my own choice of apparel, notwithstanding that the company clearly had no dress code. I had decided that wearing a suit again had too much of the supplicant about it, so I had gone with my default smart-casual combination, the same one I had worn for my first date with Debbie. Not discourteous, I had felt, but not needy. Sunil didn't comment on it, but instead ushered me to a seat by a glass coffee-table, and then sat down in an identical chair opposite me. There were cups, tea bags, sachets of sugar and pots of hot water and coffee set out in front of me, but I wasn't sure if I was supposed to help myself.

"So," Sunil began, "I was really surprised by our conversation earlier. But let's start again, bearing in mind that I've never been one who can take no for an answer."

I smiled weakly. "I'm really flattered to have been asked," I said, "and five years ago I would have jumped at the chance." I wasn't a hundred per cent convinced that was true, and hoped it didn't show. "But it would take over my whole life and give me a whole heap of stress at a time when I don't need that anymore."

Sunil appeared to think about that. "For us men," he told me, "life is either work or family. What else is there? And we are bored doing nothing. Our families understand that. What is stress? I don't get that. Worrying about failure? Stop worrying! Work hard. Succeed!"

"Stress," I heard myself say, "is the gap between what you are responsible for and what you can control." I wondered if I had read that somewhere, or had just come to that realisation for myself.

"And now," Sunil countered, making an expansive gesture with his hands, "we are offering you something with far more control than you have ever had before, Alan. So that argument falls. And on the day that you finally retire, don't you want to be proud of what you have achieved?"

"Of course," I replied almost sotto voce.

Sunil sat back in his chair. "How do I persuade you?" he asked candidly. "More money? More staff to lighten the load – we can't go too far with that. I can't believe our offer isn't preferable to spending the rest of your life in a flat watching daytime television!"

I decided to let that pass. After some difficult months, I thought that several elements of my life were already tentatively improving: the choice was no longer a life of work or a life of nothing, but none of that was really Sunil's business. Or frankly would interest him.

"How about this," I said as calmly as I could, with a picture in my mind's eye of Debbie offering her advice on Saturday evening. "I help you set it up, working with one of your existing managers, or someone you bring in. They can be much younger: they don't need to know the detail of the coding we do just to manage the department. I help them recruit the programmers, who are all going to be older and probably wanting to work part time. Then I step back, the manager manages, and I just do a couple of days of consultancy a week."

Sunil shook his head slowly. "No," he said, "that isn't what I envisaged. Not at all."

We were interrupted by Jane putting her head round the door to announce that Sunil's four thirty appointment was outside. I looked at the clock on the wall: it was exactly four thirty. Sunil nodded and stood up. He held out his hand; I stood up and took it. This time the handshake was much weaker and more peremptory. "Sorry, but we will have to make alternative arrangements," he said bluntly. "But if you change your mind in the next day please let me know."

"Sorry," I said, though I had promised myself I would not apologise. "Nice to see you anyway."

Sunil gave a slight nod. I realised that it was unlikely I would be seeing or hearing from him again, and that saddened me.

"This way please," said Jane in answer to some invisible signal from her boss, "it's easy to get lost in these corridors."

I told myself that I mustn't allow my disappointment at the way my meeting with Sunil had gone to affect my behaviour when I went out with Ella. The evening was hers: she obviously had some problems - or maybe that was too judgmental of me and she had just had one bad day - but either way it was down to me to be supportive; to be cheerful and upbeat without being annoyingly so; to listen, to offer advice where I could, but only if requested. Ella had been supportive to me during some difficult times (no doubt sometimes in unorthodox ways!) but there for me nonetheless; and now was my chance to pay her back.

One thing that did occur to me, as I got changed and freshened up for the evening, was that I hadn't heard from Debbie since Saturday. I wasn't sure what to make of that. As I've noted in these diaries, we keep saying that we aren't teenagers anymore, and she won't thank me for texting her every five minutes or sending her sonnets. But if we are in the early stages of a relationship, we should communicate most days, shouldn't we? In a way it was convenient that I hadn't heard, because it avoided any awkwardness if she asked me what I was doing tonight, or even suggested we do something together. Would I tell the truth? Should I? In the end I just sent Debbie a message saying "How's your day been? xx" having agonised for too long over whether to include the kisses, eventually concluding that it sounded too cold without them.

I knocked on Ella's door at the agreed time. She let me in, and we exchanged a few pleasantries before she told me to take a seat because she wasn't quite ready. Her manner was actually a little brusque, I thought, or perhaps just aloof, designed to forestall any too-concerned earnestness on my part. She was wearing a knitwear jumper, a pair of jeans and minimal make-up, but looked pretty good nonetheless, without a hint of the tiredness that had framed her face yesterday.

She seemed to read my thoughts. "I had to cancel my session this afternoon because I've aggravated the problem with my arm," she told me as she tried to fiddle with an earring, lost patience with it and removed both it and its pair. "So I had a nice long nap."

"Looking good on it," I told her.

"Thanks," she replied without smiling. "We're heading for the White Hart."

"Fine with me. Or there's the Coach and Horses."

"I've booked the White Hart." Still no smile.
"The White Hart it is."

The White Hart seemed particularly busy for a Monday. Or maybe, as with my meal with Lisa, it's just me being out of touch with the extent to which people now eat out. Ella had clearly been sensible to book. We stood patiently in the "Please Wait Here to Be Seated" queue until it was our turn. The young man at the desk was obviously taking Ella in as she gave him her name, even though it seemed to me that she was almost old enough to be his mother. He also looked at me slightly quizzically, as if wondering what our relationship might be. I overcame the temptation to wink knowingly at him.

We were led to our table and handed giant menus. The table was adjacent to two fruit machines, and so close to the toilets that our table was illuminated by stark blue light every time the doors opened. Ella ordered a large glass of white wine, which surprised me; the expression on her face seemed to be daring me to say something about it, and I quickly looked away and ordered a large beer, which I felt a sudden need for.

"Packed, isn't it?" I said, for something to say.

"It's always like this," Ella replied dismissively. "Listen, there's one thing I want to be clear about for this evening. I see you as a friend, Alan, which is good, but what I don't want anyone doing right now is telling me how I should be living my life."

"Completely understood," was all I could find to say.

"I'm not saying you were doing that." Finally a smile. "But just in case you were tempted."

"I have enough trouble trying to lead my own life," I said limply.

Ella nodded. She eyed me over the top of the giant menu. "What do you think of what I do? For a living? Honestly."

Happily, at that moment the waiter returned with our drinks, apparently keen to get our food order, so we spent a few seconds skimming the list of staple grills, steaks and burgers and quickly made our selection.

"It's been a while since I had gammon," I offered inanely. "I'm really looking forward to it actually."

"You haven't answered my question," Ella reminded me. She raised her glass, I did the same and we clinked them together and said "Cheers!".

She continued to look straight at me; my discomfiture seemed to amuse her.

"OK," I said. "What I think is that it is, er, unusual, you're the first, er…"

"Yes? Starts with a 'd'."

"…dominatrix, that I have met." The word sounded odd in my voice, and I was aware that I had said it quietly for fear of being overheard. "But if you like doing that…"

"I do. And not just the money, which is great by the way. I like doing it. I get a buzz out of it."

"Well, then, good for you."

"Do you think of me as a prostitute?" The piercing look again.

"No." I hadn't been expecting this. I was beginning to wonder what Ella's purpose had been in suggesting we go out, and if I should have found a way politely to get out of it.

"You don't sound sure."

"No," I repeated more firmly, "but even if you were, so what? I like anyone who is friendly to me. Anything else is too complicated. I'm not judgmental."

"Ha, ha. But saying you're not judgmental is being judgmental, isn't it? You wouldn't say that if I was a greengrocer."

"Don't talk to me about fruit!" I said, trying to lighten the mood.

Ella ignored me. "The thing is, Alan," she went on, "I make people happy. Temporarily of course. They have their daily humdrum lives, and they have a secret sexual fantasy, and I help them turn that into reality every now and then."

"Yes, I see that," I replied. "And I could get it if these fantasies were for pleasant sensations like incredible sex or, I don't know, even a massage or a bubble bath or something. But why fantasies for…"

"Horrible things?"

"Yes, exactly."

I hadn't noticed the waiter approaching with our food. The embarrassed look on his face told me that he had heard the last part of the conversation. He mumbled something about where to find the condiments, hoped that we would enjoy our meals, and skipped away.

Ella laughed. "We've given them something to talk about in the kitchen. But the answer to your question is, who knows? Of course, the large majority of people do have fantasies for what you would call 'nice things' and they can get them in a relationship, or from a prostitute if necessary. I'm there for the others."

"I get that," I said, suddenly conscious that I was very hungry as I simultaneously tried to spear an onion ring. "You like doing it, they like you doing it to them, so everyone's happy."

Ella sighed and put her fork down. "Yeah, well. Except me."

I nodded and waited for her to go on.

"Because I do genuinely like what I do, and I'm certainly not ashamed of it, and it does actually make people happy."

"But…"

"But for all that, it is an artificial world, and it takes too high a toll on normal life. So I've got guys I've never physically met paying hundreds of pounds to talk to me online and tell me how they worship me. Some even send me money just because they've seen my website, without making any contact with me at all! But if I just want a normal night out, or to sit on the sofa with someone eating chocolates and watching crap TV…"

"You have to resort to the weird old-timer in the flat across the way."

We both laughed. I had the impression I was expected to speak next. "You know my history, so I'm not the best person for relationship advice," I said, "but what about the speed-dating? I'm pretty sure most of the guys you met that evening would have wanted to see you again."

Ella exhaled. "Yeah, a bunch of guys met me once and wanted to have sex. Which is as far as it gets, because they then ask me what I do for a living, and if I tell them, that's the end of it. Or they say, OK, but you'll have to give it up. I don't want to give it up! I don't need to be 'rescued'!"

"I don't know what to suggest," I said, trying to sound thoughtful. "How about one of the guys you see, er, professionally?"

Ella shook her head. "No, most are married anyway, and the ones that aren't are often, I shouldn't really say this, a bit weird. And in any case, I'm not interested in a relationship with a submissive guy."

"OK," I said in surprise. "I didn't realise…"

"It's fun for work. But I don't want to take my work home with me."

I smiled and thought for a second. "OK, well are there other people you deal with for your business who are cool with it?"

"Possibly… But it's a very small pool. I did go out with a photographer for a while."

"Didn't work out?"

"I ended it. I didn't like the way he looked at me."

"Professional eye."

"Well, yes, but it gets a bit wearing after a while. He wanted to suggest what I should wear, how I should do my make-up."

I wondered if this guy was the father of the child that I thought Ella had had, but I didn't dare ask.

"You don't want that," I said sympathetically. "My ex-wife was a bit like that. Whatever the opposite of power-dressing is, that's what she thought I did. I just thought I was being comfortable."

Ella smiled, looked me up and down and shook her head. "Well, she may have had a point. Anyway, to go back to me, which is much more interesting," she smiled again, "I need someone to listen while I think aloud about what my options are. Which is where you come in."

"Can I eat while you do that?" I asked in a playful tone.

Ella seemed belatedly to become aware that we both had full plates of food in front of us that were rapidly getting cold. "Of course," she said. "Sorry, I'll do the same."

We set to with a clatter of cutlery. Neither of us spoke for a few seconds.

"I haven't completely ruled out a change of career," Ella told me. "But what?"

"Something using your psychology degree?" I suggested.

Ella nodded. "I'd thought of that. It's something that still interests me, and it helps me a lot with my work now, actually."

"Go for it, then."

"Yes..." Ella didn't sound convinced, "but it's not that simple. For a start, training could take years, though that's not the real problem because I've made seriously good money doing this."

If that were true, I wondered why she was living in the flat next door to mine. "What *is* the problem, then?" I asked gently.

Ella stopped eating and looked into the middle distance over my shoulder. "There are photos. Quite a lot of them. Of me. That have...escaped on the internet."

"Ah."

"Yes, 'Ah'. Mostly from years ago, because I'm a lot smarter now, but you can still tell it's me."

We sat in silence for a few moments before I spoke again. "And you're worried that someone in your new career could find them?"

"Exactly."

"Is that likely. Unless they were looking?"

"Well, there's more and more artificial intelligence that can recognise people on social media and other platforms, so I'd say yes."

"True." I decided not to say that my previous employer had a division focussing on just that, though it had been rather too cutting-edge to involve old Alan. "In that case, maybe there are other options for self-employment, something that your experience would be useful for."

"Such as?"

"Well, you run an online business, don't you? You have the skills and the connections to make that work, so maybe a different type of online business. Retail perhaps."

Ella's mood seemed to brighten. "That's not a bad idea, Alan. Maybe I'll give it some thought."

"Great. If you need an IT manager…!"

"You already have that job after fixing my camera last month."

"I was thinking more of a paid role."

We both laughed and I started to relax. The evening seemed to be going better after a slightly awkward start.

And then suddenly it wasn't.

It's strange how sometimes you have a sense that someone is looking at you, even though they aren't within your field of vision. Instinctively I turned my head through ninety degrees and saw a group of four young women at a table; one of them appeared to be telling a funny story accompanied by a lot of hand movements, and the other three were laughing. But one of the three looked slightly distracted, as though she were only half listening. She wasn't looking in my direction, but I sensed she was aware of me, in the way that you do if someone is exaggeratedly ignoring you. My eyes were unfortunately not deceiving me: it was definitely Becky.

"Problem?" Ella asked casually. "You look like you've seen a ghost."

"No, it's fine," I mumbled.

Ella wouldn't let it drop. "I'm seeing four pretty young girls," she said. "Anything you want to tell Auntie Ella?"

I decided it was easiest to be truthful. "That's Becky, Debbie's daughter," I explained.

"The tree-hugger doctor?"

"Yes," I replied more testily than I had intended.

"Oh dear," Ella laughed out loud. "What if mummy hears you've been seen with a busty brunette!"

"It's fine."

And it could have been. But then Ella decided it would be funny to embarrass me. She tried to grab my hand across the table, and in my haste to withdraw it I knocked my beer glass over, in Ella's direction. Luckily there wasn't much liquid left in it, but it soaked into the tablecloth and Ella ended up pressing her napkin against the edge of the table to prevent a small pool of beer falling into her lap. All the diners in the restaurant, it seemed, looked in our direction. I momentarily caught Becky's eye, but she flinched and looked away. I thought I should go and talk to her, but first I had to placate Ella, who clearly wasn't happy.

"Thanks a lot," she said sarcastically, continuing to dab at the tablecloth.

"Sorry," I replied, though I wasn't sure that it was entirely my fault. "Do you want the tablecloth changed?"

"No, it'll take too long. The food will get cold."

"OK. Well how about if I sit that side then?"

"Alright," Ella grudgingly agreed.

We then had a couple more minutes of awkwardly manoeuvring round each other and shuffling plates, glasses and cutlery to their new positions. People continued to stare. The waiter came to offer assistance and was rewarded with an order for another large glass of wine, and a small beer.

The result of our seating rearrangement was that I could now see the table where Becky and her friends were sitting without turning my head. And that they were each pointing cards or phones at some sort of payment machine, which meant they would be imminently leaving. I knew I really should go and talk to Becky. Except that, with the mood Ella was apparently now in, there was no guarantee that she would still be there when I got back. I caught Becky's eye again as she got up to go, but she blanked me once more and turned her back as she put her jacket on. Then the girls had all gone.

Ella thought it was funny. "Oh dear," she said, "no sex for you this week!"

I said nothing. I thought if I did, I was likely to lose my temper. I looked down at the table.

But Ella hadn't done with taunting me. "What's the matter?" she asked in a kind of baby-voice. "Can't you take a joke at your expense?"

"Of course I can, but…"

"Seeing as we are supposed to have come out to cheer me up, because I've hit a bit of a rough patch, and instead you're obsessing over yourself and what your girlfriend's daughter might do."

I decided to say nothing for a few seconds, in the hope that might defuse the situation, and in case I said something I would later regret. The waiter gave me a bit longer by arriving with the drinks. Ella sipped at her wine. "I'm just asking you to be supportive," she said quietly, without making eye contact.

That disarmed me a little. "And I *am*," I said, "it's just..."

"I've been very supportive for you."

"Yes, you have. You really have. I am grateful. It's just that I've had a strange day myself; I've got a few issues of my own at the moment."

"OK. Well, go on."

"Well, I've just turned down by far the best job that anyone has ever offered me or ever will."

"Oh." Ella put her glass down, folded her arms and looked directly at me. "That doesn't sound like a good idea. Is there still time to change your mind?"

"Yes, probably."

"Well, then do that. Problem solved. See how helpful I am to you!"

"Yes, but that's not it. I don't want the job."

"Well, then don't take it. Equally simple."

"That's not the answer either, though, is it?"

"You're not making any sense, Alan. Drink your beer!"

I ignored that. "No, I don't know how to explain it," I said dolefully.

Ella sat back. "I'm listening. Do you not think you can do the job?"

I hesitated for a moment. "I think technically I can do it, but I'm not sure of the managerial side of it, which is a big step up from what I did before. I'm not sure I want the stress."

Ella rubbed her chin. "Want or could cope with?" she asked. "I was just thinking maybe do it for a limited time, just for the money?"

I half smiled. "Those are the questions I have been asking myself."

Ella looked pleased with herself. "I have a unique insight into the male mind! So, what's your answer?"

"I think I could cope with it during the day."

"But you wouldn't be able to sleep?"

"I suspect that's the case," I admitted quietly. "I've had insomnia episodes in the past, often over things that seemed trivial in the light of day."

"I see. Well, there are things you can take, medication."

"That's a slippery slope, though, isn't it?"

Ella shrugged. "People do. I mean, if you were just looking to do it for a short while…"

"I suppose. But then how easy is it to get off these drugs?"

"Well, that can be a problem. Don't you want the challenge, though, to see if you can do it?"

"Part of me does."

"Then I say give it a go. What does the tree-hugger say?"

"Debbie says I should do whatever makes me happy. She'll support me either way."

"She said that?" Ella looked genuinely surprised.

"Yes."

"And you believe her?"

"Well, I did until a moment ago. Shouldn't I?"

Ella folded her arms again. "High risk strategy, I would say. I mean, she may even believe it herself. Feminism is still a work in progress, though, if you want my opinion. So historically women preferred their partners to be successful - caveman thing - and men preferred their women not to be: they felt threatened by them if they were. Now, with feminism and equal rights, men are more used to successful women, and I think you're actually quite proud to have bagged a hospital consultant, and why wouldn't you be? But I think successful women are still attracted to successful men, even if our intellect is telling us it doesn't matter anymore. There are exceptions and maybe it will gradually change, but for now…"

I had lost my appetite and pushed my plate to one side. "That's a pretty depressing thought, Ella," I said sadly. "So I either take this job or…"

"Risk losing out to the next airline pilot that comes along."

"Really?" I was looking directly at Ella to determine if she was just teasing me.

Ella made wide eyes at me. "I'm afraid so, Alan. Bummer, isn't it?"

Tuesday 23 March

I woke this morning at around five o'clock needing both a drink of water and a visit to the bathroom, and I didn't really sleep much after that. I felt a little dehydrated, my intake of beer having gone up substantially after Ella persuaded me to reconsider Sunil's job offer. Ella had kept me company, going from glasses of wine to a bottle (more? I couldn't remember) and the mood of the evening had improved considerably as we moved away from serious topics and instead spent a lot of time laughing at funny stories, though what they had been about and whether I would have found them funny when sober I could no longer say. Some, I think, were about the strange requests Ella could get from her clients, and what could go wrong when she tried to oblige.

I got up at seven and made a cup of coffee. I sat down and decided to be decisive. It turned out that was all that was needed. I looked at the four walls of the flat and found them mind-numbingly boring. Maybe I did need a challenge. Sunil clearly thought that I could do the job. It might be a little daunting for a while, I told myself, but only until I got my feet under the desk.

At eight o'clock I phoned Sunil to say I had changed my mind and, if the offer was still there, I would like to take the job. Sunil said nothing for a few seconds, then, when he replied, I sensed that there was still the distance between us I had experienced at the end of our conversation yesterday. But the coldness lifted as he spoke, as though a wave of relief were washing across him, and by the end of the conversation he was back to the Sunil of old. "That's great, my friend," he said. "Welcome aboard!"

"Thanks," I replied. "Sorry about yesterday. A bit of self-doubt…"

"No good in business," Sunil admonished me.

I wasn't sure I entirely agreed with him, but I decided this wasn't the time to debate the issue. "I could start some time next month," I suggested.

Sunil cleared his throat. "We need to get moving on this," he pronounced. "Next Monday."

"OK," I replied, trying to replace my audible hesitancy with enthusiasm as I spoke. "See you then."

"Seven thirty we start. I'll email you some papers to be looking at."

"Great," I said. "Thanks, Sunil. I'll look forward to it."

He rang off. I sat for a moment taking in what I had just done. I felt a few butterflies in my stomach, but when I got up and looked out of the window, saw the damp street and dark grey clouds and wondered how I would otherwise fill the hours, I became convinced that I had done the right thing. A sense of elation flowed through my body. I printed off, signed and dated the draft contract, inserted a start date of 29 March, scanned it and emailed it back to Sunil's HR department. I felt relaxed and then drowsy, lay down and had two hours of perfect, dreamless sleep, waking up more refreshed than I could remember having been in a very long time.

I thought about going for a walk, but when I idly consulted my phone I discovered there were already half a dozen emails from Sunil's company requiring my attention and, in some instances, my comments. They all had attachments, which turned out to be board and committee papers and minutes, and various other reports and procedures documents, many of which seemed to be individually more than a hundred pages in length. I turned on my laptop and opened my email account, downloading all the attachments so I could look at them more closely.

By lunchtime I had got through two but a further two had come in. I realised that my powers of concentration had waned since I had last worked, and I took to making notes as I went along in order better to assimilate what I was reading. I had lunch at the computer, and then worked all afternoon. Every now and then, though, I was able fleetingly to enjoy the spring sunshine which, now that the clouds had unexpectedly cleared, streamed invitingly through the window; it threw a silhouette of the frame onto the far wall, along which it gradually moved as the day wore on.

I stopped for dinner, making something quickly in the microwave. As I sat eating it in front of the TV news, I was simultaneously using the messaging app on my phone. First, I sent a fairly general message to Debbie, who I still hadn't heard from. It occurred to me belatedly that I should have done so earlier, before she might have had the opportunity to speak to Becky, but I had been too preoccupied with work. I also sent a message to Ella, thanking her for her company the previous evening and hoping she was OK. Ella replied about an hour later saying she was fine, and had I taken the job? "Well done!" she replied when I said I had. Debbie did not reply.

I started to fall asleep around midnight, so I switched off the laptop and went to bed.

Thursday 25 March

Feeling a bit tired and a bit sad this evening, but I still think I'm doing the right thing. Really, what's the alternative?

Lisa, unsurprisingly, was more than a little put out this morning when I arrived to look after the kids and told her I was going back to work. I think she feels that I might have discussed it with her first. Then I made it worse by admitting that I had agreed to start next Monday, which leaves her in the lurch for childcare without much time to make alternative arrangements. I would have preferred it if she'd lost her temper with me, but she just looked at me with huge disappointment in those big eyes of hers. It was a look I couldn't bear when she was little, and had to do something about if I possibly could; it hasn't lost its effect over the years. I protested lamely that I'd wanted to start some time next month, but that Sunil unfortunately wouldn't have it. Lisa didn't respond, just gave Jasmine a kiss on the top of her head and left without looking at me, calling over her shoulder that she would ring me later to see how the kids were getting on.

Kids pick up on things, don't they? Jasmine had given every impression of being engrossed in her colouring book while her mother and I had had our exchange, but when I asked her if she wanted any juice she earnestly shook her head without looking up.

"Is Mummy sad?" she asked suddenly, several seconds later.

I decided not to lie to her. "A bit," I replied.

"Why?"

I sat down next to her. I noticed for the first time how similar her serious expression is to her mother's, which wasn't going to help. "Grandpa's got a new job," I explained, "which means he, I, won't be able to come and look after you on Thursdays any more. Not for a while anyway."

"Why?" Jasmine offered me a perfect poker face.

"Why what, sweetheart?" I don't know why I asked that: four-year-olds don't elaborate, do they? "Well," I said, deciding to go through all the possibilities, "Grandpa has decided he doesn't want to be at home all the time, and a nice man has offered him a job which will pay him money so he can have all sorts of things he otherwise wouldn't be able to have, and he'll be able to buy you nice presents too." I felt a bit shabby about the last part as soon as I had said it. "But unfortunately he'll be working on Thursdays so won't be able to come here."

Jasmine didn't react at all. She put down one crayon and picked up another.

"But I'll still be able to come and see you at weekends!" I told my granddaughter with a big smile. I heard the inadvertent catch in my voice and hoped that Jasmine hadn't. Was what I was saying even true? Would Lisa invite me over in future? Would we be back to the distant relationship that had subsisted between us during the years when I had spent most of my waking hours either plugging away at work or trying to recover the energy to start work all over again? I couldn't let that happen: without doubt, the best thing that has happened in the four months since I stopped work has been re-discovering my family.

I got up. "That's a nice picture," I said, though I wasn't entirely sure what it was. Having possibly started life as a Disney princess, it was now very much a toddler abstract with bright primary colours: fierce green hair, a red face and everything else yellow.

Jasmine was used to such compliments – it was doubtful that anyone had ever told her her drawings were rubbish – and didn't visibly react. "Are *you* sad, Grandpa?" she asked diffidently.

"Yes, a little. Like your mum."
"Why?"
"Because I like spending time with you."

"Why?"

"Because you say 'why' all the time."

"Why?"

I gave her my 'gotcha' expression and she shrieked with laughter. Then she suddenly got up, grabbed my legs and buried her head against them. It was both exactly what I wanted and the last thing I wanted. I picked her up, carefully sat down and put her on my lap, facing away from me. I hugged her, enjoyed her warmth, her unique smell, the way she wriggled slightly.

"Are you crying, Grandpa?"

"Just a little bit, sweetheart."

"Why?" we both said in unison. Jasmine giggled and I cuddled her a bit tighter.

Because, I thought, I'm scared I'm doing the wrong thing for the wrong reason.

"Because I'm old and silly, that's why," I said aloud.

Jasmine sat quietly and then started swinging her legs. "Can I have some juice now?"

"Of course you can. Then I need to go and check on your little brother."

My phone pinged for the umpteenth time that morning. I supposed it was more work-related emails. Well, they could wait until both my grandchildren were asleep.

I was still feeling a bit low when I got home. When Lisa had returned in the evening, we had both behaved like people who knew there was a problem but were pretending there wasn't. She had given me the most perfunctory kiss on the cheek and no hug when I left. Jasmine waved and grinned at me, and that image seemed to have burned itself onto my brain.

I felt I needed to talk to Debbie. She had sent a short reply to my message yesterday just saying "Busy..busy...busy!" with a picture of a bee at the end. I hadn't known what to make of that, whether it was true or whether she was avoiding me, and had decided eventually to take her at her word and leave it till today.

She was making dinner when I called and put me on speakerphone so that she could continue. I could hear sizzling and the whirr of the extractor fan, and realised for the first time that I had hardly eaten all day and was hungry.

"How was your day?" I asked by way of introductory small talk. I realised that I was feeling slightly nervous.

"Strange," she replied. "All my customers kept falling asleep."

I laughed. "Successful day's work then."

Debbie said something that I didn't catch.

"Sorry, I didn't quite get that," I told her. "Noise in the background."

"It's OK, I wasn't talking to you. Becky's here. That needs to go in in about two minutes, love. Sorry! What were you saying?"

"Hi Becky!" I shouted. I thought I heard her reply, but couldn't be sure.

I weighed up what to say next for a couple of seconds, which I judged at this stage of our relationship to be the longest sustainable period of silence before it would become awkward. "Did she say we were in the same pub on Monday night?" I asked casually.

Becky said something that I couldn't make out.

"She's only been here a few minutes," Debbie replied.

So Becky hadn't called her mother specially to tell her; I supposed I owed her for that. Though perhaps, as Debbie had just implied, they had more interesting things to talk to each other about than me.

"Yes," I said, "I was there with my next-door-neighbour."

"Right."

"The one I went to speed-dating with."

"Right. Oh God, the busty brunette?"

"Yes. She's been having a few problems."

"Which I'm sure she doesn't want you to share with me. Can you turn that down, love, or it'll boil over?"

"No," I agreed. "I just didn't want…"

"Me to think you were seeing a gorgeous younger woman behind my back? Ha, ha, in your dreams, mister! Did you see the way the men at speed-dating were looking at her? Some of them had no blood left at all in the top half of their bodies by the end of the evening!"

I laughed with relief. "Anyway, I just wanted..."

"We're not teenagers, Alan."

I laughed again. "Is that going to be our phrase? Maybe we should have it in his and hers tattoos."

"We are never ever going to have his and hers tattoos, Alan!"

"I suppose then we *would* be like teenagers, wouldn't we?"

"Exactly."

I paused for a second to steel myself. "My other news is that… I've taken the job."

"Oh, OK." Debbie sounded a little cold. "Well, that is a surprise. What made you…?"

I had been trying to come up with plausible justifications all day. "The possibility of a comfortable old age rather than just an adequate one," I offered. "The challenge, maybe…"

Debbie didn't sound entirely convinced. "OK," she replied, "well as I said, it makes no difference to me, but if it makes you happy."

"I start on Monday," I said, just before the two-second permissible pause had elapsed. "But I'm wondering when I can see you next."

"Er, well, I'm not working on Saturday."

"That would be great."

"Saturday it is, then. Unless you get a better offer from Miss Wet-Dream obviously."

I laughed politely.

Saturday 27 March

I spent the whole of today (and yesterday) reading up for work. Sunil rang twice to discuss two separate potential new clients for legacy software work, asking me to look at their RFPs and draft a suitable response for an initial pitch. At the end of the second call I had to confess that I had no idea what an RFP was ('request for proposal' apparently). Sunil didn't sound pleased.

I was both hugely disappointed and hugely relieved when Debbie messaged me to say she had to work after all and would have to cancel. She suggested Wednesday, which I accepted without any great confidence that I would actually be able to make it.

Sunday 28 March

I need to put the light out or I won't get enough sleep before tomorrow's start in the office.

I spent all day on the potential client RFPs. I wasn't sure I fully understood either of them. I wonder if anyone will be able to help me? I also have no idea how to even start putting together a response. I understand the software they are using, but how do I estimate the resource we would need to manage it, or how much we would need to charge? I assume (hope) I will at least get assistance with that.

Ella came round earlier with a 'Good Luck with your New Job' card, which was really sweet of her, but I think I may have offended her by talking to her in the doorway for a couple of minutes but not inviting her in, forgetting in my self-absorption even to ask if she had had any more thoughts on her own future plans. I had things going round in my mind and just wasn't relaxed enough.

What I will remember about today, though, is that at nine p.m. Lisa phoned me to wish me all the best for tomorrow. I had had no inkling that she would do that after the way we parted on Thursday, and I think I embarrassed her by becoming overly emotional.

What is done is done. The pictures of Lisa, Neil, Jasmine and Alfie that usually live in the lounge are next to me now on the bedside cabinet as I write.

Monday 29 March

A LOT to write about but no time. I will try to catch up tomorrow.

Wednesday 31 March

I want to keep this diary going, but am not finding the time. Hopefully I'll catch up on it at the weekend. Along with some sleep.

I cancelled my evening out with Debbie, which was just as well as I didn't leave the office until gone nine. She didn't sound too displeased but did ask if I was OK. I said I was fine.

Sunday 4 April

Early hours of Monday 5th actually. I have some time to do this for no other reason than that I can't sleep. I could do some work, but I'm kidding myself that writing my diary instead might actually make me drowsy, even though it's a forlorn hope, as I have to get up in two hours. I had about thirty minutes' sleep when I passed out in front of the television last evening, then I went to bed at eleven thirty and slept till two, so I've had three hours' sleep in total, which has been about the average for the last week. I mentioned this in passing to Sunil last week and he said he makes a point of always getting four hours. I did a bit better last night, which I put down to it being the one night of the week when I hadn't been in the office that day and wouldn't be going in the next day. Though to be honest, with constant emails and access to the company's remote desktop on my home computer, it hardly makes any difference.

I've heard of imposter syndrome before, where people think they are in a position that they don't deserve to be. Mostly you hear it talked about by ridiculously talented people who clearly are where they are on merit, and for them the syndrome is just a delusion, a psychological insecurity. But with me it seems all too genuine. There is so much of this job I don't know how to do, and I'm just bluffing my way through. Very badly. Colleagues at all levels seem to have picked up on it; at the moment no one is saying anything because I'm seen as Sunil's man, and they don't want to look like they are questioning the boss's judgment. But it can't be long now.

For the last twenty years of my previous job my work hardly changed at all. Maybe if, instead of remaining in technical work, I had made a gradual progression through management grades, I would be ready for this new position by now. Maybe, but I'm not sure. I'm not sure I am cut out for the loneliness of decision-making at this level. Or the sheer volume of work that seems to be involved.

At my old employer I was always a little resentful of people who did very well for themselves without any obvious talent for the job, or appearing to produce very much. I always thought their secret was talking a good game and delegating to more competent subordinates. Could I try that? Maybe, but I don't think I could carry it off. It's like wearing your coat with the collar turned up and your glasses on your head: you either look the part or you don't, and I don't.

I spent a lot of time last week with Sunil's CFO, an earnest but nice young man, who was going through budget projections, a departmental balance sheet and the profit and loss account with me. There were several items I didn't understand at all, but I didn't feel able to say so. I made one suggestion for each, hoping it would sound like I was in command of the subject, so perhaps I am learning. But suppose the numbers are all wrong, and we quickly run through the budget and lose shedloads of money? What then?

Would people respect me if I say I have looked at myself in the mirror and concluded that I am not the right person for the job?

No, of course they wouldn't.

I'm still asking myself if Ella is right about all women wanting to be in a relationship with a successful man, even if they don't admit it to themselves. I hated having to cancel my night out with Debbie again yesterday, but I was expecting two calls that I would have had to take, which would not have pleased her, and I don't think I'm very good company at the moment anyway. So cancelling seemed the least bad option. Except that Debbie just said in quite an offhand way that I should get in touch when I'm definitely going to have some time, because cancelling on the day isn't giving her enough time to make alternative arrangements. Which told me on all fronts. I can't blame her at all, and worst of all I've no idea when I might next have time for an evening out.

I've re-read what I have just written and am now wondering if I'm just feeling sorry for myself. Surely this workload is only temporary? Hundreds of thousands of people cope with senior management positions quite happily every day; it's just a question of adjusting. Sunil thinks I can do the job, and he's a successful, unsentimental man who wouldn't have hired me for old times' sake! It's simply a question of self-belief. In a year's time I'll be much happier, and much richer! I probably won't even be able to remember what I was so worried about. I'm sure, if Lisa has told her, that Anne will be adamant that the man I have become is not up to this, so wouldn't it be great to prove her wrong? And my anxiety seems to be far worse at night – during the day I literally don't have time for it – so maybe the solution to that is, as Ella suggested, to get some medication. Just temporarily, obviously, until my new responsibilities become routine.

Five o'clock and there goes the alarm. Time to find out what Alan Brierley is made of!

Wednesday 7 April (1)

I'm going to do what science has failed to do, and make time run backwards, then forwards again. I'm having to write this on a scrap of notepaper because I haven't got my diary with me, but hopefully I will get time copy it across later.

The light isn't very good and I'm doing this quite furtively, feeling guilty about it, though I can't for the life of me think why I should. Aren't we all encouraged to talk nowadays?

Monday 5 April

I got up and did everything automatically, the way I have for years. I must have showered and made breakfast and coffee, and eaten it and cleared it away, and got dressed and left the flat and walked to the station. But any memory of it I think I have could just as easily be of another day.

I got a seat on the train which, I thought, was one of the few advantages of travelling much earlier than I used to. I regretted no longer having the time to read books on my commute. I worked through emails, which seemed to be popping up on my phone as quickly as I cleared them, and remember thinking that to be more productive I really needed to travel with my laptop in future. I felt tension rising in my chest, an aching hollowness in my stomach, and a curious desire to cry. I gazed out of the window and took a deep breath. I looked back at the phone. Someone needed me to make a decision about something. Urgently. And I had no idea. I couldn't understand the question, still less provide a satisfactory answer.

My heartbeat began to rise and I started to feel a tightness in my chest. I blinked two or three times and took another deep breath. I looked around me. Everyone else seemed to be engrossed in their phones too. Some people looked very serious, and others looked bored. But no one looked happy. For the first time in forty years of commuting I felt an almost overwhelming desire to strike up a conversation with another passenger. I made eye contact with each of the three people sitting closest to me, but they all looked away.

I went back to my emails, scrolling up and down, trying to use them to create a plan in my head of how my working day should be structured if I was to achieve something, push my projects forward, and not just add to the backlog. But I couldn't hold onto any clear notion: numbers and words swam in front of my eyes, even when I closed them. I wondered if a few minutes' sleep would help, but my body showed no sign of being willing to relax and shut down.

I opened my eyes. My vision wasn't as clear as it should be, and I blinked frantically to try to clear the fog, without success. The train had arrived at the terminus and stopped. Everyone around me was standing up and getting off. I could hear the hubbub of their voices, but although I could see the people close to me, the sound seemed to be coming from a very long way away. I didn't move. I wasn't paralysed, but felt weighted down by an unbearable sadness.

Time passed, but not smoothly. I smiled at a woman who came through the carriage emptying the bins into a large black sack. More people got on. The doors closed. The train started to move, back in the direction it had come from. I looked at the floor, which was dirty, and at my shoes, which were admirably clean and shiny.

Immediately, or perhaps hours later, we arrived back at my home station. I looked at my watch. I was supposed to be in a meeting. Someone from work rang. I declined the call and then turned the phone off. We set off again. I remember worrying that my train ticket wasn't valid anymore, and that I would be fined if an inspector got on.

We arrived at the terminus at the other end of the line. I wondered if I had ever been here before. I thought not. Everyone got off. Some noisy schoolchildren got on. Two of them looked at me and then exchanged wary glances before moving further along the carriage. The others followed. I had only the mildest curiosity to know what it was about my appearance that was worrying them. I went to wipe my eyes and found that my whole face was wet.

We set off again. I started to think more clearly, but doing so just increased the all-encompassing melancholy that was gripping my head and body. It was all over. I would be the laughing-stock of the London IT market. Ruined. Failed. And I could hear Anne's derisive laughter echoing in my head already.

We reached my home station again. But I didn't get off. The doors closed and the train set off, and I was starting to feel numb, wondering if I was just going to keep travelling back and forth all day until… until what?

And then I had the most amazing stroke of luck. The tightness in my chest spread to my left arm. I started to yawn uncontrollably, which, bizarrely, made me laugh. Then laughing made me laugh harder. My heart sped up then started to add and miss beats. I felt a need for air, but however hard I gulped at it I couldn't get enough. I started to get spots before my eyes, which grew in an instant so that they completely filled my field of vision. My heart gave a final lurch, like a washing machine with a load out of balance. And that was that.

Wednesday 7 April (2)

This entry is going to contain some stuff on yesterday and Monday because it gets too complicated otherwise, and it's too fragmented to try to split out accurately. And frankly I haven't the energy to try.

Reader, you will have gathered that I had a heart attack. Though it appears that 'heart attack' is a layman's term that the medics around here don't much care for. So I've had an 'episode' or one of a small number of Latin phrases I've been hearing today, though unfortunately not sufficiently clearly to be able to render them in writing.

The point is that my heart stopped doing what it is supposed to do and as a result I lost consciousness. Did I nearly die? I don't know, and it seems vain to ask when all the staff here are obviously so overworked. What does 'nearly' matter? I'm not intending to dine out on it: everyone thinks their own medical problems are interesting but absolutely no one else does. I suppose the only thing that really interests me is will it/ could it happen again, and so far they haven't told me that.

I'm not really sure how I got from the train to here. I seem to have some bruising on my arms and head which suggests I may have fallen off my seat onto the floor. I don't know who raised the alarm, how long the paramedics took to arrive or what station they took me off at. I have a vague and fleeting recollection of an oxygen mask and the back of an ambulance but nothing after that until I woke up here. I have no memory at all of whatever was done to get my heart going again, though serious bruising (much worse than from my tumble) to prove that a fair amount of effort must have been required.

Here at the hospital I was initially in some sort of high-dependency unit (I'm not sure if it was 'intensive care' as nothing here seems to be known officially by the same name as it would be in common parlance, and they love a set of unexplained initials) and I'm now in the cardiology ward but in a bay with three other people. I am the youngster of the group and the only one currently awake. The old white-haired chap opposite me has his mouth wide open and reminds me of one of the old men in the Muppets. I suspect the man to my left dyes his hair. He also has ostentatious stripey pyjamas. Which leaves the man on the diagonal, a slight, little mouse-like figure with a face dominated by a long aquiline nose. When awake he looks permanently terrified, as well I suppose we all might.

None of us is very sociable, which suits me fine. Being sociable with strangers requires energy, and we don't have much of that. And I have no interest in comparing symptoms and prognoses to establish a pecking order of near-death experiences.

There is a one-upmanship in visits, though, it seems to me. Ostentatious-pyjamas man had six visitors this afternoon (which had me wondering grumpily why the hospital doesn't enforce its own rules, there being a big sign on the wall stating that the maximum number of visitors per bed is four.) Mr Diagonal has a wife who dutifully visits every day and provides practical assistance without ever showing any visible signs of affection. The old chap opposite doesn't seem to receive any visitors in person but, fair play to him, is a whiz on his iPad with several Facetime calls each day, whether with the same or different people I can't tell. Waving seems to be involved, so I assume there are sometimes children at the other end.

Which leaves me. I have had one visitor. Poor Lisa got involved at a very early stage because the paramedics found her named as my next of kin in my wallet. Bless her, she was sitting there on an uncomfortable plastic chair the first time I woke up after admission. And almost the first emotion I felt, when I realised what had happened to me and where I was, was guilt. I started apologising to Lisa for whatever I had put her through, and for being a burden, and asking how she had got here and who was looking after the kids. She just smiled and said it was all fine, and ended up shooshing me the way she would Alfie. Which, much as I appreciated it, only increased my sense of guilt. I ended up telling her it was nothing, and that I would soon be as right as rain, and that they had no business bothering her. She just stared back with those beautiful eyes of hers, giving me a smile which tried unsuccessfully to mask her worry. I hate causing her any sadness or anxiety.

She contacted work for me, which was a huge relief. Apparently there were a series of increasingly shrill then downright rude emails on my phone at my failure to appear for meetings. Lisa did not reply to any of them but just rang Sunil. She said there was that awkward momentary silence after she had said who she was and before she explained that I was not dead. By her account Sunil said all the right things, and Lisa thanked him politely but asked him not to call me. Which is fine with me. I will call him, but don't feel in any hurry to do so. I expect he knows the score.

Lisa came back this afternoon. We chattered about trivial things and tried to make each other laugh. I did an impersonation of the rather grand cardiac consultant, which Lisa dutifully sniggered at, but I had the impression, just by looking at her face, that as soon as the preliminary niceties were over, there was something that was worrying and preoccupying her, and that she wouldn't be able to leave without discussing it.

"Dad," she said finally. "I'm worried about you."

"Oh, that's kind, sweetheart," I replied. "But I'm on the road to recovery now, and they tell me there's no need to suppose…"

"No, not your physical health, Dad, though that as well. I'm worried about your mental state."

She looked close to tears and for a second I struggled to breathe. "Well, I admit I'm not as sharp as I was," I replied carefully, "but that's the ageing process, I suppose! I am still Emperor of France, aren't I?" I laughed at my own joke.

Lisa wasn't listening. "I went round to your flat," she told me. "The woman opposite had to let me in because I didn't have a key. I was in your bedroom looking for clothes to bring in, and I discovered a diary by your bed."

"Ah."

"And I know I shouldn't have, but I started reading it to see if there were any clues as to what had happened to you. And then I couldn't stop, and now I can't unread it, can I?"

She was beginning to well up. "I can explain," I said quickly.

She shook her head. "I'm not cross about anything you've said about me, Neil or the kids. I'm worried that you're just making stuff up, making people up…and treating it as real."

"It's not really a diary…"

"I had a nice chat with your neighbour, Daphne. Does she know you've moved her out and replaced her with a dominatrix?"

It sounded preposterous and I laughed. "No you see, as I was trying to explain, it's part diary, part novel. I've always been something of a frustrated writer, ever since school really."

"But why a dominatrix of all people, Dad? Is that secretly your thing?"

I looked round to ensure that no one was eavesdropping and laughed again. "If you've read it, you'll see it isn't. No, I just saw somewhere that to get published you need an angle, something unique that will pique people's interest. So that was going to be mine. She's someone who asks the right questions, the ones that I actually ask myself in my head, so that I/ my character can work through the options, decide what the best answers are and move our lives in the right direction. Which I'm going to start doing as soon as I get out of here. But that was a bit one-dimensional from the point of view of the novel, so then I tried to flesh her out a bit."

"And the hospital consultant you met speed-dating?"

"Did you like that?"

"The dominatrix is more interesting."

I smiled. "Everyone's a literary critic! I know what you mean, though. Still, I've got plenty of time for a re-draft now, haven't I? Or, now I'm in here, it's the ideal opportunity to turn fiction into reality and meet the consultant's real-life equivalent!"

Lisa now looked puzzled. "So why is there real stuff in it about Neil and me, and the kids?"

I scratched my head. "Well, you're interesting already, nothing needed to be changed. I like writing about you. And if I ever get round to sending it to a publisher, I'll obviously amend names and details so you wouldn't be embarrassed."

Lisa shook her head. "I'm confused, Dad. I just don't know what's fact and what's fiction. Did you go to France last year, for example? And if you did, why on earth didn't I know about it?"

"Yes, that is true." I shifted awkwardly in the bed. "I didn't tell you because, well, it was a bit of a fiasco."

Lisa said nothing. I felt the need to cover the awkward silence. "France is true, and everything to do with work is true, and the charity shop, and you of course. And then all the parts where I'm on my…"

"Oh, Dad. That's so sad. Imaginary friends at your age. Are you very lonely?"

"They're not imaginary friends!" I protested. "I told you, basically it's a novel."

Lisa didn't look convinced. "Daphne said she was worried about you. She thought she heard you crying in your flat on New Year's Eve."

I floundered for a moment. "Well, it's a strange time to be… God, what is it with that woman? Has she got her glass against the wall of my flat all the time? No wonder I wanted to move her out and replace her with someone more interesting!"

That broke the ice and we both laughed. But Lisa quickly reassumed her serious expression. "You need to get well, Dad," she told me. "So, like it or not, you're going to be seeing a lot more of me in the near future."

"I'd really like that," I said. "But I'm fine. The diary has helped me work through some ideas, and once I regain my strength I'll start putting them into practice. Very soon you won't recognise me!"

Lisa looked at me questioningly with those big sad eyes, but my beaming smile was contagious and soon we were hugging, neither of us knowing if we were laughing or crying.

Thursday 17 June

It's a paradox of diary-keeping that when your life is at its most interesting you don't have the time, or even often the inclination, to write it down. So the worst periods of your life get set down in elaborate detail and the best go unrecorded. I have a free day today, so I'm going to try to correct that a little. There's no point trying to reconstitute two months of diary entries, so the best thing is to write down where I am now and what my plans are. I may then start making daily entries again.

I am still convalescing, officially. I feel fine, but this status means I can feel completely guilt-free about not working, and about spending so much of my time with my daughter and her family. I sometimes stay over, which is nice, though there is always something to be said for the comfort of your own bed, so I'm usually happy to return to the flat.

I have spoken to Sunil. He has offered me consultancy work, two days a week. I have agreed to give it a go, starting in September. No minimum period if I don't like it, and I will be sharing expertise, not managing. So no stress but I will be able to exercise the grey matter, which is exactly what I want. Sometimes things accidentally work out for the best. My 'heart attack' has given me a cast-iron alibi to accept this change of role without any loss of face, and in many ways it is the same for Sunil. Without that, despite the enlightened times we supposedly live in, failure due to mental frailty would have earned me no more than a certain amount of professed sympathy, together with a 'well-earned retirement.' The world is what it is, not what it should be.

Today I have been on light duties, helping to look after the grandkids, and the big news is that the Maserati has a new fan in the shape of Jasmine!

In her own way. She actually called it "Grandpa's funny little car", which amused her mother, but I've decided to accept that as a compliment. I even searched online for FLC numberplates for sale but did not find any. So instead I photoshopped one of the pictures I took of Jasmine in the passenger seat, and added an FLC1 plate that way.

It turned out to be quite an undertaking to get her into the car. When Lisa was little, I just used to put her in the passenger seat, tighten the belt as far as possible, and off we would go. Now you have to navigate child seats and the law and regulations for using them. I couldn't put Jasmine in the back seat because there isn't one, or switch off the airbag because there aren't any, but even so it took an hour of sweat and swearing before the seat Lisa had lent me would fit. Even then the car looked as though it was embarrassed by the affront to its interior aesthetics, but I didn't care. For reasons that I couldn't fully explain, I found that I had really been looking forward to taking Jasmine out in the car. It had taken a while to plan: surprisingly you're allowed to drive four weeks after a heart attack, but I'd decided to wait a bit longer, even though the specialist assured me (I got her to put it in writing for Lisa) that I was now no more likely to have another one than my general demographic, whatever that is. It needed to be a day that was warm and dry, and one when someone else was able to look after Alfie for a while (apparently putting babies in the boot is an infraction of the Highway Code, even with two-seaters.) Today the stars aligned: it was a cloudless summer's day and Neil was working from home.

For a moment I thought Jasmine was going to refuse to come out. She had a big frown on her face as I knelt by her side in the hallway trying to get her into her shoes and jacket. Endearingly, since Alfie had started to say a few words, his sister had shown an increasing unwillingness to be parted from him, something I guessed might well intensify further once his faltering steps supported by an adult turned into actual walking. I had explained why Alfie couldn't come, and that we wouldn't be long, but I was aware that logic wasn't necessarily going to win the day. Jasmine started to make a snuffling sound which was generally the precursor of tears, but at that moment Neil came out and, in a stroke of parental genius, persuaded her that Monkey had been looking forward to this and would be disappointed if it didn't happen. So, with Jasmine clinging tightly to me with one hand and to said fabric primate with the other, we finally got through the front door and into the street.

It was a beautiful July day. The air smelt warm, and there was only the ripple of a breeze disturbing the neatly trimmed hedges we walked past. In an immediate change of mood, Jasmine began skipping along, and I struggled to keep hold of her without squeezing her hand so tightly that I would hurt her. Monkey tried to walk along the top of a short brick wall then fell off it into someone's front garden. Grandpa tried to retrieve it and found himself on the end of an angry stare from the owner, who happened to be looking out of her front window at that moment. Miraculously, the angry stare turned into a big smile and wave as soon as she caught sight of Jasmine and her infinite, liquid eyes. I retrieved the toy, smiled and waved back in acknowledgement. Maybe the world would be a kinder place if we all went everywhere with a four-year-old.

We drew up alongside the car which, apart from the indignity of the child seat, was really looking its best in the summer sunshine. I opened the passenger door. Jasmine looked at me uncertainly and then clung to my legs. This was potentially a setback, but I remembered last Christmas, when she had clung to her mother on seeing me standing on her doorstep, and thought how far my relationship with my granddaughter had come since then.

"There's nothing to worry about," I told her soothingly. "Look, there's your seat, see. Just that it's in Grandpa's car and not Mummy and Daddy's." She still didn't look completely convinced, but she offered no resistance when I picked her up and gently placed her onto the seat. She didn't take her eyes off me as I carefully strapped her in, fixing me with the same trusting, and occasionally overwhelming, expression that I was familiar with from taking stones out of her shoes or reuniting dolls with their temporarily severed limbs. "There you go," I pronounced definitively, giving the side bolsters of the seat a final tug and finding no movement, "safe as houses and snug as a bug in a rug!" I closed the door gently and waited for traffic to pass so that I could walk round to the driver's side. It really was a nice day; I was sorely tempted to put the roof down, which after all is the point of a car like mine. But I remembered that Lisa had said it was a bad idea, at least until Jasmine had got used to the car and the motion, otherwise the rush of air would probably terrify her. Then there was a good chance she would be sick.

There was finally enough of a gap in the traffic to allow me to open the driver's door. I sidled into my seat and pulled the door towards me. It didn't close, as it often doesn't, so, without giving it any thought, I opened it again and gave it a proper slam. I turned to Jasmine, who to my relief was completely unfazed by the sudden loud noise. "Sorry about that, sweetie," I apologised to the toddler, who for the moment looked as though she would believe anything I said. "1980s Italian build-quality."

I started the engine. To my pleasure it fired first time, and I couldn't resist the temptation to give a little blip on the accelerator. No reaction from my granddaughter. I tried again, longer and more revs. This time Jasmine obliged by squealing with delight. I beamed at her, and tried to lean over to give her a kiss on the head before I realised that the seat belt wouldn't let me. I revved the engine again. Same reaction. I was about to do it for a fourth time when I noticed a woman outside a house opposite giving me a disapproving look. "I think we'd better go before we get told off," I told Jasmine with a conspiratorial wink. She nodded her head gravely in agreement.

We eased out into traffic. And there was a lot of traffic, bumper to bumper. It wasn't a surprise in the part of London where Lisa lives, and it's all thirty or twenty m.p.h. limits in any case, but it seemed a disappointing anti-climax. The last thing I wanted was for Jasmine to be completely underwhelmed, just bored by the experience.

I headed for the only bit of dual carriageway in the area. It took almost ten minutes to reach it, during which I was constantly confirming that we would soon be there.

And finally we were: a short, straight stretch between two roundabouts, with the speed limit at a heady fifty m.p.h. "Hold onto your bolster seat," I told Jasmine as I kicked down and the engine surged, giving that exhilarating shove in the back that I never tire of. I backed off at fifty and looked around for speed cameras. "You OK, sweetheart?" I asked. I couldn't take my eyes off the road to look, but the sound I heard, a cross between a sigh and a gurgle, I knew usually indicated approval. I couldn't believe how happy I felt.

We did a couple of laps and then on a whim I decided I wanted to take the chance.

"Shall we put the roof down?" I asked unfairly.

"Yes," squeaked Jasmine, obviously completely unaware of what she was agreeing to.

I pulled into a lay-by and got out. The Maserati has a manual roof, which is probably infinitely preferable to thirty-five-year-old Italian electrics, but a bit of a pain nonetheless, even when none of the parts falls off. I usually end up swearing at it, but I was aware of the need to be on my best behaviour today and not accidentally teach Jasmine words she might repeat in front of her mother. I turned unclipping the roof from the windscreen into a game of peek-a-boo, which seemed effectively to counter Jasmine's bewilderment at suddenly being able to see the sky.

Happily, the hood was in an unusually cooperative mood and was soon safely stowed behind us. I got back behind the wheel with some relief, having been wondering what I would say if a police patrol car pulled in behind me.

I smiled again at Jasmine, who seemed to be squinting a bit in the sunshine. Reproaching myself, I put her sunglasses on for her and marvelled at how she could simultaneously look so cute and so cool. I took a photo on my phone. She should have a hat too, I thought. Yes, but it would blow away. I settled for applying a small amount of extra sunscreen to her face, more to assure myself that I was a responsible grandfather than because I thought it was really necessary for a journey of a few minutes. Jasmine thought it was a funny game and kept moving, so quite a lot ended up in her hair.

We set off again. Down to the roundabout. Back to the other roundabout. Round again. Speed didn't matter with the roof down, so I didn't push it, let other cars past, just had the odd burst of acceleration when I could, and listened for Jasmine's approval. Someone in an Alfa gave us a thumbs-up as they passed. Jasmine waved at them, and they waved back and honked their horn. Round again. And again. Jasmine squealed with delight at every surge of power, and I looked at her and stored the moment and wished that it would last forever.

And then, with regret, I decided we had better go back before Jasmine got tired, or bored, or started to miss her dad and brother and the familiar surroundings of home. The famous Maserati clock doesn't keep accurate time in my car, but I guessed we had been out of the house for the best part of an hour. "Time to go back to Mummy's," I told Jasmine, who happily did not protest. I stopped again and put the roof up: I wasn't going to lie about it if Lisa asked, or Jasmine told her, but why go asking for trouble?

We navigated the side roads back to the house. Jasmine was singing a song that I didn't think I recognised. A lot of the words didn't seem to make much sense; I suspected she had misheard them or just made up her own. Monkey was being made to dance along.

And then we were outside Lisa's house again. To my great relief there was a space to park in that wasn't too far away. "So that's that," I told Jasmine as I prepared to back into the gap. "What do you think of Grandpa's 'funny little car' now?"

There was no reply. I looked to my left and realised that my granddaughter was fast asleep. I parked and, without waking her, gently extracted her from the seat and carried her back to the house, enjoying the warmth of the summer sunshine, listening to her rhythmic breaths and wondering why on earth anyone would be working in an office today if it wasn't a financial necessity.

Monday 12 April

I don't think I will be putting this entry in my 'official' diary. But I am (as you will see remarked on a few lines further down) nothing if not an accomplished scribbler by now, and don't have much else to do here; so I thought I would write this down and then revisit it as necessary, as I do with my diary itself.

Who should visit me today but my ex-wife of all people.

One of the nurses brought her round, and they both approached very slowly, as though they would rather not be doing this at all. Anne particularly had a strained expression on her face, which looked flushed and shiny in the stark hospital lighting.

"I'll leave you to it," said the nurse and she quickly beat a retreat. I smiled at that and looked knowingly at Anne, hoping for a similar reaction, but there wasn't a flicker. I inadvertently made eye contact with Mr Diagonal, who seemed to sense some sort of tension and quickly looked away.

"On your own?" I asked breezily.

Anne seemed surprised by the question. "Er, yes," she replied, almost in a whisper. "Well, Howard is outside in the car."

"Getting his money's worth, considering how much they charge for hospital parking. Very sensible," I joked.

Anne looked uncertainly around her. Mr Diagonal smiled and pointed at the chair next to his bed. Anne nodded at him, went and fetched it and brought it back. The legs grated against the floor as she sat down on it, and set my teeth on edge.

"To what do I owe the honour?" It sounded more sarcastic than I had intended, so I tried to make amends with a big smile.

"The hospital contacted me," Anne began quietly. "They said you had named me as next of kin."

"Oh, that," I said, trying to wave a hand dismissively before realising sheets were in the way. "Yes, sorry. I kept telling them I didn't have one, but eventually they wore me down. Some bureaucracy whereby they need a next of kin in order to discharge you. Covers their back, I suppose. But don't worry: as you can see, I'm almost fully recovered physically, and fully *compos mentis*."

Anne chewed her lip, which is what she always did when something was worrying her. "They're concerned about you, Alan," she said.

"Who is?"

"The hospital."

"Well, they needn't be. I feel ninety-five percent back to normal, and just need some time at home to get back to a hundred. I'm not sure why I'm still here now, when you always read how desperate they are for beds."

Anne looked particularly pained. "It's not your heart they're worried about, Alan," she told me.

I tried to sit up. "I'm not sure what to make of that," I replied a little nervously.

"They say that you're spending all your waking hours scratching furiously away at any scrap of paper you can get your hands on."

My handiwork surrounded me, so I could hardly deny it. "Oh, that. It's so boring otherwise," I explained. "And I've always wanted to write, so this is my opportunity."

Anne picked up a couple of pages before I could move them out of her reach. "What are these?" she asked in a tone that seemed to accuse me of something.

"It's a sort of diary," I replied, trying unsuccessfully not to sound defensive.

"Why are you writing a diary entry now for June?"

"It's just something.." I tried to remove the paper from her grasp, but she moved it out of my reach.

"Oh, God, she's called Lisa."

"I could change that if anyone ever wanted to…"

"The nurses told me you said you had a daughter. That she was going to come to see you. That's why it took them so long to contact me."

I tried to laugh it off. "I don't think so, unless I was completely delirious when I came in."

"Alan, for one last time: we don't have a daughter!"

"Keep your voice down," I said calmly, putting my finger over my lip.

Anne moved closer to me and grabbed my arm. She looked directly into my face. "We. Don't. Have. A. Daughter," she repeated slowly and breathlessly.

"Well, that's where you are wrong," I replied amiably. "We have one: Lisa Amelia Eloise Brierley" and I gave her date of birth.

"She died, Alan. For the millionth time."

I shrugged. "We all die; it doesn't mean we didn't live."

Anne moved back. "That's so cruel, Alan. I'm her mother. I gave birth to her. Don't try to cast me as the uncaring one. But we lost her. It happens. And eventually we all need to move on, or we lose our own lives as well."

"And you have. With Howard."

Anne looked at me resentfully, as though she were trying to measure her words. "It's called closure, Alan."

"I don't care what it's called."

"Come to the grave, please. With me. Just once."

"No."

Anne threw up her hands in exasperation. "I gave you... wasted another ten years, just trying to get you... and all you would do was work. Work, work, work. No family, no friends. And it's thirty years now, Alan. And look where it has got you! A heart attack, and living in a fantasy world in your own head!"

"It's not a fantasy world," I explained patiently. "As I told the HR woman, I'm a coder. It's about the 'if statement': if this, then that. So, I'm just exploring different 'what-ifs', you see. It's all perfectly logical."

Anne looked anguished and slowly shook her head. "Will you just listen to yourself, Alan Brierley?"

I didn't want to argue anymore. "It helps," was all I said.

Anne just sighed, then stood up and started towards the door. "Please," she said, "just find someone. And be happy. I want you to be happy. It is possible. I'm living proof of that."

"Thanks for coming in," I replied, and I gave her retreating form a cheery wave.

I felt a bit sad for a couple of hours after she left, and couldn't really settle to anything. "Cheer up," said the woman who brings drinks round. "It might never happen."

But I am, as I have noted before, by nature a positive and optimistic person. I have now regained my composure, and it's time to get back to my proper diary, I think. A bit of a re-write for Wednesday 7th April is clearly in order:

Lisa has correctly deduced that Ella is an invention; Debbie, however, is in fact a secret that her father has been keeping from her. Fast forward to July and the picnic they all have together. Start with Jasmine sitting patiently while Becky plaits her hair. Debbie and Lisa laughingly trying to direct all the wasps in Alan's direction. What would be a funny thing for Alfie to say?

Printed in Dunstable, United Kingdom